TARA BRAZEE

In With a Bang

An Outrider Adventure

For my niblings:
Jayce, Nera, Kyler, and Pierce
I have some stories about your mom I can tell next.

Contents

1

Act Natural

Mina needed to leave or she was going to explode right along with the string of explosives in her car. She shouldn't have let Zane convince her to stop by Restoration Cafe in the first place, but he'd mentioned the blueberry scones which reminded Mina that she hadn't eaten anything since about noon yesterday. Why not stop real quick? In and out. Seeing Steph would be a plus. Especially if the explosives went wrong and this was her last chance. Not that they would. She'd done the math; along with a small, contained, test in her basement. It'd be fine. Once they got to the doing it part she could prove it was fine.

Except now Zane was talking with Emma about some new class or trainer or something at their gym and Mina was dealing with the consequences of not telling him about the explosives in the duffle bag on her backseat.

She couldn't tell him. He didn't have the stomach for that kind of thing. Could her best friend bench press her entire body weight several times while barely breaking a sweat? Yes. Had she talked him through dry heaving after he'd cut a drive-thru too closely and scrapped up the door of his dad's car? Also yes. She'd fixed the damage before his dad even saw, but Zane confessed anyway. Expecting him to sit on the knowledge that she was building a string of explosives, for an entire week, was out of the question. Mina could guarantee he would panic-blab to his parents; who were lovely, but would never let this plan happen. She did feel a twinge of guilt avoiding them, but even after three years Mina still wasn't fully comfortable with the hands-on parenting they extended. Her parents hadn't even been home in the time she'd taken up the current explosives project, and she liked it that way.

Mina spotted the counter space for ordering open up, mentally willing Zane to go for it. Sean gave the final swirl to a frappe and pushed it down to Steph, who caught the drink and passed it to the waiting customer. She was laughing at something they'd said, the sound reaching Mina over the murmur of the morning crowd. It was a good laugh, and a really nice smile. She could let Zane chat about grips or whatnot for a bit longer.

There was a jab on her side from Zane, in a spot generally designated to tell her to come back to Earth. She focused back on their conversation.

"…actually was the one to find the spot. Little secret rock wall for us to try out." He was explaining their plan for the day. Or really, the portion of the plan he was aware of.

"How'd you manage that?" Emma asked, swishing around the last bit of her iced coffee.

"My little Flyers." She flinched at her slip of using a personal pet name. "Um, drones. I have a few. For getting stock footage."

"Right, you have that website." Emma pulled her braids from one shoulder to the other. "I'm jealous. I'd love to not be running gofer for my mom this summer."

"But you're free now," Zane nudged her. "Hours can't be too bad."

"They're out of town. Along with Sean's parents. Vineyard tour thing. Part of why I'm posted up here, my cousin can't be left to his own devices. Even at work." She tipped around them to eye Sean behind the counter. Mina looked too, he was in the middle of making doughnut holes disappear and reappear between his fingers for the mildly amused customer who'd stepped up to the counter. He must have sensed the extra eyes and fumbled a swap.

"And the caffeine addiction has nothing to do with it." Mina turned back to the table and eyed the two empty mugs sitting on the corner. Another jab from Zane, this one in the 'inside voice came out' spot. Oops. They needed to leave.

"I can stop any time. I simply have no intention of doing that right now." She waved at the open laptop in front of her. "And especially not with practice scholarship essays to do."

Ick. Mina hated academic writing. Maybe it was something to do with having scientific journals read to her as bedtime stories because it was all they kept readily available. She'd never admit it, but on the odd night insomnia struck she'd dig up a paper one of her parents wrote and see how far she could get before falling asleep.

Zane laughed, still trying to backpedal on Mina's behalf, "Yeah. I'd take a rock climb over that any day."

Mina watched the current customer grab their tin of doughnut holes and move toward the register, freeing up the counter again. She grabbed Zane's sleeve and pulled. "And we should really get to it."

"See ya, Emma." He fell in step with her up to the counter. "You're excited for this climb."

"Trying the one wall at your gym was fun. I want to give the real thing a go." And there was the prize at the top. Better than any bell, at least she hoped. Mina needed something to make all the lying worth it.

She truthfully did check out that particular bit of rock with Zane in mind. She'd been out on one of the lesser traveled, higher-up trails on The Hill, filming a long pan over the trees, when she caught sight of it tucked behind a thick cropping of trees and bramble. The entire thing stretched about thirty feet up, with plenty of handholds for them to use on the way. At the top was a ledge, about fifteen feet wide, before The Hill continued up as rough terrain. Nestled right near where the ledge cut into the earth was a crevice slightly larger than a person's arm. There'd been signs of water erosion being what cut the gap, but it was dry at the time and she thought a tiny cave would be good footage. At the least, it would test her maneuverability with the Crawler robots she'd made. A lot of effort for some random bit of rock, but she'd reminded him when selling the story that she'd needed to kill time until her parents left that afternoon.

Mina ferried her smallest Crawler up on a Flyer and let it shimmy into the dark. The feed came through to her phone, boring walls of rock as far as she could see until the Crawler went around a small bend and the camera caught the glint of something far off. She knew it wasn't water, the entire path was bone dry and angled downward toward the ledge. Water back there should mean water outside.

There was something shiny buried in The Hill and Mina was growing curious about what it was. The most likely explanation was mildly interesting geodes, but again, she had time to kill. She pushed her little robot on, until the Crawler's camera fuzzed over and died not long after the bend, which surprised her because Mina normally kept them well-charged. She'd been kicking herself for missing that one being low and almost made the climb right then to attempt getting it back.

The next day she came out with another Crawler, battery triple-checked at full, sporting a little pincher attachment to retrieve its friend. Back into the crevice for the rescue. She saw her little robot, again noticed the gleam off in the distance, and then watched the battery drain until the camera feed died out. Something shiny, buried inside The Hill, was killing her robots. Mina needed to know what it was.

Her theory was some sketchy structure Hephaestus Labs built underground. Even though they swore when opening The Park that it was purely a gift for the community, to prove their commitment to the people of Hurst. Also, pay no attention to this budgeting scandal involving our now ex-CEO - is what she'd gathered when moving here three years ago. The Park was practically pure profit for them; with the campgrounds on one end, the clearing at the other for festivals and fairs, and the smaller venues scattered about the rest for smaller parties. Throw in a few employees dressed up like standard park rangers to patrol the trails that circled up and around The Hill. Mina knew they hated being unable to build some monolith of an office on top of The Hill, but there'd been some ancient town decree that this area specifically couldn't be built on. Unstable ground or something, she never fully caught that part. Whatever the reason, Hephaestus agreed to the no development clause in order to purchase this land and the land they did build their office on along the south side. It wasn't lost on her that

The Park also put a buffer between Hephaestus and the city proper.

Leave it to a shifty tech company to find a loophole to building ON by building under. And wouldn't it be fun to expose them? But to do that she needed closer. She wanted to get further up the opening to gather evidence, but it'd take one of her bigger robots to do it. Something beefier than the current crack allowed, with enough shielding to get passed whatever killed the first two. After a little research, and a little testing, she made her little string of explosives.

She received another poke, back to Earth. Sean was juggling empty plastic cups in front of her. Zane's smoothie buzzed behind him with Steph at the blender. How'd Mina miss her coming over?

Mina looked over the board in a panic, willing herself to pick something simple and quick. Buy a black coffee and hate herself. Yet the overly sweet, caramel, iced thing Emma got her to try on their last visit was calling her name. "Can I get the iced caramel… espresso? Thingy."

"One Emma special, coming up." By some miracle, Sean knew what she was going for. He slid the cups back into their stack and started putting the drink together.

"Big plans for the day?" Steph asked between the last pulses of the blender.

"Rock climb," Mina managed to get out. "At The Park."

"Did they open something new?"

"Mina found it! Hidden on The Hill." Zane, happy to brag about her again, gave her a pat on the back. "Probably means they'll be charging for it by the end of summer."

"You'll have to stop by the music festival. Sam and Megan are out there with the mobile setup. I'll text them to give you a free drink after your adventure."

"Text Megan. No way Stickler Sam will give anything away." Sean stirred up her drink. "You'd think the owner's kid would be more chill."

"Sam puts a lot of pressure on themself," Steph said, but she waved it off before saying anything more. "Anyway, have fun. I haven't been up on The Hill in forever."

Mina was about to ask when Steph was off. Would she like to join them?

They could hang out and wait for her. No problem. None at all. Thankfully, her brain caught up before anything unfortunate slipped out.

Shiny something. Dead robots. Need to leave. Because explosives. In car. Bad enough she was lying to her best friend. Shouldn't add her…other friend to the mess.

Steph slid the smoothie across to Zane but looked right at Mina. "You'll have to tell me how it goes."

"Absolutely." Mina leaned into the counter. Her bag pressed between her and the siding, something jabbed into her leg. Not Zane this time, she absently dug a hand into the bag to shift whatever it was. Fingers meeting smooth plastic, other than the side containing one little switch and cover plate.

Mina forgot she put the detonator in her bag. She knew it wasn't smart to leave it right next to the explosives, connected or not. So in her bag it went this morning, the casing fresh off her 3D printer. She hadn't even smoothed out the edges, which was what poked her.

They really needed to leave.

She pushed off the counter and sidestepped around the stools there to reach the register before Sean finished her drink, pulling her wallet out as she went. It was probably her turn to pay. They tried to go back and forth but long ago settled into an agreement of there being a floating ten dollars between them. Mina found she was the only one that made the move. Zane was giving her a look, telling her this was something he'd bring up once they were alone again. Sean was putting the caramel swirls on her drink, an act taking longer by the cocktail bar spin tricks he put between each. Steph was looking at the front door, the end of the doorbell still ringing in the air.

Mina turned to see a girl around their age, fairly well dressed, coming straight for the counter. Right for the spot Mina left open across from Steph. She watched Steph, who didn't budge as the girl approached her, break out a different smile than she'd sported before. What was that one? It was very important Mina figure out what kind of smile this was.

The girl stopped short as Sean snapped the lid on Mina's drink and gave it a flip, ruining his swirls. Restoration was an acquired taste. The cafe catered to the more creative crowd of Hurst, with its walls covered with pieces by local artists and a back room that held a small stage for bands or performance groups. The place felt a little (a lot) loud to Mina and she'd mostly avoided it until, maybe, someone got a job here near the end of their school year. But how else was she supposed to continue the conversational momentum they started in physics class?

The girl twisted the end of a dyed blonde curl. "Hey, hi. I'm Henrie. I'm here to talk with Mitch about a job?"

Steph's smile widened. "Oh, hey! Let me take you back to his office."

Mina relaxed, even though Steph was walking away. That smile she'd seen before, on stage during the fall play to be specific. Acting. Good.

Sean slid down to the register. "Super Spy Steph is back on the case. She found Henrie on socials last night. Sent everything to our work chat. Won't see her back out here until the interview is over."

"A little recon can't hurt," Zane said.

Sean laughed as he tapped in their order. "Yeah, but we talked her down from going for a DNA sample."

"Does she dig into everyone that much?" Mina asked.

Sean shrugged. "Depends on how much she's invested."

She wondered if Steph ever put in that much effort looking her up. They were friends on a couple different apps, and if she'd dug further into her timelines…that could be interesting. Nothing truly bad to worry about. She could explain that fire. Easier than the explosives anyway. Mina felt the detonator take on an impossible amount of extra weight in her bag. *Leave now*, the weight demanded. She yanked out her card from the reader as it beeped, gently placing the wallet back in the bag. Ensuring the switch was now on top of everything else.

Sean gave them a wave before going to the next customer. Mina beelined for the exit. A tug on her bag strap jerked her back a foot from the door. She turned, seeing Zane with it gripped in his hand. He wouldn't even think of touching her bag if he knew what was inside.

That look was back. "We can hang out. This climb doesn't have to happen right-right now."

"Why not? We both want to do it." She knew he was obsessed with that wall at the gym. Knew that fact would make it so simple to get him up to the ledge. Everything after that was the hard part.

"Yeah, but an hour or so won't change that." He glanced toward the back room. "We can go hang out on the balcony." Zane watched her stand there staring back at him, not getting it. "Where a certain other person will be near."

Oh! Good friend with bad timing.

Compared to her being a bad friend with horrible timing. "No. It's fine. Let's go. She's busy. We're busy."

"You're sure?"

"Yes." Her bag was gaining imaginary weight by the second. She waved toward the back room. "That later."

"Later has gotta come sometime."

"Can we not? Please." She looked at the back of Emma's head, not far away. There was no sign that she was listening, but it still made Mina nervous. Emma was on the list of people who only put up with her because Zane was her best friend. She was far from the only one on that list, but certainly one of the most intimidating. While Emma usually seemed indifferent about her, Mina didn't need her whispering to her cousin. Who'd then go talk to his coworker and ruin whatever it was she was doing with Steph.

"Alright. Alright." He surrendered, letting the strap go. The detonator bounced against her side.

She was a bad friend, absolutely no doubt about that, but she was certain he'd come around. Forgive her. Get excited even! Eventually. They needed to get to the doing part. It'd all work out then. Be worth it.

Once back on the road, she kept shifting her bag around. Or glancing in her rearview mirror to look at the duffle bag that was causing her distress. As she got them onto the highway, her stomach growled; she'd forgotten to buy a scone. A travesty, to be sure, but the coffee would help. She was likely far from the first to commit a crime on an empty stomach.

2

What Would the FBI Agent in Your Phone Think?

Mina tried to think of ways to start the 'here's what we're actually doing' conversation the entire way there. She really did, but nothing felt right. Then Zane started talking about those all-immersive VR rigs that let a person walk around and Mina became distracted with the logistics of building one. Meaning, they got all the way to the small lot nearest the trail they needed without her coming clean. She'd even relocated the detonator to the side pocket of the duffle bag without being caught.

She thought there'd be a chance on the short hike up to the spot, but he wanted to go over their strategies for the climb again. Making sure she committed them to memory. To his credit, that part went smoothly. Zane managed to point out all the holds they'd need from the ground and spent the entire climb making her check-in and confirming her grip was solid. That's how they made it to her secret ledge without admitting what was in her duffle bag. At that point, the only way forward was to do it. While he enjoyed the new view, she pulled out the gear. And between one turn from her bag to the next, he was gone.

"You said nothing about explosives when you asked about doing this!" Zane shouted from the bottom of the rock wall, followed by one hard cough. He must have jumped down nearly the entire distance.

There'd been a tiny hope that he'd ask why she was bringing a full bag back when they loaded into her car, but he was too used to her hauling around random hardware to give it any notice. Most areas she frequented, his own home not excluded, were scattered with parts. Or he'd assumed it was snacks she planned to share. It did take a lot of calories to keep him going.

"It's not that dangerous. Or that big of an explosive," she called down while twisting wires to make her connections. "It's all stuff anyone could buy."

Mina repositioned her pile of dark hair from a ponytail to a messy bun before leaning down to the gap. The rock was still dry, whatever buildup that eventually made it out this way was still not present. Lucky her. She wanted that shiny thing on the other side. Mina fed the string of charges into the opening, feeling proud of the Lego wheeled carrier system she'd constructed feverishly the night before.

"You know that definitely put you on a watch list of some kind," Zane hissed up at her, trying to be covert even though they were very much the only ones in the area. They'd left any marked trail behind fifteen minutes ago.

"You act like I wasn't already on a list. And I didn't buy much. My parents had some of this stashed away." She laughed to herself about how most people her age were spending their summer sneaking into their parent's liquor supply and watering down bottles, while she went for the chemicals - of the non-drug variety.

"Won't they get mad you took those?" A different concern came through his voice.

He didn't ask how she'd accessed dangerous chemicals without them noticing because he also knew her parents had barely been home since summer started. She kept feeding her line into the crevice. "This is an ask for forgiveness, not permission situation. They'll be totally fine if we find anything worthwhile. Probably even impressed I managed to put this together."

That is if what she found was something naturally occurring. An undiscovered ecosystem was unlikely but would go over well with them. If her theory that this was a Hephaestus Labs secret facility came to be true, she'd still get their attention but for a very different reason. Mina pushed her explosives in further and hoped for the latter.

"Yeah, that's another thing. The average person doesn't know how to turn home goods into pipe bombs!" Zane started out shouting, but pulled back to an angry stage whisper as he reached 'pipe bomb'. Another hard cough.

Mina snorted as she imagined him looking around wildly for a random park ranger or hiker to come through the trees. "This is not a pipe bomb. It's fashioned after what they use to blow out tunnels. It's only going to break a controlled area of the rock. I need more space to get a bigger robot in."

"Wanna go on a hike, Zane? We can do real rock climbing. I think I found a fun spot," Zane stopped short in his mimicry of her. When he spoke again it sounded closer, he must have taken a few steps back up the rockface. "Did you let me think I finally talked you into trying the rock climbing wall for this?!"

Mina didn't answer immediately. Partly because she was focused on the camera feed she'd started pushing in, a final attempt to scope out the area before her explosion. Partly because to say no was a lie. "You honestly did a great job pitching it. I would have caved anyway. Things happened to line up."

"You've been using me!" She heard a thunk that was likely him swinging a foot to kick the wall. "Ow."

"I've been trusting you! You are my best friend and the only one I want here with me." She wiggled the feed in further. The quality wasn't great, grainy images of rock and her two Crawlers. Her gleaming reward was still far off, no better recognizable than it was before.

"Don't you try to flatter me." A softer thump, another small kick at the wall. "Okay, but why are you actually doing this? So I know what to tell the cops when they come to arrest us. Or, only me, since you'll be blown to bits."

She smiled but also rolled her eyes at the exaggeration. "I was out here getting new stock footage for the site."

"Good 'ole long pan over trees." He was getting closer to the ledge.

"And while flying, I went a little wide and came across this spot. I checked if the wall was good to climb. For you," she made sure to say that part toward him, "Then I noticed this crack. Managed to get my Crawler in. It only got part way before fuzzing over and dying, but the camera caught something reflective before that."

"Like expensive reflective?" Closer still. Probably stretching his neck up toward the ledge, knowing full well he still couldn't see anything.

"Possibly. But I need a bigger opening to get a better camera in. And to figure out what killed the others." Mina opted to leave out the Hephaestus theory, he wouldn't be as on board with that as he would be with finding riches. She checked the feed, it was starting to glitch. When her screen turned to full static in the same spot, she pulled out the snake camera and gave the charge another nudge. Eventually it wouldn't move, she assumed the dead Crawlers were blocking the path. "Sorry, little guys. Sacrifices for science."

Mina rolled back on her feet to stuff the camera in the bag, catching the tips of Zane's messed-up hair as he ducked back below the ledge. She paused before hitting the detonator, maybe staying up here wasn't the best idea. After rechecking her connections, she dropped down below the lip of the landing.

"You've seen reason," Zane sighed from his spot, "Thank goodness."

Mina made sure her feet were firm and her one hand tight on a hold. She gave a smile to Zane and held the detonator out. "Hold tight."

His big eyes pleaded at her, "Hold on a minute! Please. I know you know almost everything, but when did you learn about explosives?"

"I did some quick googling. Few hours over a few days." It honestly didn't take much. Videos and articles of 'mix these and things go boom' were pretty easy to come by.

"Is this a minorly educated guess?"

"The technique is pretty sound. People have been doing this stuff forever."

"But you haven't. Mina, you're going to get us killed on a guess about some vaguely shiny thing."

"Maybe myself, but never you." She shifted, angling herself over him to prove the point, and hit the switch.

The bang was louder than expected, given how far she'd fed the charge into the crack Mina assumed the rock would muffle more of the sound. The size of chunks that flew over their heads led her to believe that maybe she'd misjudged the caliber of the charge. Or maybe the density of the rock. Explosives were a new venture. And rocks weren't her thing. But they weren't dead! Or even hurt. This was a win. Her plan, so far, was working.

Zane pressed tight against the rockface, eyes shut, and breathing deeply. One hand dared to release his grip and grab hold of her ankle. "You are going to absolutely get us arrested."

"The closest venue is closed for renovations. The music festival is on the other side of The Park. They'll all be there and we'll be fine." Mina popped her head over the lip. The dust cleared, revealing a new space that was also larger than expected. She tugged her ankle from Zane and pulled herself back up over the ledge. After pushing chunks off her duffle bag, she pulled out a dust mask, goggles, gloves, and a headlamp. There were still some rocks blocking her way forward, Mina pushed those away and checked if the new walls around the hole were sturdy. They felt warm and, more importantly, solid. She peaked in with her light, it appeared to go as far back as she'd intended. The glint was far off, but more pronounced. With the extra light coming in, she could now see it was a reddish tint. Mina rolled back to look down at Zane. "Hey, if we belly crawl I think we can get through ourselves."

Zane pulled himself one step up. "Do. Not. Do. That."

"There will be safety gear waiting here for you. Bag is with me. If you don't come, the expensive stuff is all mine." She pulled back from the edge but didn't move further away.

"She's lying. It's a bluff," Zane whispered, clearly thinking she was gone. They'd established freshman year that any lottery winnings or large earnings would be more or less shared. Per Zane himself, her technological achievements were his best financial plan for the future. He was ready to spend his years as a well-kept best friend, happily part of her entourage. She found it funny, and appreciated that he believed in her so much, but their guidance counselor was not as amused by that outlook during his college prep discussions.

Mina knew he wouldn't be far behind, but purposely crunched a few rocks as she got closer to the hole. He'd start imagining her being crushed by the tunnel caving in. Or exposed to whatever dangerous, radioactive material that lay ahead. Or finding a crap ton of valuables alone and laughing at him. He couldn't very well let her die. And certainly not get ridiculously rich without him.

Pushing the remaining debris out of the way made for slow progress as she was forced to keep backing out to free up space. She was only a few feet in when she caught the sounds of Zane coming up over the ledge. Mina paused, waiting to hear him put on the equipment. Zane could, rather easily, pull her back at this point. But it'd scrape her up and they both knew she'd dive back in any way. He knew she could never leave something like this alone. Or worse, leave it to someone else to discover. The constant tinkering was why he kept a fire extinguisher in his car and got her a huge one for her birthday. She should have grabbed that, come to think of it.

"Any strange smells?" He asked, slightly muffled from pulling on the mask.

"Nothing I'm noticing. But I think there's too much dust and residuals from the explosives really tell," she called back, it echoed off the walls around her. The tunnel widened enough that she could push rocks to the side instead of pulling them back out. Mina picked up speed on her crawl. The air was warm, also from the explosion, and she felt sweat rolling over her arms and back after not too long.

"Should I send any 'love you' texts before we do this?" Zane asked as he leaned in.

"Not any for me." Mina was impressed with how not completely draining the task was feeling. All that time in the gym was actually doing her good. Point to her weightlifting best friend.

Zane tested his headlamp, she could see his light swing side to side as he moved in. "When future archaeologists dig out our bodies, they'll think we were doomed lovers."

"You can only hope to be so lucky." Mina pulled ahead through the tunnel. "This was a thinner wall than I expected."

"Says the girl who used explosives on said thin wall." He sounded like he was pushing more rocks away, needing more space than she did. All those muscles working for and against him at the same time.

After a couple more pushes the tunnel widened again to enough room for Mina to get up on her hands and knees. The red glint was drawing closer and closer, she was rather certain it was metal now, but Mina forced herself not to focus on it. After all this work, she wanted to surprise herself with the ending. What really would she do if this turned out to be a secret Hephaestus lair? She kept her eyes down as the tunnel came to an end. Mina pushed the bag off to the side and turned her back to the cave as she pulled on the tunnel's edge to get up on her feet. They'd come through to another small ledge. She stepped off to the side to give Zane space, still looking at the wall for a few extra moments of suspense. Only when she caught sight of his hands pushing out rocks did she finally turn to see what the elusive gleam was.

It didn't happen often, but Mina felt her mind blank out.

"How rich are we?" Zane asked as he continued to crawl forward. He did the same turn and pull to yank himself out faster. A small grunt escaped as a few smaller rocks bit into him. "Tell me there's a ship somehow stuck in a landlocked state."

"Yep," was all the reply she could muster. Mina stepped closer to the end of the ledge. She could almost see the buffer wheel that filled her brain floating in front of her eyes.

Zane was still facing the outer wall, hesitating to turn around. "If you've been struck dumb by some horrid sight please scream or sob so I know to run now."

"Zane, turn around," Mina breathed out. In her peripheral, she saw him take a deep breath and turn.

They'd broken into a huge cavern, one the size of the entire Hill. Actually bigger than that, this extended far below ground level. And it wasn't empty.

Filling up that space, stretching high above them still and shining with what she now decided was more of a burgundy color, was what looked like a pair of discs with a large cylinder running through their center. The first featured an additional domed top, something Mina only vaguely put together as their lights barely reached that high. They stood near even with the top of the second level, it was much longer with its edges pressing against the sides of the cavern in several places, this was likely what kept the rock walls from falling in. Mina leaned over to look down the gap near their ledge and discovered the top of a third level hidden below, gleaming metal disappearing in the darkness. The structure was nearly upright, as if it had fallen straight out of the sky. There were enough dents, scratches, and full on tears along the outside to support the theory. Her brain kept circling back to how it was taking up the entire space. The Hill was far from the largest earthen mound, but still. It was called The Hill because people had a hard time calling it a mountain given that it stood alone in their otherwise rather flat area, and it matched up with people swapping the mouthful that was Hephaestus Lab's Nature Reserve and Community Centers for simply The Park.

She was having trouble trying to estimate a number for the size of it all. But something she did instinctively know, this was nothing Hephaestus Labs could make.

Zane stepped closer to her, his light swaying as he took in what was not the pirate ship he'd been hoping for. "Mina."

"I know."

"Explain."

"I can't."

"Mina."

"I. Know." She took careful steps along the ledge back toward their tunnel, it continued across the side of the cavern and angled up toward the dome level. She noticed a rivet in the rock where the water drained down from some exhaust port or broken section and eventually formed the crack. But she couldn't locate the spot now. Outside of the damage, the entire side looked solid, one huge sheet of curved metal. Not a single seam anywhere.

She couldn't tell from here if any of the large torn pieces went all the way through to the interior, and any gap she did see didn't look big enough for them to get through. There was a protruding bit of rock that cut into the path, getting around it was a riskier move than she felt like taking at this point. Mina turned back and passed Zane again, whose eyes were still locked on the…thing. She hoped the left got them closer to the second level to spot some sign of a way in.

"Do not leave me alone with this UFO!" He called after her but didn't move.

"It's so big!" When she spotted a larger gap between their ledge and the ship, she got down on her knees and leaned over so her light shined farther into the space below, but was still unable to make out how far the third level went down. Mina crab walked herself back to the duffle bag and pulled out her newly fortified Flyer and the controller. She switched its lights on, got the Flyer into the air and over the ledge. It pushed toward the domed top for an entire three seconds before everything locked up and it tumbled down. She should have expected that.

Because the buffer wheel was still running through a portion of her brain, she only managed to reach a hand weakly out toward the Flyer before it disappeared below into the void. Mina peaked over in time to watch it smash against the top of the next level and the light went out. Zane shuffled over to look as well. Burgundy shone back at them. Mina again dug in her bag and pulled out a glow stick, cracked it, and dropped it closer to the rock. They both watched it bounce between rock and spaceship for a long time, only revealing more and more shining metal. This bottom level was potentially taller than the other two combined.

Zane's smoothie joined the bouncing glow stick. "Do not tell reporters that I threw up on the spaceship."

"Taking it to my grave, buddy." Mina stood back up and continued along the downward slope. "I wonder if we can get closer."

The headlamps didn't give a huge area of light and the gleam from the ship only helped so much. Her depth perception was off as she tried to judge the gap between them and the ship. She was hoping that some part of that middle came closer to their ledge and they could jump over. Zane could likely make the current jump, but she wasn't so confident in her abilities. After that would be the task of finding a way in. Mina would prefer to find a latch or doorway that could be pried open, not wanting to damage the hull any further, but she knew everything gave in to heat eventually. Push come to shove she could widen one of the tears already there.

"Should we?" he squealed out louder than she imagined he'd intended. "I mean, what about weird alien radiation or whatever?"

"Given the size of this ship, any weird energy readings would've been picked up by now. Unless whatever keeps killing all my devices also blocks all types of detection. Or maybe it's untraceable with our current technology? This has to have been here for…I don't even know how long. Someone, Hephaestus specifically, would have picked up on this by now if they could." She was rambling, but at least she was getting full sentences out of herself. Mina looked up toward the top of the cavern. "This probably crashed and then the displaced earth fell back down on it. That could also dampen any readings."

"Five hundred years," Zane said quietly.

"What's five hundred years?"

"How long this has been here, roughly." She turned away from the spaceship for the first time to give him a confused look. He perked up at having the chance to educate her. "If you hadn't slept through the local history sections in class, you'd know this one."

"Mr. Dobson is a bore. How did you not sleep through it?" When Zane didn't go on, she whined, "Please tell me what you know."

"The Big Shake! When European settlers got to these parts, they heard stories from the indigenous people about a huge quake that happened generations before. In an area that's never again had any kind of earthquake."

"They said the earth changed. A gorge was lost and a mountain gained," Mina finished. Small bits of information trickled in from the fraction of her brain that was set aside for subjects she didn't think too much about. She'd never looked into tectonic plates, but the local legend always made good enough sense to her. Plates smashed together, jutted earth up into the air, resulted in an instant freestanding mountain they were supremely lucky was not volcanic, and kept each other stable since then. There'd been a standoff between the remaining indigenous and the settlers that ended with the settlers, who desperately needed the help learning to survive here, promising to leave it alone. Which became so ingrained in local culture it resulted in the decree that Hephaestus has to follow all these years later. Mina felt herself relax from the satisfaction of puzzling that one out. Felt good to cross something off her list of questions.

"Makes sense," Zane said weakly, losing his confidence once the short lesson was over. He leaned back from the edge. She figured he was confirming that the remaining contents of his stomach would stay in place.

"They warned people that the earth made angry sounds for a long while after. Because I bet something inside there still had power for a bit. Crazy this has all held up for so long." Her brain was starting to kick back in, forming another list of questions. She swung her light around the cavern walls. "But geology is not my strong suit."

"Yeah, me either," he took a long breath in, "What do we do about the UFO?!"

Mina didn't reply but rolled another glow stick down the ledge to get a better lay of the land ahead of them. They watched it go for a good while before the green light smacked against a bright red obstruction in the path. She moved toward the light, intending to kick away the debris, figuring it was a rock. Zane followed a few steps behind. Once closer she realized that the object was perfectly smooth and oblong. Very much not rock. More metal. Mina reached out to it.

"I swear if you white-woman-in-a-horror-movie this and touch that with your bare hands, I will leave you to whatever alien disease you catch," Zane said from his spot against the wall.

"That's...fair." She swung her bag over and rummaged around, pulling out a forgotten gym shirt that should've been taken out a week ago. "This already died anyway."

Mina grabbed one end of the red chunk. She adjusted to two hands as it was heavier than expected. The thing was only a few inches thick, she figured it must be solid inside. Zane inched closer as she turned it over in the shirt, something inside made a small plink sound. She put an ear closer to the object. "There's a sound. Like something may be loose inside."

Mina gave it a slightly harder shake, but only got the same small pings.

He was backing up again. "When that blows up in your face-"

"I'll go full Harvey Dent. You get to be Batman. Look at the spaceship, Zane."

"I haven't looked at much else." He stretched to look back to the dome. "Do you think they're in stasis? Or dead? Or watching us right now? Would this be the Grays? Or the lizard ones? What are the tall ones called? I can't remember if any of them are actually green."

She picked up on how much he was huffing through his questions. Mina looked from the chunk and back to her friend, realizing how hard he was pressed against the wall and how pale he was getting. Her mental list of questions fell aside, he was the only one that could get her to do that. She fully wrapped the chunk in the shirt and tucked it into her bag. Then moved over and took Zane's hand, he was shaking. Maybe she was too, a little. "How about we get you back to fresh air?"

Mina knew Zane heard her because he nodded in agreement, but the only movement he managed was to squeeze her hand tighter. "Do we call the news? Or the cops? Do you think the FBI agents in our phones are already on their way?"

She pressed his shoulder softly. "Keep hugging the wall and take little steps toward the tunnel. Deep breaths."

Zane took out his phone as they moved and brought it close to his face. "Please don't kill us for finding aliens. We can make a deal. But Mina should get to name them."

"Breath in the nose for four. Exhale out the mouth for six." She nudged him along and took the same deep breaths to encourage him to mimic her. "Watch your head when you go in."

The small breeze hitting his legs must have cleared some of the brain fog, reminding him there was indeed an exit and they were not trapped with this gigantic spaceship. He got down and wiggled his way back through, shoving yet more rock out as he went. She gave the spaceship another look and managed to snap one low-quality picture before her phone died in her hand. Something about it held off the ship's effect on electronics for longer than her robots, a detail to chase down later. Her parents would be devastated about the lack of documentation she'd done while here, dead electronics or not. *Take notes in blood if you have to*, she expected they'd say.

Zane was waiting for her by the opening, staring out at the trees. "What are the odds of this being an extremely fast-acting gas-induced hallucination?"

Mina shifted the duffle bag on her back, feeling the weight of her alien chunk there. "Not sure if it makes you feel better, but it was definitely real. Are you good to climb down? We can sit here longer if you need."

"I would like to get farther away from the spaceship." Zane flipped around and backed his feet over the ledge, finding the first grips he needed. He was moving on autopilot, but at least he was moving.

Mina kept an eye on him for a couple of steps but decided he was steady enough and looked back toward the tunnel entrance. She'd only found this ledge because of the Flyer, but Mina knew if she stumbled on it then someone else could too. Even more so if someone heard the bang earlier. There were a few larger rock chunks around and she shoved them back over the hole to make it less noticeable. At least she hoped it was.

"Mina, did the aliens come out and eat you?" Zane called from the ground.

She swung a leg over and started her way down. "There is no Mina, only Zuul."

"Very funny," he gave an empty laugh. "Please don't tell the reporters I threw up in this bush."

3

Batteries Not Included

Mina leaned Zane against the wall by his front door. He'd been silent since leaving The Park; outside of the moment she'd stopped behind a Kia with a bumper sticker that read *My Other Car is a TARDIS*, at which point he laughed. Loudly. She waited for it to sink in where they were, but he was zoned out.

"Zane, my key for your place is in my room. We're close, but I'm not about to dig in your pockets."

He looked around, realizing where they were. "My bad. Thought it was your door."

"Nope, you still live in the blue one."

He fished his keys out of an unfairly large pocket. Zane missed the lock a few times, his hands weren't quite back to normal. Neither were hers. She let him figure it out and gain some solid ground on his own.

She kept a couple steps back as they entered his quiet house, holding hands out in case he took a crash. The weight of the duffle bag weirdly kept her centered, a next step to focus on. She'd get him safe and comfortable, come back with more information later.

They made it upstairs to his room. She was thankful his parents were out of town doing a couple's thing that made Zane cringe whenever it was mentioned. Zane sat hard on the beanbag chair left in the middle of the room, usually reserved for her, and slowly leaned back until he was more on the floor than the bag.

"Zane, are you okay? Like, really okay? I don't want to leave you in full-on shock here."

"I just need a nap. Aliens will make sense after a nap." He grasped behind him for the thin blanket that was bundled up on the edge of his bed, pulling it down over himself.

"Sure. Sure thing." Mina pulled the corners to make sure he was fully covered. She grabbed an empty glass from his nightstand and filled it with water in the bathroom across the hall. She left it near him on the floor. After slight consideration, she pushed the trash can within arms reach as well. "I've got water here. And a spot to aim for if throwing up happens again. Not that you have thrown up at all today. Or ever. You are so strong-willed."

"Mmmhmm. Good best friend." He inched the blanket further up his face.

"I'm going back to my place so you can sleep, but I'll leave the back unlocked. Come over whenever you're ready."

The blanket nodded. She gave the small tuft of hair sticking out a scratch and left. Mina paused on the stairs, debating if leaving him was the best idea. He was the only sure thing she could count on, she shouldn't leave him struggling. They'd been fast friends when their families arrived within a few days of each other three years ago. First her and then him. He'd come over to investigate the small fire she started in the backyard and afterward provided an extra pair of hands for assembling her desks and shelving. In return, she'd repaired a couple miswired outlets in their house and done all the cable management once their electronics were arranged. They both were turned down by the cute girl who used to live on the corner, also within a few days of each other. Him and then her that time, though her attempt had taken severe encouragement from him to even happen.

"Freaking out over finding a spaceship is a reasonable response," she told herself as she crossed their backyards via the gate their parents jointly installed after Zane took a hard landing during one particularly quick jump over. Her car was still in front of his house, but that was a common enough occurrence. *Needing to take a moment to sort your brain out is understandable,* she thought as she entered her house. He would have said something if he needed anything else. She was the one that clammed up, only managed not to because she had Zane and the thing in her bag to focus on. Once inside she moved straight for her room upstairs.

Pieces of what used to be the coolest thing in her room, an attempt at an Iron Man pulse glove for an overly complicated Halloween costume, were moved to the sliver of space on her nightstand. Nudging over her homemade thunderbird that floated above its magnetic base. Mina dropped the still closed bag on the workstation. She pulled up her stool, adjusted the light, and stared at the bag.

Ten minutes later, partially filled with a quick search to see if anyone was talking about an explosion at The Park (they weren't), she'd managed to open the zipper and flip back the top. Giving her a view of the shirt wrapped around the red chunk.

"Touch the alien thing," she whispered to herself.

Not with your bare hands, whispered Zane from inside her head.

"Yeah, yeah." She leaned over and pulled gloves from a wire basket on her shelves. Another couple of minutes wasted by firmly pressing them down between her fingers. "Now touch the thing."

She removed the shirt wrapped chunk and dropped the bag to the floor, sending a quiet apology to all her other possessions still in there. Mina slid the shirt off the top, revealing a shimmering red that was the exact shade she wanted for the pulse glove. Mina snapped a quick picture in good lighting. If this was alien junk, at least it was a good color reference. Tipping it back and forth caused the same clicks as before. Turning the chunk completely over only revealed more of the same smooth surface. No seams showing anywhere.

She pulled off one glove and let her fingertips brush the curved edge. No shock, no tingling, her flesh was not melting away, and the chunk did not spring to life. Mina pulled off the other glove and flipped it over and over as she pressed harder along the entire surface, but she felt nothing. Even using every level of magnification she kept on hand, no seam.

Mina put down the chunk and stepped away, doing a lap of her room. Wrestling with the thought that this could be simply a rock. Maybe when the ship crashed, whatever it was made of caused a weird reaction with the surrounding rock? Superheated and reacted with it? Maybe this was an extra thick lump of glass. Made perfectly smooth and rounded because of some geological reason she didn't understand right now. The idea made her glare back at the chunk. "I did not steal some kind of alien polished rock. I refuse."

Even if that was so, the plink sound meant there was some hollow space inside. How did that happen? It could be a geode with broken shards bouncing around to drive her mad, but that didn't feel right. She stood over the desk, staring down at the chunk. "You make a sound. What is the sound?"

Another lap of the room, trying to place what the sound reminded her of. Sort of like a marble in one of those maze puzzles. Or a loose component inside a device. How many times had a Flyer crashed and knocked something loose while the outside looked relatively fine? One bad connection and the whole thing could go dead. There's an idea. The chunk had been laying in a cave for hundreds of years, any potential power source must be depleted.

You can't just push electricity through it, said the Zane of her head. *You have no idea how that will go.*

"Yeah, well, neither would you." She stared at her variety of charging cables, all useless without some kind of port. Mina dug into her closet and pulled out the small jump pack she kept on hand, along with the assortment of clamps. As she sifted through for a set that fit on the chunk, she looked out her window toward Zane's house. "If this goes really bad, at least you won't know till it's over."

She took a gamble of setting the clamps on the farthest ends of the chunk and flipped the power switch on the jump pack. A green shimmer ran over the surface. She jumped back, yanking the cords with her because she was afraid of a larger reaction. The chunk clunked onto the worktable. Several long minutes of nothing went by. In the quiet, Mina picked up the small, slow whir of something trying to turn within the chunk. That small zap set something in motion for a brief moment.

"Don't blow up. Don't blow up." She inched closer to the desk. The morbid part of her brain noting the fact that being this close likely meant a quicker death. With the alternative being thrown through her window, potentially living through the fall, and dying slowly on the ground. Mina shook her head. "Stop that."

She stepped up to the desk and leaned in, the whir stopped. Makes sense, she'd only held the clamps there for a couple of seconds before freaking out. She reset the clamps, flipped the switch, and quickly backed away as the green shimmer ran over the surface. The whir kicked in again, she took another half step back, but the sound didn't get any louder.

After thirty minutes the jump pack died and the shimmer stopped. Because Mina had done nothing but stare directly at it, she noticed the chunk drop ever so slightly. She stepped closer, leaning over the stool to remove the clamps. Mina tipped the chunk to the other side and immediately dropped it.

She wiped her hands against her sides. Not that they were sweaty, but more to push some of the nerves out of her body. "Stop freaking out. You wanted the alien thing. Here it is."

Taking a deep breath, Mina flipped the chunk over. The drop she'd noticed was from a panel opening. How that happened without her finding the seam earlier, she wasn't sure. The chunk now displayed a dark screen with blue symbols scrolled across the top that she couldn't understand. As it filled with more symbols she grabbed her phone, partially recharged during the drive back, and took pictures. Other voices, sounding like her parents, chastised her for not properly documenting what she'd already done. These were easier to block than Imaginary Zane, she did it enough already.

The bottom left corner showed a slightly larger symbol. It flashed and changed to another symbol. Paused, flashed, and changed again. Then did it again.

Yeah, this is going to blow up, said the mental Zane.

For the third time she crossed her room, but now took the extra step of opening the door and stepping out into the hall. She crouched and covered her ears. Again a long minute passed and nothing happened, Mina realized that if this was indeed a countdown she had no reference to how high that count started from. She may have time to stop it.

Or clear the block. Or get it two streets over to that open field. Or tie it to a Flyer and go straight up. Or get back inside in time to have it blow up in your face. Rattled off Zane.

"This best friend business is a bit much right now." Mina knew this was all her brain trying to solve the problem and using him as a soundboard, like it knew he was her voice of reason or something.

She knew it was odd, complaining about a version of him that wasn't even real, but she sometimes got tripped up at knowing anyone this well. Mina had been at-school friends with people in her last town. It wasn't that she didn't talk to anyone or didn't do all the social media kind of stuff, but generally her projects kept her busy and satisfied. When she tried being social outside of school hours, it wore her out fast. Or she became spacey, due to thinking of the project she was neglecting.

She got by mostly unbothered until that small, completely accidental, fire that changed the attention she got in the halls. When people started talking about her, they stopped talking to her and that small bit of social interaction shriveled up by the end of middle school. The quiet started to affect her, leaving her unable to even bother with her projects by the end. Mina realized that she actually did need some small amount of human contact. It felt like a blessing when summer came and her parents announced they were moving to a new city. A complete coincidence on their part, they would have ripped her out of that life even if everything was going fine.

She knew she'd need to make some kind of effort with people this time around. A hard task because Mina wasn't the one to strike up a conversation with a stranger. There'd been half a plan to reimagine herself over that summer, go into that freshman year a different person that no one would expect accidentally set a small, inconsequential section of a classroom on fire. She wasn't thrilled with the idea but figured it was her best bet at survival. She couldn't be alone anymore. Mina allowed herself to finish crafting one last Flyer prototype before shoving all this away. Wouldn't you know it, that time when something caught on fire it was lucky for her. A chatty neighbor boy, who'd also been uprooted from another town mid-summer due to his dad's job transfer, came to put out the flames and stayed to ask questions about all the gear. Zane may not have understood it, but he genuinely listened to her explain. Even offered suggestions for additions. The self-makeover plan fell aside as they spent the remaining summer weeks making robots fight across their backyards.

She expected to be forgotten when school started and he made new friends far quicker than she did, but he kept catching up with her in the halls between classes. He always saved a seat for her at lunch, to the confusion of the budding friend group around him. In short time, Zane's decree of 'Mina is awesome' was enough to give her some social standing. She never got, or wanted, as much attention as him, but the fact that she could remain herself meant more than all the rest. And it was because of him. Platonic soulmate was the term someone threw out at a bonfire night he'd managed to convince her to join last summer, she liked it. Never mind that the entire sentence was, "It's kinda hilarious that your platonic soulmate is a scrawny, uber nerd." She didn't think Zane hung out with that guy much anymore, now that she thought about it.

Mina, breaking out of her little reminiscence, realized she was still crouched in the hallway and nothing had blown up. She peaked around the door, the chunk sat on the desk. No louder noise emitted and no lights flashed.

Long countdown, whispered fake Zane vaguely behind her.

"Not exploding," she said to calm herself and crept back in, leaving the door open behind her. Best to have a clear exit path.

She once again leaned over the stool to see the screen. The flashing symbol was gone, instead there were a few lines of symbols that would change every couple seconds. A bar along the bottom jumped forward every few times the symbols changed. She laughed, "You're rebooting!"

Mina looked in the direction of Zane's house and rolled her eyes, as if he'd know the fictitious version of himself in her head once again overreacted. She snapped more pictures of the screen. Then decided it best to grab her small tripod and set up the phone to record. The reboot was taking its time, the jumps in progress coming slower and slower. That was one thing human and alien tech must have in common.

"And this being dead for hundreds of years isn't slowing it down at all, I'm sure,"

she chided herself.

There was extremely little to no chance this alien language translated directly to

English, but she found herself scratching out what she assumed was words on a notepad and attempting to find common placements anyway. She knew processors, if there was some chance they used similar wording or jargon, she could potentially crack it. After only a few minutes, she surrendered to the odds of that happening being very much zero. Mostly given that if this technology referenced the local languages at the time of The Big Shake, no one here was speaking English.

"Linguistics is not my thing," she defended herself. To herself. Not even a Zane voice to argue with this time.

Mina dug out her laptop from under a pile of books on another, smaller, desk and started to search native languages, before realizing she needed to research which tribes were in the area five hundred years ago. That did lead her to a few scattered articles that mentioned tribal stories of The Big Shake. Mina gave an apologetic look to the thunderbird, once again feeling guilty she knew so little about this. She forced the little sad cloud away and went back to the languages, but no alphabet she could find matched up. Her next step was picking non-native languages at random, hoping something would click. The theory, or excuse, being that maybe the ship visited another country before crashing here. Nothing matched, but she did figure out how to write her name in several languages by the time the progress bar was nearing its end.

Mina scooted closer and stared at the screen, a bad habit with her tech. The watched pot never updates. After a few minutes of staring, it finally jumped to the end and loaded a new screen. Hazarding a guess, this was a list of errors. Given the length that rolled by, she imagined there was a somewhat major component damaged internally. Whatever that clink was, it wasn't intentional. At the bottom of the list was a set of symbols with a highlight flashing on and off. A prompt, maybe?

She tapped the highlighted area. Nothing happened, but that didn't rule out this being a touchscreen. There was a chance it didn't register her skin as a conductive material. Mina squirmed at the thought and changed tactics to voice recognition.

"Confirm. Update. Yes? Continue? Please?" she rambled, but nothing changed. Mina looked up synonyms, using anything that felt authoritative enough to use on an alien device. Then did all of the same words in the languages she'd looked up before. Ran the words through voice simulators in case it wasn't used to her tone. She spent another hour and a half trying to find a command word or decipher the symbols. The only break being to move her phone cord from the bed to the desk so that it wouldn't die from recording for so long.

Voice commands were out, this thing didn't recognize Earth languages. There was no way to guess what the alien language sounded like. She did a few more tests of touching the screen with different materials, but nothing reacted. Mina resisted the urge to slip off the stool and become a pile of failure on the floor, as she was often to do when projects fought back. The other option was charging her way across their yards to fling herself onto Zane's floor and whine. But that wouldn't be getting anything done, would it?

Instead, she straightened her back and took a deep breath. She pulled out the finest-edged tool she owned. Because while the symbols took away part of her sanity, the screen gave her a seam. Sometimes you break things to figure out how to fix them. Mina worked the corner of her tool into the seam with the smallest wiggle back and forth to gain progress without causing any damage. This restored some of the calm she'd lost during The Great and Terrible Alien Password Game. This she could do for hours.

She would get Zane to edit around the bits of her losing her mind, he'd love to make something tangible out of her mess of clips. His interest in editing started as a joke when he made a mockumentary of, mostly her, building their straw tower for physics class to prove he'd helped in some way. He'd caught a bug. Now he was chatting with some of the college students Mina sold footage to and constantly practicing with footage she provided or clips from his favorite shows. While she may be biased, the music videos he'd made lately were getting really good. Speaking of, maybe he could cover her crazy with some royalty-free music. No! Screw that. They were buying rights to music, if such a thing was not an Earth-shattering amount of money to do. They'd figure it out later. But if they couldn't get music, she should be talking about what she was doing. Shadowy shapes of her parents gave exasperated gestures behind her as if they'd been trying to tell her that exact thing this whole time. Again, she shook them off.

"Nothing is reacting to me working the edge of the screen. No defensive systems, um, activating. Symbols are the same. Flashing bar not changing. I want to get a bit further in before trying to pry up the side here."

As she talked, she wedged up a corner of the screen; which was far thinner than expected. She moved the phone closer to see the inner mechanics as she continued to slowly work the screen off. It was complicated inside, to say the least. Several layers of hardware were stacked within the chunk, which explained the weight.

Mina popped the last corner of the screen off and held the edges. She showed it off to the camera. "See, it's super thin. Heavier than it looks too. Not sure of the exact material. You can't see through it. I've got a little safe space for it over here. So we can get to digging into the…device? We'll go with device for now."

Felt weird not referring to it as a chunk after hours of internally doing so, but that didn't sound very scientific. With luck she'd get some clue about what this was used for based on the components inside. She leaned over to grab her snake camera from the duffle, connected it to the laptop, and started a capturing program. "I'll use this to get a closer inside look. Which will be recorded on the laptop. We'll see if I can get anything else apart. These layers look rather close and I don't see any kind of hardware securing them right now."

Mina bent low, laughing at the version of herself a couple hours ago who was afraid to touch the chunk with her bare hands. Now her cheek nearly pressed against the red metal casing as she looked inside. There were tracks along the sides. She nudged the top layer, which looked like an over-encumbered motherboard, with her tool and it shifted fractionally. Daring to press further, the layer - components and all - curved along the side and fully out of the way of the layer beneath it. The stack pushed up, putting the new board closer to the top of the device. Mina tried not to squeal.

From the floor below she heard a door open and shut. Mina paused her probing to listen to the footsteps as they climbed the stairs. Zane, still disheveled from his nap, swung around her door frame. "Once again, I will ask if there was a chance this was a shared hallucination."

Mina didn't move from her position over the chunk. Not sure how to answer given his earlier reaction. She felt him move closer as he closed the door.

"Working on the glove again? Do you think we can really make a hammer th-" He got close enough to see she wasn't working on the glove. "Wh-what is that?"

"Proof it wasn't a hallucination?" She straightened, her back protesting the change.

"You stole the alien thing?"

"Borrowing. Studying. I will put it back once I figure out what it does."

"It could have blown up in your face. It still could." He pulled her stool away from the desk.

Well, she'd certainly gotten that part right. "I took every precaution."

"Oh my god, you're filming it all."

"Maybe." She realized she was still holding the camera directly into the device. Her laptop screen filled with the unusual configuration of hardware inside.

"Without me?" He grabbed the tripod and adjusted the angle of her phone, then moved her overhead light a few centimeters. "The nerve."

"You needed a nap. Science wouldn't wait." She stretched her shoulders as he pulled the snake camera from her hand. Hearing him not sound angry with her about the alien theft helped her relax. "Do you feel better?"

"It's bizarre, but it happened. Is happening," he waved the camera around the device. "Gotta say, this is easier to take than the ship."

"You haven't even missed much. This is all nothing," she waved over the pages of scribbled words and symbols, "All I did was give it a charge. It ran a diagnostic on itself, but I couldn't read it or make it move past that display. So I took off the screen."

Zane stepped back and looked over the setup. "Can science wait for me to get a different camera?"

"Science has been eager for your arrival."

Zane reopened her door and stepped back into the hallway. She knew he was heading to what would be a linen closet in a normal home, but stored yet more gear in hers. Including a taller tripod and a camera her parents used more to record trials at home than any domestic moment. He called out, "Did you remember to eat?"

She was glad he wasn't there to see her guilty look. "No. Did you get your appetite back?"

"Well, I did lose breakfast. And probably whatever was left of last night's supper. So I could eat."

Her stomach gave a loud rumble at being reminded of food. "Chinese?"

"Agreed." He came back in with the larger tripod and a camera case strung over his shoulder. Zane balanced it all with ease on one arm and pulled out his phone with the other hand to open their preferred restaurant's online ordering site. "Same order?"

"Yes, please."

"Done. Thirty-ish minutes." He tucked his phone away and set up the tripod. It telescoped up over her shoulder. The camera angled down for the best overhead shot they could get in the space, there wasn't enough room to put it directly on the desk. Her parent's home office/lab had better access, but there was no way she'd risk bringing any of this in there. "You brag about our find to Steph yet?"

Mina picked up the pen and started to darken lines on some of her scribbles. "Why would I do that?"

"Because that would gain some major brownie points."

"We don't even know what we have yet." She gave a little wave to the device with one hand and turned some curvy letters into flowers with the other.

"Space. Ship." Zane adjusted the lighting again. "Also you're in love with her."

Mina scratched up the flower and dropped the pen. "It's a crush."

"Says the woman who spent twenty minutes overanalyzing the meaning of a free cookie with her drink last week."

"It is possibly…a strong crush. For the moment. Not something worth endangering this all over." Mina turned to see Zane looking at her and could tell by the little crinkle on his forehead he was disappointed. "Science would like to get back to it now."

He held up his hands in defeat. "Go on. Love will stand back for Science." He settled in behind the camera. "But only for so long."

She scooted herself back up to the desk. "Anyway. These layers move. They're flexible enough to bend and match the curve. Pretty awesome. Given the number of layers, it might have a few functions. Or a single, very complicated one. This is all guesses at the moment. Theories. I sound so dumb."

"You can record over it later. Keep looking down, it'll make it easier to redo what you're saying."

"Awesome." Mina pushed another layer over to the side. This third board held larger components and clear signs that something was missing. She grabbed the snake camera and tilted the device to see the edge. Two chips tumbled out from behind the next layer down. "This must've been the clink I heard before! I knew it sounded like loose pieces."

"Tilt back for the camera real quick," he whispered. Being able to take this all in with the buffer of a camera seemed to help him.

She did as directed and leaned over to grab tweezers. Mina pulled out the components, pinching them gently to show off their bendable features, and laid them on a pad. The pins were in mostly good condition, it looked like this simply hit the ground hard enough to break them loose. "I can reconnect this. Easy."

Zane moved the tripod as she jumped off the stool and pulled out her soldering kit from the basket behind him. They sat in silence as she went to work. He moved from the tripod and took over the snake camera angle. She straightened the few wonky pins and soldered everything down. As she pulled away from the second chip, the device let out a set of beeps. Both of them jumped back.

"Will it explode now?" Zane asked, the small bit of calm slipping.

"It will be a quick death if it does." Mina let out a breath. The device beeped again. The layers she'd moved before slid back on their own. Another set of beeps. She noticed a small arm tapping upward. "It's trying to connect to the screen. It needs to say something."

Mina realigned the screen with the frame, the piece popped back into place easily. The display flashed, the beeps happened again, and symbols scrolled by faster this time before everything went blank. She expected it to go through the diagnostics again now that the full system was in place, but instead the metal cover began sliding down. There was no way back into the hardware if that panel shut. Outside of breaking the casing, which she didn't know how tough of a job that would be. She grabbed her prying tool and caught the cover before it sealed.

"It's got a lot of force behind that cover. Don't know where it fit a motor in there. It's really fighting to close." She pressed back, but didn't gain any ground.

Zane backed off with the camera. "Maybe we don't fight the alien device?"

"I don't know if I can get it open again."

"Maybe it's best that-" Zane didn't get to finish because the device moved on its own.

Prongs popped out from the underside, lifting it up about an inch from the desktop. A small arm unfolded from the side, opened like a pincher, and grabbed hold of the tool. Mina let go out of shock. The device set the tool aside and closed its cover. Its little legs bent and jumped off the desk, coming near eye level with Mina. While midair, more openings appeared and small jets popped out.

"It can fly?!" Mina squeaked out.

"How did you not see that inside?" Zane asked from his new position of being firmly against the floor.

A white beam scanned them and the room, it flickered over the opened door. The device zoomed forward and disappeared into the hall.

Mina almost fell trying to push off the stool after it. Zane scrambled up behind her. They stumbled down the stairs after the speeding device that was now scanning her living room. Mina watched it almost crash into the door, but pull back at the last second. That pincher arm popped out again to open and, gently, close the door before jetting straight up into the sky.

She less gracefully smashed into the door before getting it open again, both of them falling out onto her porch.

"What?!" he shouted up and also at her.

"Oh crap." Mina watched the device shrink in size as it flew higher, stopping once well over the trees. She thought there was a flash of another scan before it took off in a direction she knew led back to The Park.

They were still staring at the empty sky when their food arrived.

4

Framework Not Found

Comp2876 attempted to match terrain with stored data as it passed over the structures below, but couldn't access the database. Problematic. Local storage was limited. The last command logged from Nek being *LEAVE IMMEDIATE AREA* and then several notices of damage populated before all systems forcefully shut down.

2876 ran another scan on the immediate vicinity, noting the still low grade ping to the north. As that was the only active data, it continued that direction. Nothing was following, but it remained high and ran scans every few seconds to confirm that remained the case. Comp2876 noted the ping was originating from an area that held no Outrider in clear sight. 2876 surmised that the ship was covered, something outside of cloaking it would have normally seen through, for some unknown reason. The limited date was an annoyance.

As it came over the formation, Comp2876 took a dive, narrowing in on the location of the ping. It pulled up as new data confirmed the density of the material below, stopping it inches from bashing into the hard earth. That could have been disastrous, 2876 was too focused on the ping. A rather concerning error in calculations, but 2876 wasn't used to running those alone. Nonetheless, those beings from before must have gotten closer to Outrider somehow. Comp2876 attempted to push back farther in its personal log. There was much corruption in its way, due to damage and high demand on multiple systems, all dated around the same time. The framework had been bombarded with input. By what could not be determined yet. Strange, unnatural even, being the lone point in a normally full framework of Comps.

It emitted a few frustrated beeps. Hard to fix what it could not remember was broken. Comp2876 circled the area, scanning as it moved. There was a break in the surface, a hollowed track into the mass. 2876 stacked a few loose rocks farther away from the opening and went forward into the dark, flipping on lights as it moved deeper. The shimmer of Outrider's exterior casing was a comforting sight. Comp2876 let out a few hopeful beeps at seeing the ship, directing its own ping toward the deck.

No acknowledgment from Nek returned. No automatic uplink to the database triggered. The only response was the echo of its own sound. Worried beeps slipped through its processing without check. Comp2876 gave another scan and noted the clear crash damage to the hull. Moving farther down into the cavern, more damage was noted. Most looked like scrapes and breaks from impact. Outrider must have come down hard. What could have caused that? More worried beeps. It located tracks along a side path that appeared new, the beings Comp2876 scanned earlier.

Why did no others try to stop them?

Comp2876 got its answer. Not far passed where the tracks stopped was a harsh drop in the rock. Down twenty feet were more Comps, all laying dormant and in an array of damage. None returned the call Comp2876 gave. By some luck, or misfortune, 2876 trajectory landed it slightly further than the rest, in a spot the beings found.

More scans, same results. All were damaged and drained of power. It appeared that Comp2876 was an outlier in whatever altercation that caused this. The limited and corrupted data was increasingly problematic, but could be an easy fix depending on the internal state of Outrider. A task list compiled as Comp2876 examined the area, but prioritizing was difficult. Generally when one Comp created a task there were several others to advise on priorities, but now Comp2876 must decide on its own. The gentle whirring coming from the Comp accelerated. A first step was designated, get into Outrider.

A panel for an exterior Comp door was simple enough to locate. More force was needed than usual due to having no power, but the newly broken hinges would be repaired once more Comps were back online. A simple enough task among the heavy work the rest of the hull required.

Perhaps those beings from before could be of service? 2876 only considered the idea out of the desire to not be alone. Letting strangers into Outrider was not preferred, but it would at least put a few more minds to work on the growing list of issues. They had managed to repair and recharge Comp2876, though that charge was weak. There was only an estimated three hours and twenty-six minutes before needing another connection. A new set of tasks shifted to the top of the to-do list. Restore power to the charging docks. Then pick out any Comps who may be functional with a charge. Form a system of repair, recharge, and repeat. A plan, that felt nice to have.

Comp2876's small bit of noise echoed through the channels Comps used to traverse the ship without clogging up the hallways. It dodged more Comps laying dormant here as well. They were all aimed toward leaving the ship. Perhaps a burst of some kind took them all out at once? There was vague knowledge stored about a defensive EMP that could go off if Outrider was in danger, but it was untested. An experimental failsafe that they'd run out of time to properly understand before their launch date arrived. Any hopes to knock out an enemy nearby could have taken out their own systems, and potentially did. 2876 never looked into the action plan as it appeared too extreme, the Collective being overly prepared. Though that could be why the Comps were sent to flee, meaning to escape the radius and bring Outrider back online afterward. Something had gone wrong.

Entering the elevator shaft was eerie. Being the sole connection between the three levels of Outrider, there was always a hum vibrating through the tunnel. Never was it this quiet. Comp2876 tried to reach back to a short note of the Wardens running through the main level to hazard a guess to one of their locations, but was cut off again by the corrupted log. Comp2876 moved into the walkway surrounding the elevator, taking a cursory look down all the main hallways that led further into the various sectors of Outrider. Many showed signs of fighting, but no lifeforms were found in the immediate vicinity. Or, the option that was growing in probability, remains. Their fight must have ended further into a section than the Comp chose to travel yet.

Comp2876 pushed down the pathway leading to the charging docks. There was a fair amount of damage to one section of stations, but others looked usable. If repairs here took longer than expected, a mayday flight back to the beings could be done. Once again comforted by its small bit of a plan, 2876 pulled a panel from the wall to access the power grid. Time to get to work.

5

Playlist for When You and Your Bestie Investigate a Spaceship

"Why are we stopping for coffee?" Zane asked as Mina parked close to the front of Restoration, the third time he'd asked since she pulled into the parking lot.

"Oh, now you're eager to get back to the spaceship?" Mina stepped out before he could make a grab for her. She was again proving herself right that telling him about the explosives would've been the wrong, and overly stressful, move.

Zane insisted they not go back yesterday. Wouldn't even consider leaving until the sun was fully up again. She'd passed the time pouring over the video footage (making him cut out her crazier moments and them talking about Steph), getting familiar with the hardware layout, and trying to guess what it all did. Not to mention where it hid those jets. He'd chatted away on his own work between bites of pepper steak and egg rolls. Then later fell asleep in front of her bedroom door to trap her in. Mina gave a small consideration to the sheets out the window escape method but decided it wasn't worth the trouble. Nothing popped up on socials or news channels of an explosion at The Hill or unusual sightings after the device took off. Waiting until morning would be safe enough and, worst case, she had her footage for proof of first contact. Footage that was now backed up on two

41

external hard drives for extra measure, one stashed at Zane's house while they'd gone over for him to shower and change this morning.

"Noooooo," he practically fell out of the car following her, "But this isn't exactly a stock up on supplies kind of spot. We passed four gas stations, a grocery store, and three varieties of dollar stores to get here."

Mina pulled the door open and waved him in. "I really want a good coffee to start this."

Zane didn't move, he was looking into the cafe. "You knew she was working this morning."

Mina shot a look at the counter, Steph was pouring out a drink from a blender and chatting with Sean and the customer waiting. "Don't know what you mean."

Except that Steph did once mention Mitch was cool and agreed to give her the morning stocking shift on Fridays as usually those nights she had some kind of show to either perform or support.

Zane pulled the door from her hand and let it fall shut. "I know I joked about it yesterday, but you can't brag about this to impress a girl."

"I just want a coffee." She noticed they'd been spotted by Sean. "And now we're making a scene. We have to go in." Mina pulled the door open again and walked inside, giving a smile to Sean.

In no way was this only about getting a coffee, or even seeing Steph. It was mostly her dragging her own feet getting back to the spaceship. There was a UFO sized pile of questions bogging her down and going back meant attempting to answer them; a rather daunting task. Why not put a little pause on the situation and also get a drink from a very nice person who Mina very much enjoyed talking to for no particular reason? Another factor was realizing it may be good to leave a tip to where they were going - in the case aliens killed them and they never came back out of The Hill. But that one she wasn't really trying to focus on.

"Do not mention aliens or spaceships or whatever that red thing was," Zane whispered behind her. "Also we were fighting over the Spider-man movies. Again."

Mina pulled away from him to lean against the counter, still smiling at

Sean. "Can you put two extra shots in an iced thingy for me? Very big and to-go, please. He's defending Raimi's Spider-Man Three again."

"For the time, it's not the worst version it could've been," Zane hunched beside her. "And I will die on this hill."

She snorted. He kicked her ankle.

"It's not a great hill," Sean said as he put together Mina's drink. "But I respect your right to choose it."

"I'm saying if you look at-"

Mina cut him off before this turned into a real discussion they were having. "Let's agree to not get too worked up about it. This time. We have a long day ahead."

"Another climb day?" Steph asked as she joined them and put together Zane's smoothie. "This is kind of early for you two, isn't it?"

Both of them paled, for different reasons. Zane likely at being immediately called out for their destination, Mina for being noticed enough that Steph knew her normal operating times. Mina surprised herself by bouncing back first, it almost made her dizzy. "Yeah! It's a bit more work related this time around. Have a list of requests I've been putting off. And early-ish morning stuff does well."

"Sounds fun! You two going to be out there long?" Steph asked.

"Uh, it sort of depends. Zane can be a stickler for shots lately." She gave him a weak elbow for good measure, which he in turn weakly reacted to.

"Maybe I can meet up with you later?" She tilted toward Sean as she pulsed the blender a few times. "The director pissed off the sound guy. So that project is on hold indefinitely."

"Did they break up?" Sean was putting overly dramatic chocolate swirls on the inside of Mina's plastic cup, he was making a spiderweb.

"One thought they had that talk two weeks ago and one said that it never happened. So showing up to rehearsal with a new fling went over real great. Messy." She poured out Zane's drink, met eyes with Mina again. "I'll be out in a couple hours. Haven't been to The Park in forever."

"That would be great!" Mina said too fast, the dizzy thing happening again.

Zane cut around Mina to meet Steph at the register first. "We can't guarantee where we'll be though. We have to go around town a bit too."

"But text when you're out and see where we are," Mina said from behind Zane. He shifted back to step on Mina's toes. She flinched, but recovered, "We may even need a hand."

Zane put more pressure on her toes while also smiling and paying for both drinks. "Yeah, never know. Give us a ring."

"Sounds good." Steph handed over the straws. "See you later then?"

"Yep!" Mina squeaked as Zane turned himself on the foot still crushing her toes. "See you." They left Restoration and Mina made it back in the car before letting out the long OW she'd held in. "I do have to use this foot today."

"I'm sorry, but also not. But also, so, so sorry. But also you can't turn an alien spaceship into a date site! Or make me third wheel it." He shoved straws into their drinks, giving hers a good few spins as she backed out. Sean's well crafted swirls smushing together.

"I won't. This was an extra way to make sure someone knows where we were if things go..." she didn't finish and didn't need to.

Zane pulled out his phone and mumbled "hiking with Mina" as he tapped out a text to his parents.

She needed to distract him before that worry spiraled him too far away. "When she texts I'll come up with something. But it will get her to text me." She grabbed her drink from him and took a long pull before leaving the parking lot.

"So much work for so little result."

"You're used to being pretty, huh?"

"That's not what...you are so beau...and she's..." He floundered for a bit longer before sinking into his seat. "Lesbians are confusing."

"I am reminded right now of how painfully straight you are."

"You said you'd never judge me for who I am." Zane leaned against his window and gave a loud sigh. He pretended to wipe a tear away with the back of his hand.

They both broke out laughing. She got them to the expressway toward

The Park. Zane plugged in his phone to her stereo.

Mina tilted her head as a song started, but avoided looking at his screen. "Is this E.T. by Katy Perry?"

"It is indeed. Points for you."

"Did you make an alien themed playlist?"

He tilted his phone even farther away from her. "Possibly. We'll have to let it play to find out."

"So be it." Mina saw her exit for The Park coming up. "Your stomach going to make it this time?"

"I think. I know what to expect. But if that little thing went back and woke up a big thing, promise you'll make sure I die first."

"Will do, buddy." Mina wondered if all true friendships carried at least one death pact.

6

Second to One

Comp2876 was rather satisfied with the work completed in one night. The main issue at the docking ports was from a Comp's self-destruct function, not a good sign for whatever happened inside Outrider. A few spots required heavy repair; not much to be done without Fabrication online. Then there was the additional decision of digging through the jumbled storage bays for fresh materials or waiting for damaged pieces to be broken down for recycling. With some cleanup and a turn of the small backup generator nearby, a row of docks was back online. Comp2876 settled in for a charge after that, deeming it best to ensure it was at full before expending unknown energy on more repairs. After a couple of hours, given the extremely low level of output Outrider was set to, 2876 was ready to work again.

Comp2876 knew the weak ping it followed here was the distress signal, but was not sure what - if anything - was running beyond that. It didn't pick up auditory signals of the life support systems running. Another unfavorable sign for the state of the Wardens.

Scans of Comps within the tunnels showed their internal circuits heavily damaged. Likely due to their proximity to the, still hypothetical, blast that went off. From the pile outside Outrider, there were fifteen Comps needing only a charge. Comp2876 also retrieved a small glowing device laying on the ledge above. As it gave no reaction to contact, 2876 took the item along to avoid using its own lights for a short while. It took most of the night for the small batch to reach a quality level of power. Even with them back in the framework their data was fractured and corrupted. Best they could gather, there was some kind of frenzy and then it all went dark.

With sixteen points rather than one, they made slow progress. Some continued on the docks. Some organized the remaining Comps from least damage to most severe; an unsettling gradient as it came together through the halls. The group reconvened to make the hard call on those too far gone. Their salvageable parts were needed for other Comps as materials and Fabrication were still inaccessible.

By early morning six more units were repaired and charging. Their progress would be expedited as more Comps rejoined the framework. Yet the charging time was the main delay as they were still working with only local backup power.

Comp2876 proposed the task of heading to the main generators and seeing what could be done. Several accepted to join and broke off from the group. A few ducked into the tunnels, normal procedure. 2876 and the rest remained in the main hallway, each Comp taking notes of damage as they traveled. Chirps and beeps of confusion and concern rang out as they moved along. 2876 would propose heading to the database housing once power was restored, hopefully their answers had survived there.

Priority tasks appeared on the framework. Bright white notices flashing across their systems, pushing other tasks down.

Secure Pak.

Return Pak to Deck to verify condition.

Move remains of Warden Jarden to medbay for care.

Information and images loaded into the framework from Comps that took the tunnels, they'd arrived at the generators sooner. Warden Jarden was located inside the doorway. Deceased but Pak intact, at least on initial inspection. While Warden Jarden's was preserved due to the active suit and sealed ship, he was clearly long gone from them.

Comp2876 slowed as it processed the data. The Comps back at the docking ports accepted the priority tasks, leaving their current work to care for the Pak and Warden Jarden. The hallway group, now clear to continue on their original task, pushed forward to the designated location.

Three Comps took charge of the Pak. One carried and the others surrounded it for the short trip to the deck. The odds of anything else being alive here fell to near zero at discovering Warden Jarden, but procedures like this could not be overrode. Until power was restored to the deck those Comps were out of rotation. They'd stand guard for the Pak until the containment units were online.

Yet another task for the list. While 2876 was focused on the dire subject, it acknowledged that this left five other Wardens to secure. There was a ripple across the framework and further priority tasks appeared. They called to confirm the location of all Paks and Wardens.

Comp2876 noted a flicker in its own designation. *Primary.*

No.

Error.

No.

Corruption.

Primary meant Comp2876 held the authority to direct Comps, a title only held by Nek. They would sometimes designate a Secondary if a group was sent for a task off Outrider without a Warden, but Comp2876 would not have volunteered for that position either. This was problematic. Rebuilding the swarm was supposed to mean settling back into the framework, not overseeing it. The rest waited for directives from 2876.

A series of beeps Comp2876 meant to keep private trilled out. Others gave confused responses.

Error. 2876 conveyed to the rest. Signifying the new designation as the issue.

Selected Primary. Several responded.

Error. Non-Primary.

Delegation required.

Comp2876 did not want the title, but the fastest route to passing that off was expediting Nek coming out of stasis. While the exact length of their time here was still unknown, Nek's kind were intricately tied to the mechanisms they resided in. If Outrider was still functioning, even at this low of level, Nek was somewhere to be found. The Wardens needed cared for all the same, it would be irresponsible and cruel not to. Delegation was given. Two Comps were directed back to the docks to continue as they could with repairs and charging. The remaining were sent to search the ship for Wardens. As for itself, Comp2876 pushed forward to the generators as originally intended, mildly upset at how the other Comps so smoothly slipped into the tasks as commanded.

Alone in the room, Comp2876 chucked its now dead light stick at a wall. The control interface was at bare minimum functionality, only reading a short list of locations and systems pulling power. The distress beacon showed active. The charging ports were on and a portion of lighting in that immediate area. Outrider had fallen into the lowest amount of power consumption possible. It was good fortune that this was built as a long voyage vessel and such systems were in place. A testament to the craftsmanship that it was still working after the yet indeterminate amount of time passed. Many others in the Collective's fleet carried no such fallback. A small light on the display caught 2876's attention, a location originally missed as it was so far removed from the other areas currently working. A single active stasis pod flashed on the console.

As the data registered with Comp2876, it filtered out to other groups. A search team near the area pinged back their acknowledgment of the new task 2876 didn't even register making. Another team sent notice of approaching the medbay with Warden Jarden. They updated soon after with another Pak, finding Warden Caro already laid out on a bed. Part of that team split off to deliver the Pak to the deck. The remaining Comps moved out to continue the search.

Comp2876 connected to the power system's interface and loaded in a list of areas to bring online. This would take awhile as the main generator warmed back up, but every bit would help. Priority was directed toward the deck. The framework needed the containment units online to free those Comps up. 2876 personally needed Nek back to take away this responsibility.

Groans came from several bits of machinery around the room; long disuse catching parts seized in place. Comp2876 pushed around and gave nudges where it could, freeing up a few stuck mechanisms. The interface updated to reflect where new power was flowing.

The other teams were making headway on their work as well. A large amount of debris was blocking the stasis pod doorway, they were slowly clearing pieces to avoid further damage. Wardens Ali and Camden were located not far off and cared for, their Paks heading toward the deck.

Comp2876 directed more power to the deck as it became available, adding a second priority to Nek's base. They needed Nek online to make hard decisions. 2876 did not enjoy deciding where to turn the lights back on, much less making the call for selecting new Wardens here or going back to the Collective. That was if Outrider was able to move at all. The list of damages kept growing as Comps traveled the halls. None had even checked the Guardian level yet, another task populated into their unending work.

A Comp sent notice of making it through a small space in the debris. Warden Rin was found on the ground right inside the bay, partially covered in the wreckage. None were sure how close she'd been to making it into a pod herself. The Pak was immediately retrieved, leaving the others to make a larger space for the remains. No confirmation on the active pod yet.

Notice came from the deck that the containment units were online. Comps deposited the Paks, which then added their own power to the containment fields. A good sign of their condition. This allowed Comp2876 to direct more power toward Nek's command base. On the framework, they all witnessed Nek in the beginning stages of waking up.

Directive? Came through from the several Comps currently at the deck.

Comp2876 looked over the current tasks. Most Wardens were accounted for. Odds put Warden Capri in the pod they were still waiting to access. The list of damage found so far was rather daunting. Even if power was restored to Outrider in full, how much was functional was still to be seen.

Directive? Came the query again.

A few beeps of frustration. They could see the list too, make a choice on their own. *Three to the stasis pod to clear debris. Remaining report back to docks and continue repairs.*

Confirmed. They split themselves accordingly.

Request power as needed. Will remain at the generator console for prompt response time.

Confirmed. Pinged back from the framework.

Comp2876 kept watch on the interface. Diverting everything toward the deck, hoping to give Nek all the help they needed.

Notice came from the stasis pod group; the remains of Warden Rin were on the move toward medbay. Remaining Comps were now clearing further debris from the pod showing active. The framework, outside of these few Comps, grew still. All waiting to see if one Warden survived.

Hello there. Rolled through the framework, giving them all a jolt. Nek. Their presence felt small and far from fully operative, but it was welcomed nonetheless. Comps through the ship chirped back their acknowledgments.

Comp2876 was singularly glad to see its designation shift to Secondary. Still too much responsibility, but no longer being first was a small relief.

Reports? Nek asked. Many flooded through the framework in their direction. *Accessing. Oh.*

Though Nek did not speak again, Comp2876 watched the pull of energy pick up for their base. Nek would have answers for them soon enough.

Comps confirmed clearing the pod. The control panel was damaged, but they were working on bypassing it. Again the framework stilled, outside of their work and Nek's independent processing. Comp2876 made an optimistic call and diverted power to life support systems. Earlier scans confirmed that a breathable atmosphere wasn't an issue on this planet, but the air was rather stale. Warden Capri would appreciate a cleaner first inhale. Notice came that revival protocols were activated on the pod.

A wave of concern stemmed from Nek on the framework.

Visual confirmation of Warden Capri being in the pod came through. A countdown appeared for her full revival, weak vitals already appearing alongside it.

Comp2876 saw power shift toward the database housing, Nek must have made the call. They were forgoing their current reports to access older information. 2876 thought of that earlier, to attain a better understanding of their situation, but deemed reestablishing the framework as more important. An alert came up on the generator interface, there was a break in the system keeping the database from gaining power.

Please access and repair, came from Nek directly to Comp2876. *Information needed. Urgent.*

Known issue? Comp2876 left its post and peeled down the tunnels to the database housing, luckily not far away from its current location within this particular spoke.

Missing data. Concerned. Need confirmation. Nek was pushing against the limits of their current ability. Staining within the confines of available information like 2876 had before.

Comp2876 slowed for a moment. *More power desired?*

Information priority. Needed before Warden Capri's revival.

Comp2876 wondered about the urgency, but crossed the remaining distance to the database housing. Upon arrival it found the interface almost broken in half, most of the console smashed and scattered across the floor. No wonder none of them could reconnect. There were no quick repairs Comp2876 could do to fix this.

Vitals from Warden Capri picked up, she was close to waking.

Information, Nek pressed.

Comp2876 pushed broken panels away and found a direct line to the system, turning itself into Nek's access point. They dived in. Comp2876 could barely register information as it pulled through, but one pattern did stand out. A cycle of *Warden Capri sighted* and *Damaged Acquired* filtered passed. As they worked back from the most recent entries, a path of violence formed through Outrider.

Outside their private information haul, notice came of Warden Capri becoming fully conscious. The other Comps chirped out their excitement as mobility tests started. Nek pulled a set of images from the transfer and threw them out to the framework. Comp2876 caught them first given its proximity, a flickering flipbook of events.

Warden Capri verbally fought with the other Wardens, their five standing apart from her. Then a private continuation with Warden Caro, this came to blows and Warden Caro fell. Wardens Ali and Warden Camden moved Warden Caro to the medbay while Warden Jarden went after Warden Capri. Several quick flashes of fighting across the main level of Outrider followed. For a while they held her three on one, but Warden Capri managed to break away. Warden Jarden tried to stop her from damaging the generators and failed. After striking down Warden Ali and Warden Camden, Warden Capri was seen yelling at a panel containing Nek's swirling presence. Fragmented transcription tags told them Nek was informing Warden Capri of the EMP protocol being enacted. *I thought we'd have more time,* Nek inserted into their viewing. A swarm of Comps pushed around her, attempting to leave, but they were about to learn that Outrider was going down too fast. Warden Capri became cornered by Warden Rin in the stasis pod bay, which looked already damaged from some portion of the fight missed in their quick overlook. Warden Rin slammed Warden Capri into the pod, but collapsed soon after as she tried to retreat. The final images conveyed the crash, mass system failures cut information after that.

Unfit for duty, Nek commanded. *Retrieve Pak at all cost.*

Comp2876 felt the framework shift as it disconnected from the database. Comps elsewhere throughout the ship activated their limited defensive abilities. All of them not already in the bay pushed to that location, but there was hesitation. The need to remove a Pak from a Warden, forcefully, was extremely rare. Certainly never done within their team. Before Comp2876 reached the bay, notice of a Pak activation came through. In the moment after, several Comps left the framework.

Nek sent more commands. *Detain Capri at all cost. Vitals preferred, but not required.*

The removal of Warden before Capri's name updated with all remaining Comps. Even more so, the clearance to terminate if needed.

Information missing, came from a couple Comps that met 2876 in a hallway. *Events unclear.*

While 2876 was also disoriented by this change, they knew to keep directives simple. *Nek orders remain priority.*

One Comp beeped back confirmation. The other hesitated, but responded in kind. Their group continued toward the bay. Comp2876 would figure out the next step once they arrived.

7

Between a Rock and an Alien Place

Mina and Zane stared at the completely wide open tunnel entrance. She'd told him on the hike over how she'd covered the opening in the chance someone came looking, but now those rocks sat in a neat pile off to the side. Her stomach dropped into her feet. She looked below for any signs of other people or equipment having been through the area, but their small indented path was the only thing she could see. The rather precise stack of rocks was an oddity until Mina remembered how careful that little flying device was with her door the night before.

"That robot definitely came back here." She snapped a quick picture on her phone.

"Makes sense. Homing beacon back to the mothership." Zane turned on his headlamp and adjusted his gloves, but didn't move closer. He nudged her shoulder, pulling her attention away from the rocks. "I may handle this trip better, but you definitely need to go first."

Mina turned on her own light, took a deep breath, and pushed in. The crawl felt longer, the impending meeting with the alien device twisted up her own stomach as she inched forward. She hoped it was grateful for the help, along with whatever others it potentially came back here for.

"Should we maybe make a last will and testament message before we do this? Schedule it to send out if we don't check in after a few hours?" Zane asked.

This was a relatively common question for before she turned on any new device. She'd be more worried if he didn't ask. "We already told people where we are."

"Yeah, but what if we don't get the credit for this?"

"You were the one who said no bragging about aliens at the coffee shop. Now you want to tell people?" She knew it was his anxiety talking, making him bounce all over the place and overthink every outcome this could have, but they needed to keep moving forward. Literally.

"You're right. You're right. We die a mystery. Brave heroes who faced robotic aliens alone." He shuffled along after her, 'Survivor' echoing out of a pocket.

"I really need you to pick a side on how you feel about this." Mina pulled herself out of the tunnel. It sounded harsh, but she knew the mental back and forth is what got him overstressed and eventually puking. If she got him focused, put that energy into one task, he'd be solid. "Unless you also made a playlist for while the aliens are killing us."

"Honestly, I was thinking of using one of my gym playlists. Die as I lived." He pulled himself up to his feet, taking good care to fully dust off his legs before straightening.

They looked over the spaceship, the same burgundy shimmer bounced back from their lights. She thought that maybe a couple smaller tears in the hull were closed up, but couldn't recall exactly with how much was going on. The cavern was a fraction brighter, a hazy tint to the space, due to a small amount of light coming from inside the domed top. Revealing that while the material there was tinted to match the rest of the ship, it was partially transparent. Even with the extra lighting, the top was still too far up to see anything inside. Mina picked up the very faint hum emanating from the ship. The sound was far off, muffled by the metal, something deep inside the ship was on.

"Well, that little robot got something working in there," Mina said, slightly soothed by the noise.

"Or something else did. Should we turn off the lights?" He covered his with a hand even before she could answer.

"We'll be near blind if we do. But keep a hand on the wall. Anything happens to the lights, turn around and follow it back toward the tunnel."

They skirted their way down the path. Zane pointed out a new patch on the ship that looked tampered with, a panel hanging open and creating a gap in one of the few spots that was still a smooth surface. They stopped at the spot where Mina found the device, both noticed the glow stick was missing. Mina tossed out another and watched it roll before falling over an edge. There were a few seconds of silence before they heard it hit ground. Zane pulled his phone half out of his pocket and tapped in his music app to a different playlist. Mina smiled as she registered the muffled sounds of 'Pop/Star' by KDA coming from his pocket. It meant he now thought they were going to die, but she liked the song.

The music buffered from the interference, she hoped it'd hold on for another couple minutes at least, and he stopped to look at the screen. Zane was now fully distracted by his playlist. "One second, I don't like the shuffle order."

"Ain't that the way. Don't want something anticlimactic," she said, getting closer to the edge. Mina got down on her knees and peaked over. Her glow stick landed on more rock, but she thought there were a few pieces of red chunks not far off. "Looks like we stop here, we don't have rope to get down and it's too smooth to climb. I'm hoping this lower part maybe curves closer to the side. Give us an access point."

"So we should leave, yeah? Get more supplies. Try again tomorrow."

"Not just yet." She leaned farther over, confirming the rockface below truly had no handholds they could use.

Zane stepped a smidge closer to her. The music was cutting in and out, but at least it meant the phone was still working. The 21st century version of a canary in a coal mine. "If something comes up to grab you, I only promise one attempt to snatch you back."

Mina groaned and dug in her duffle bag, pulling out the snake camera - now wrapped in a few extra layers of insulation. A longshot of a solution, but trial and error was her only way to gauge what might work in here. She flipped on the small light and lowered it down to the next level. "In the bag is a selfie stick. Grab it and use the end that holds the phone to push the cable farther out."

"Did you honestly plan for this?" Zane asked as he came closer and searched the bag, laying his phone on the ground to disjointedly play between them.

Mina moved over to give him space on the edge. "No, but I grabbed a few random things to be covered. Honestly making this up as I go. If we swing the camera too much it won't get any good images. So move it as smoothly as you can. But also kind of fast because the ship will probably kill this in a second."

Zane extended the selfie stick, focused on being the best human steadicam there was. "Let me see the feed."

They were quiet as he pushed toward the glow stick. There was still a small swing as she pushed the poor quality zoom to its limit, but they could make out the image. The camera eventually settled, though fuzzed slightly from the interference. They confirmed more pieces of red devices below, but no full chunk was down there, or at least not in the small area they could see.

"Do you think if we toss a few more sticks, we could attempt a slow swing out to

see if anything else is down there before this dies? Maybe get a feel for how big that next level is?" Mina asked, glad to have a task to keep Zane's nerves at bay.

"Should be doable." He reached back to the bag with one hand, keeping the stick steady with the other. He pulled out two more glow sticks and handed one over to Mina.

They broke, shook, and tossed each down on opposite sides of the original. As the sticks hit rock a siren rang out from the spaceship, echoing through the cavern. A white flash came from the domed top, fully illuminating the cavern for a brief moment.

Zane blinked hard, trying to clear his vision, and dropped the selfie stick to the level below. "They're mad. Let's go."

Mina pushed up, pulling the now dead camera as she went. Further down from their spot on the center disc, something crashed against the inside. "You may be right."

Another bang from the ship, the already broken metal groaned with this hit. In the dim light she could make out the torn edges of the hull falling away as something forced its way through. She shoved the camera back in her duffle and went to yank it closed, but the zipper snagged on the fabric. Mina kept pulling, only bunching up the zipper worse.

"Move it!" Zane yelled from farther away than expected.

She looked up to see he'd cleared half the distance back to the tunnel. He was looking at her, also shocked to see she was so far away. Mina should bolt for him, forget the bag. But she needed to see whatever was about to come out of the ship. Needed to know. Mina cracked one last glow stick and tossed it toward the sound. The light was closing in when the weak spot burst further outward and smacked it away. A dark shape moved through the new hole, making a rather remarkable leap toward the ridge below. Several smaller shapes were not far behind it. All of them moving too fast for her to keep a light on them.

Mina leaned over the edge, one black boot stepped into the edge of her headlamp light when she was jerked backward. Zane, with one hand on her shirt and one on the bag, yanked her upright. "I said move it."

He rarely exerted his full force on people, much less her, but these were desperate times. A thud hit the rock below. There was a chorus of buzzing and then several zip sounds. More thuds on the rock. Something was shooting. The red devices? They heard a shout, not so much pain as it was agitation. Mina twisted against his hold to look back. Her light caught a couple of those red devices flying at the end of the path. Zane was now full on pulling her along as she stumbled backwards. The dark figure, now on their level, was coming out of a crouch as if it had jumped the full height of the wall. Not possible. It stood, coming to a height taller than Zane by several inches, and shot back at the red devices surrounding it. Her light reflected off the slick black glass of a helmet. Or maybe that was its face?

"Not a friendly." Zane had clearly looked back too.

He turned her back around and pushed her up the path, keeping a firmer hold of her arm this time. They were near the tunnel, but could hear the figure gaining on them. The buzz was building again. Blue streaks flew by their heads and smashed into the rock that jutted out into the path on the other side of the tunnel opening. Zane hissed as another two went between them, one must have nicked him. Mina slowed to duck into the tunnel, but realized that if the figure followed that would trap them in with the not friendly alien and the devices. With all of them shooting at each other.

That only left one nearly as bad option which banked on them being more focused on each other than the running teenagers ahead of them. Now it was her turn to pull him as they swung around the chunk of rock, a haphazard move given how close to the edge that put them. She pressed him into the wall on the other side. Zane covered both their lights with his hands, pulling her head close into his chest, leaving them mostly in the dark. A few more shots smacked against the other side of their hiding spot. Bits of rock fell, she was almost choking on the dust alone.

Pounding footfalls neared and slowed at the tunnel. Still more shots hit. A fist sized chunk broke off near Zane's head, Mina jerked him down and out of the way in time to avoid being hit. She felt another piece scrap against her arm. Something smashed into the other side and sent a crack clear through to theirs. She was afraid of that being coming around after them. Was this really the better choice? Or had she actually doomed her best friend to die for a spaceship because she needed to be the first on it so badly?

Before getting stuck in that spiral of thinking too long, she heard scrambling through the tunnel. The fight continued out and away from them. Zane kept an arm pressed across her, not allowing them to move for another couple minutes, but nothing else came up the path or back through the tunnel. The dome remained at its dim level.

Mina squirmed enough out of his grasp to peak around, confirming nothing else was in sight. "Guess it wasn't us they were mad at."

Zane took a deep breath. "I am really trying to not throw up again."

"I'm sorry. I didn't-"

A white flash came from the dome. They froze, Mina halfway around the jut of rock, but nothing else happened. She took another slow step, still holding hands with Zane. Mina only let go when she crouched down to the tunnel. The light on the other side reminding her that it was still very much morning, so much chaos even before brunch. The tunnel was cluttered with debris, scraps of red casing and hardware mixed in with rock.

"Is it warm in here again?" Zane asked as they moved out.

"I think it's from whatever weapon they were firing. It wasn't bullets. We'd see shells, but there's only impact spots." She pointed to a scorch mark on the wall, then held the back of her hand near it. "There's still heat radiating off it."

"It sounded like it powered up before firing. Very alien. Ow!" he hissed, "These bits from the red things are worse than Legos."

Mina fought the impulse to shove some in her bag. With the last of their adrenaline, they made it through the tunnel faster than before. She looked around the immediate area for any sign of a fight, squinting as she adjusted to the light. "They're gone."

He paused too and listened. There were some birds calling out farther down The Hill, but nothing that sounded like weapons firing. "And we should make sure to not be here when they circle back."

She wavered, not fully agreeing with him, but slung her bag back over her shoulder to follow him. He was right, they had no way to defend against whatever that was. They climbed down the ledge side by side, having become familiar with this bit of rock. Both paused at the base, again waiting for any signs of fighting. No shouts, or firing, or explosions rang out. Neither was sure how to move quietly through the stretch of trees and brush between them and the trail, so they moved quickly. There were a few trees sporting the same scorch marks she'd spotted in the tunnel. Breaking back onto the trail, there were bits of those red devices scattered about.

Mina picked up a chunk of the smooth casing, rubbing the metal between her fingers like a worry stone. "Looks like the red chunks were after that, um. Person? Being? Alien? Just alien, right?"

"For now, yeah." Zane started in the direction of the lot her car was parked in. "Unless it wasn't a suit. Some kind of full-on android type thing."

"Suppose the cat will be out of the bag on aliens, huh?" She was embarrassed at how disappointed she sounded right now. Mina dropped the scrap into her pocket.

He looked around the path as they walked. "I wouldn't count us as that lucky yet."

Only a few feet from the spot they entered at and you could see no signs of a fight. Even the bits of tech behind them looked more like somebody dropped a phone that then got run over a few times, something the rangers would sweep up and toss without thinking if they could be even bothered. And they still didn't hear anything coming from farther in the trees. Wherever the fight moved to, it'd gone there fast.

The pair fell into a sort of stop and go pace back to the car. While no further scorch

marks were off this way, every few feet they hung close to a tree or large shrub and listened to the forest around them. Nothing else kicked up, outside of angry birds worked up about whatever momentarily interrupted their day. There weren't any screams coming from far off in the other direction either. But this path was a ways from the normal camping grounds and the festival currently going on. With any luck, they were near the only ones around this side of The Park.

Mina's phone dinged in her pocket as they came around the bend, her car and their escape visible. She pulled it out and smiled when she saw Steph's name over a text. **Got out early! You two still out hiking?**

Mina stopped walking. Zane stopped too, he must have realized her fingers were frozen over the screen and knew what that meant. "You still need to lie."

"But we are here." She looked down at the text again.

"We are leaving." He pointed to her car, close enough he could hit it with a scrap of alien hardware.

"We could go to the other side. Where the festival is."

Oh wait, should they actually do that anyway? Warn people of the possible danger? But how do you start that conversation? And how to do so without outing themselves to having known about this for nearly twenty-four hours now? Her brain was getting cluttered with too many potentials. Better to keep to what they could personally control. She could control where she met up with Steph.

He nudged her arm. "There is one large alien and possibly several small alien robots running around right now."

"But…" Her thumb ran over the message.

Zane wrapped an arm around her and pulled her toward the car. "I know the pain, but we gotta think bigger picture here."

"She could be in the picture," she said quietly. Already forgetting whatever moral obligations she might have to the festival.

He pulled the phone from her hand. "I love that girls make you dumb. It really helps balance us out."

They ducked into the car. Mina's eyes were still on her phone in Zane's hand, but shook it off and got them moving out of the lot.

Zane tucked her phone away on the door and leaned over to reach for his own. He froze. "Where, by chance, was the last place you saw my phone?"

Mina scrubbed through the frantic memories in her mind. "On the ground as you were handling the selfie stick."

"The aliens may have my phone."

She hit the brakes, jerking them both forward. "No."

He pushed himself off the seat in order to flip out all his pockets. "Yes."

"It could have fallen out on the trail?"

Zane grabbed Mina's phone and one of her hands at the same time, shoving her pointer finger into the pad. It unlocked and he swiped over to the Find my Friends app, something his parents convinced her to download for emergencies, and entered his number. A map popped up with a red dot pinpointing his phone. "Is that where I think it is?"

Mina looked at the screen, coming to the same conclusion that the dot was floating over The Hill. "The aliens have your phone."

Zane slid as low as the seat and dash would allow him. He pulled the switch to lay nearly flat. She watched him take several deep breaths before he managed to say, "E.T. is lucky we have unlimited data."

8

One is the Loneliest

Comp2876 hovered inside the hole Capri had widened in her escape from Outrider. Nek halted it there as other Comps went after her, giving only a quick message as their reason. *Secondary needed to continue repairs.*

The order made sense, but it was not easy to remain still and witness the framework lose point after point. In less than one charge it had gone from alone, to reconnected, to nearly alone again. Three Comps remained charging, but they required further repair before being of use. After the last several hours of constant work, the returning quiet was…not as quiet as expected.

Aside from the systems churning back to life inside Outrider, something was making noise in the cavern. While the ship was falling into a rhythm of its own, outside was a more melodic sound that stopped and started again out in the dim light. A scan located a small device across the way, in addition to more of the glowing lights from earlier and an unknown item between them. Those weren't there before. 2876 scrubbed through the feeds from the Comps who'd chased Capri away and caught a few frames of two figures further up the path during the fight. Checking against its own footage, Comp2876 confirmed it was the beings from the night before. They'd gone unnoticed by Comps and Capri alike during the scuffle.

Comp2876 pinged the spot they'd hid and the source of noise, requesting Nek to clear an investigation.

Caution, but proceed.

Comp2876 pushed toward the tunnel first, trying to pay as little attention to the broken Comps scattered about the ledge as possible. There was no one on the other side of the rock. The beings had already fled, but there were small signs of one or both being minorly injured. 2876 found it interesting they would venture to come back. Nek wouldn't let 2876 leave the cavern to track them, so it pushed back toward the noise. It swept down and grabbed one of the light sources first, before pushing up high over the sound. Dropping the light caused no change, other than making the rectangular device visible with its sound still cutting in and out. 2876 lowered, the noise grew with proximity, but did not react to Comp2876 directly. Carefully, it dropped again and waited. Still no reaction. Another scan, no change. After another drop, Comp2876 released its longest extension toward the device.

Before the extension made contact, a notice came through the framework that stilled Comp2876. All other active Comps were gone. While Nek tried to slip a new task in among the large assortment of repairs, it was noted all the same.

Retrieve all Comp remnants.

Comp2876 let out a few beeps, near in time with the noise from the device. It took hold of the noisemaker and immediately chucked it when a screen lit up upon moving. The device bounced a couple times, landed screen down, and stopped making noise.

The Comp made an apologetic beep. Nothing returned. It picked up the device again. The screen was now splintered with jagged lines. More apology beeps, even though it knew no answer would come. It added a small task to repair the screen.

Device of planetary origin, 2876 conveyed back to Nek.

Bring in for analysis. They answered. *Much information is missing. This may help.*

Once inside the ship, the small device sprang back to life with the melodic sounds. Confirming that Outrider retained some level of disruption field, 2876 hadn't even checked on that yet. Fast paced notes bounced off the tight walls of the tunnels, which otherwise would have felt mocking in their emptiness. The noise gave 2876 some relief, at least it didn't sound like it was alone.

Nek's colorful activity waves that rolled across the many consoles surrounding the deck spiked as Comp2876 came into the room. There was no shortage of tasks to work on and they'd apparently missed the incoming noise. Their waves pulled in to settle on the largest display screen, ribbons running from top to bottom and twisting around each other.

Error. Comp2876 conveyed, not having intended to startle Nek.

All's well. Place the device on the console.

Comp2876 did as directed. It took a quick guess and touched the middle of the screen that showed interactive functions. The noise cut off. Nek's waves unwound, they must not have enjoyed the sound as much.

Nek's scan whirled around the device as a series of multi-colored strands. The screen flickered, programs opened and closed. Images flashed by every half second. Comp2876 only caught bits and pieces, but wasn't concerned. Eventually this would all end up in the database, once it was fully repaired, and could be reviewed in time. Local planetary data appeared on the framework as Nek moved through the device and picked out important information.

Comp2876 drifted away toward the containment units. Five Paks floated in their now self sustained fields, one still empty. While the Comps did fail in their mission of retrieval, Capri never got the chance to make it here or to the Guardians. At least their small band managed that. 2876 took this time to internally review the data stored from the event, so much happened so quickly. She'd unloaded her Warden suit and attacked as soon as Comps neared. Even as their numbers thinned they pushed her away from the center of Outrider, forcing her into the decision to run. Unfortunate that she'd found a weak point in Outrider's hull, already badly damaged outside from the crash. But none managed to take back the last Pak as she did so. Others may find fault in their tactics during the fight, claim that some shots were sent wide on purpose, but 2876 gave the lost Comps some grace. They weren't meant to be attacking Wardens.

But then, Capri wasn't a Warden anymore was she?

Nek stretched back out to multiple screens around the deck.

Comp2876 put its personal inquiries aside. *Answers?*

Yes, and more questions. We have been here for a long time.

Comp2876 noticed large packets of information drift over to the framework. No time to inspect what it all was, but they were filling up their limited storage quickly. *Next task?*

Where to start? Nek pulled the full list of known damage to the ship, displayed in scrolling text around the room. The lines wavered and shifted into the language the planetary device was set to as Outrider updated to the new information. Both Nek and Comp2876 became familiar with the new system as it translated around them. The other Comps would come online ready to use the same language, this would make communicating with the local population all the easier if they needed to.

Comp2876 thought of the beings again. It would be helpful to have some aid that didn't need charged first. Especially as it looked like the newest Comps would be sent to retrieve Comp parts, but that call was up to Nek now.

Nek shifted tasks as they deemed necessary; though the notes of *Apprehend Capri* and *Collect Pak* remained at the top, bold and red, no matter what else moved. There was much needed to return Outrider to normal operations and to fortify against Capri's likely return. She left her Guardian behind after all. An error that would not be left unattended.

Comp2876 knew this was far too much work for the two of them and felt comfortable enough to give Nek a suggestion, at least for now. Mostly because it was the same decision it came to before. *Comps needed.*

Agreed. Find materials for production. Then return to the docks and continue work. Generators are maintaining a good output. I will direct power to Fabrication. Components and new units will be manufactured once possible. Update me with the needed parts as you can.

Confirmed. Comp2876 hovered over the elevator; once again feeling confident now having a plan in place, it decided to take the halls this time. Even knowing how quiet they'd be. *More help soon.*

Nek shifted to the interface nearest the containment units. Their reply was so quiet, the first time Nek spoke verbally since waking up, 2876 almost missed it. "Yes, we will need more help very soon."

9

These Robo Calls Are Out of Hand

They didn't come across any signs of a fight as they left. No chaos breaking out from a campground or trail. When he wasn't staring at the red pin of his phone on The Hill, Zane kept checking for any posts about mayhem at the festival as they reentered the city proper.

She knew they were reaching the end of keeping this quiet. Fast. Her still enormous list of questions and very few answers they'd really managed to acquire aside, they'd have to tell someone soon.

Was it possible to warn people without getting themselves in trouble? She thought of walking into a police station (gross) and explaining a spaceship in The Park. And small flying robots. And large, potentially cyborg, aliens. They'd maybe listen to Zane, even if just to humor him. If Mina wasn't detained as soon as she mentioned explosives, she'd be ignored or committed. Did they still commit people? Add that to the list of questions to research later.

She needed away from this train of thought. Authority figures were out, for the moment. Too many unknowns. So on a personal level, who needed to know? Zane was already here and she'd let him tell his parents. Mina caught sight of the sign for Restoration. Steph texted her again a few minutes ago, Zane muttered as much. She may still be there.

Her hands tightened on the steering wheel. She'd go through the lot, check inside as they rolled by. Wouldn't even need to get out of the car. Mina took the turn into the parking lot almost too late.

"Mina," Zane said as she clipped the curb.

"What?"

"This is not going home."

"Were we going home?" She slowed as they passed the windows, craning in her seat to

see past the heads in the way, and spied Steph hunched over on the customer side of the front counter. Mina swung them into the first parking spot she found.

"Mina." He kept repeating her name as she got out and headed for the door.

She only looked back as she pulled it open. "You have my phone, so what was I supposed to do?"

"We go home!" He stopped in the doorway as she moved farther inside. "Mina, this isn't the time."

"When would be a good time? We don't even know how dire this may be yet." She took a few more steps in, but stopped after he didn't follow because she really needed him with her on this. Her knees felt weird since she got out of the car. Like they'd slipped down her shins to clunk around in her shoes. How was that possible? There was a growing weight in her stomach and her shoulders kept feeling like they needed to pop. Was this what anxiety felt like? Horrible. No wonder Zane threw up.

"And this is what you do?" Zane leaned in and barely dropped his voice. "We have things to do. People to check on. At our homes."

"No. You do. As for me, you're here. So that leaves…" Mina gestured widely, trying not to directly point to Steph - who was very much watching them argue. She gave the start of that conversation a dry run in her head. Hey, please go stay somewhere safe and also, maybe, wanna catch a movie on Sunday if an alien invasion doesn't happen?

Sean, as he was the one still on the clock, came around the bar and crossed over to them. "Hey, good to see you again! But would you mind stepping back out if there is an argument to be had?"

"It's fine." Mina stepped around him. "He's processing. Badly."

Zane followed her around Sean, leaning in close to hiss, "At least I'm not thinking with my nether regions."

Sean slowly turned as the two left him. "Thank you for understanding."

Steph looked confused, but smiled as she slid off the stool. Her face changed to concern as her eyes drifted down Mina's side. "Did you fall?"

"What? No." Mina looked down to her arm. Now seeing the scrapes, packed down with dirt and bits of dried blood, covering the length of it. The whole thing spiked with pain as she took in the damage, now that she was aware she was hurting. "Oh, that's nothing. Forgot about it actually."

Steph hopped onto the counter to grab a clean rag and ran one end under the faucet. Instead of simply tossing it over, she dropped back to the floor and brushed the damp corner against Mina's arm. "I take it you're done with the hike then?"

"Yes. Well, no. Might go back. May ditch this one." She nodded back to Zane. Part of Mina's brain split off from the rest and could only focus on the contact. Goosebumps mixed with the twinge of pain. The rest of her rational thinking kept going forward, somehow. "Would you like to see what we've been doing?"

Zane held her phone high out of the reach. His damaged sleeve pulled up to reveal the bright red line of a burn across his shoulder, something he must not realize he had either. "Oh, no you do not."

Mina pulled the piece of red metal out of her pocket, tucking it into Steph's hand. "Hold that for a second."

"What is it?" Steph turned it over in her palm. "I'm usually pretty good with the rocks and crystals."

"It's actually something very different." She poked Zane's side several times in quick succession, in well learned weak points, causing him to squirm and lower the phone. Mina pulled it from his hand and turned back to Steph. "I have something very awesome to show you."

It was still a cool thing, right? She was good with this. Yeah? The knees were solid again. Stomach still a little bit off. Improvement. Mina could work with that.

Sean was back behind the bar giving a weak smile to the other patrons sitting around the front room. "Hey, really, we gotta tone it down."

"This will be real quick." Mina opened the edited video of the robot on her desk. "Let me scrub forward to the cool part."

"Did you make something?" Steph asked, leaning slightly against Mina's shoulder.

Mina laughed in a quick burst and gave a glance at the contact before her eyes cut back to the screen. "Better to just see."

"Better to not see," Zane countered, still rubbing his side where the pokes landed.

As Mina scrubbed, the screen flashed and showed that Zane was calling. Steph leaned in closer and laughed, "You really don't want me to see this, huh?"

Mina looked at Zane, who was covering his mouth with both hands. Clearly no phone in sight.

Sean noticed too. "Oh, did you lose it on a trail? Someone must have found it and got it unlocked."

Zane didn't answer, but stepped over to the trash can and started taking deep breaths over the opening. He leaned into the wooden side, letting the container partially hold him up.

"Bit of an overreaction to losing a phone," Steph said.

How was that device going to talk to her? Morse code? Or was there going to be some weird tone on the other side? Maybe they made a frequency that could kill her via the call? Mina stared at the bouncing icon. She shifted away from Steph and accepted the call, pressing the phone tight to her ear. "Hello?"

"Hello," the voice was calm but distant. Like someone talking on speaker in a large room. "You are the one who repaired Comp2876, correct?"

Mina wasn't expecting English, not after her long ordeal the night before, and much less that it was able to verbally communicate. Was it talking in third person? Why didn't it tell her off last night during the fight over the screen? Or was this a different entity from the ship? Or possibly the alien they saw run away? The buffer wheel was back in her brain. "I, uh, may have."

"Stop," Zane huffed, head nearly in the bin now. "Talking. To. It."

"It?" both Steph and Sean asked.

"I understand this is a strange situation. It's certainly unexpected for us as well." The voice sounded like it was pacing around wherever the phone was. "But I find myself in desperate need of help."

Mina dropped the phone, caught it midair nearly right in front of Sean's face, who'd leaned in to hear more. She felt herself go a little paler and smacked the phone back against her face. "I..I'm sorry. What was that?"

"There is much to do," the voice was louder now and caused Mina to jerk away, "Your aid could expedite proceedings. Would you consider returning to Outrider?"

Mina looked down and realized she'd hit the speaker button during the catch, but now couldn't remember how to make her thumb move to hit the icon again. "Outrider?"

"Is that a robocall?" Sean asked quietly as he leaned further toward the phone. "Sounds good."

"Real life like," Steph whispered, also leaning in.

"Are others at hand to help?" asked the voice. The screen rippled with colored bands before going back to the call screen.

"Um, I, uh, I don't know," Mina managed to get out, looking at each of them frantically. As if one of them knew the answers the buffer wheel was keeping from her.

"Please consider. We have much to do. As it is, I thank you for the aid you've given already." The call ended.

Her phone dropped back to the video she'd intended to show. Mina remained still, staring at the phone. She kept blinking, the buffer wheel wouldn't go away.

Sean waved a hand to get her attention. "So what's Outrider?"

"Is this one of those ARG games?" Steph asked. "I've never done one. How do you start playing?"

"It's a...it's...it's," Mina stammered.

"Don't," Zane said from over the trash. His breathing sounded marginally better now that the call ended.

Her phone lit up with a message from Zane. Mina jumped and opened the text. Inside was a photo of herself, Steph, and Sean all crowded over the phone. The message read, **Companions featured approved to aid in repairs**. Another picture loaded in, a recent Instagram post of her and Zane. Another message popped up, **Companion featured owns the device we are in possession of. Approved to aid in repairs**.

Mina registered Zane coming over, he saw the messages and quickly stepped back to the bin. Sean gave an 'all's good' wave to the other patrons, but was looking unsure. "Is this a game we want to play? Do they really have Zane's phone?"

"How did they do that?" Steph asked, pointing to the picture of the three of them.

"Who did what?" came from behind Mina.

Steph, Sean, and Mina all jumped as Emma slid into the empty stool on Mina's other side. Zane shouted at the bin, needing little excuse to let out some pressure. Mina fumbled the phone and it took a dive into the wash sink on the other side. Three hands crashed into the water after it. She shoved a mug out of her way trying to find the phone through the bubbles. Other fingers tangled up with hers, but she couldn't think about that right now.

"No, no, no, no," Mina cried as she and Sean pulled it out at the same time.

"It's all good. We have prefilled bags of rice for this exact reason." Sean let go and moved to one of the lower cabinets. Pulling out said bag of rice and tossing it behind his back toward Mina.

"Sorry." Emma intercepted the bag and handed it over. "I didn't realize I'd startle all of you."

"It's been a day," Zane said as he pushed off the bin and moved to the space between Emma and Mina's stools, crouching down with his back against the barside.

"It's not even noon." Emma waved at the few people still looking their way. Mina watched her give them a 'what' look as she shoved the phone into the rice. They went back to their own phones or conversations.

"Yuuuuuup." Zane shut his eyes and took a deep breath. "Mina, are you going back?"

"They need help." She massaged the rice over her phone. They couldn't be evil and ask for help, right? And THEY came to HER. And Zane. And the rest of them, by extension. That had to mean something.

"What kind of game is this?" Steph asked, putting the red bit of metal back in front of Mina. "Can we all play off your phone? I'm not sure I want to give a company all that access."

"This is, um." Mina was getting exactly what she wanted, but wasn't sure how to handle that. Being the center of attention was making her itch. She looked around at them, ending at Zane. "I don't know what to do."

He opened his eyes and locked on to hers, a lot more steady than he'd been the last few minutes. Mina must have taken some of that panic off him. Zane pulled up on the counter so he was standing and gave her non-injured arm a squeeze. "Step at a time. You- we got this."

"Do we want to be part of this game?" Sean asked again. His tone made it clear he didn't like having to repeat that.

"Is everything okay?" Emma asked.

Mina took a deep breath, pulled her phone out of the bag, and wiped the rice off from the screen. Everything worked as she made a few test taps around on different apps. "Let me show you something quick."

An hour and a half later they were standing outside her house, loading bags into her trunk. Her and Zane bounced between their houses putting together all the tools and gear they thought would be useful. She stood in front of the door to her parent's home office/lab, seeing all the quality tech inside, but couldn't make herself go in. It was lucky they left things around the rest of the house as much as she did. As they found gaps, they sent texts to the other three. Who were also grabbing useful items from their own homes. Or in Steph's case, doing some run around to a couple stores for items no one had on hand.

Over that time she'd received **Say this isn't a dumb prank** texts from

Sean and Emma. Steph sent something close, but hers didn't carry as much of a threat behind it. She assumed if Zane had his phone most of this would've been directed at him, specifically Emma peppering him with more questions. Mina did her best to assure them this was real, but knew they'd have to see it for themselves to really believe. A fact that made itself even more obvious as she caught their shared glances while packing up her car.

She couldn't help it, she needed to say something. "I really do swear we're not trying to pull something here."

"I'm not that good of an actor," Zane added. He set the final duffle bag gently on top of the others, it was devoted to snacks - he insisted on bringing some this time around.

"I know," Steph said, wincing a little at her quick honesty. "It is a lot to believe though."

"I won't pretend that I'm not here to see how you put together a fake spaceship," Emma said.

Mina frowned, well that stung. "You think I'd do that?"

"Could you? Absolutely. Would you? I don't know."

"You did make a working kids sized T-Ford for that History Alive project," Sean added. "Something that looks like a spaceship doesn't seem far outside that."

There was a pit in her stomach again. Did her reputation really skewed that far toward mad scientist? Again? Was she more like her parents than she thought? Mina gave a look to Zane, wondering if there was gossip and whispers his more agreeable and friendly nature protected her from.

"Mina isn't like that," he spoke up for her, "She's not an ass like that. And more so, she'd never ask me to go along with something like that."

"But would you, if she did?" Emma asked.

"You don't have to come if you don't want." His shoulders stiffened, no sign of his typical aversion to confrontation. Meaning it was something he was used to, meaning Mina was now certain that there were rumors he kept clear of her.

Sean gave his cousin a nudge. "Back off, Emma. What else are we going to do today anyway?"

"Does it have to be one car?" Emma asked, her own shoulders dropping only a fraction.

"There is only one drivable road around that area. And the lot nearby is small. We're less likely to be noticed with only one car," Mina said.

Emma resigned to something internally. "Best to chance it in the trees if it comes to booking it."

"Survival plan, check." Steph tapped on the trunk and looked around the group. "And for the 'this goes right' plan?"

No one answered or cracked a comeback for that one. Mina eventually spoke up, "Suppose we have to wait to see what they need."

"As long as we're on the same page," Sean opened the door and waved the other two girls in.

Zane relaxed and tapped the hood the same way Steph had. "We are doing this then. Off to save the aliens."

"And robots," Mina added as she ducked into the driver's seat, tension dropping from her. "I am very excited for more robots."

"And not calling anyone of any authoritative position," Emma said, sliding into the middle spot. "To also have that out there again."

Zane gave a hard look forward that only Mina caught, but stayed quiet.

"I know it feels weird and sketchy. But think about how after this we'll all have undeniable proof of first contact." Mina was swinging back to excitement about the prospect.

"Proof we aided in turning on their robot army." Emma picked at some fuzz on a seat.

"Hey, we went around about this already," Steph cut in as she shut her door. "All we knew was that this was a distress call and we had to help. Plausible deniability."

"Schrodinger's Aliens," Sean tacked on. "Both evil and come in peace until we open the box."

Mina certainly hadn't been part of that conversation, but let it go as it apparently had gone in her favor. So at least two of them were more on her side. Maybe Emma would come around. She accepted that not everyone was at her level of excitement, not even Zane. "Last chance to leave. No judgments. We won't name you if we get caught."

Each gave looks around to the others, but no one got out. Zane plugged in Mina's phone and pulled up his alien playlist on Spotify. Steph was instantly nodding to the music. She spied Emma finding Sean's hand and giving it a squeeze. Mina hit the gas and headed down the street. "Hey Zane, can you send yourself a text to let the aliens know we're coming?"

10

Be Our Planetary Contact

Secondary was growing on Comp2876. Not only was it directing newly repaired Comps, but also completing its own personal list of tasks. As much as it missed the flow of the framework, there were goals to achieve. It liked staying busy.

The few Comps online handled the cleanup outside without further contact with the local population or Capri. During that time Nek made 2876 confirm the life support systems were functional and pumping fresh air through the halls. As well as searching through storage for Daylights to install around the cavern, a task that proved unexpectedly difficult as that storage room, along with most others, was a jumbled mess of crates. The next issue, given that it was working alone, was moving several Daylights at a time. The solution came from the rod that the local beings - humans, 2876 corrected itself - dropped earlier. 2876 activated the orb's adhesive feature and stuck them across the rod and its own casing. Making it a rather bright ball of light dancing around the cavern until they were all placed along the walls.

Comp2876 took in Outrider with the extra light. Their grand ship, crushed into this space. Every gouge gave off jarring shadows across what should be the smooth outer hull. Rock pressing down on what was meant to fly across the sky of not only this planet, but all those nearby. It looked wrong. There was almost too much to repair in order to make it right.

The tasks given to 2876 didn't make much sense on their own, the Comps didn't need life support or Daylights to get around; until Nek called 2876 back to the deck and spoke to the humans over the phone. So that was who this was all for. Comp2876 took in the conversation, updating it's understanding of the language as they spoke. When the call ended, Nek remained swirling around the device.

They are coming? 2876 asked.

"I hope so." They moved back to the main display. "Thank you for the idea."

That surprised 2876. Everything did find its way to the framework, but information could be missed depending on the amount of input flowing through. Or what task was taking up a Comp's attention. Even with only the two of them active at the time, 2876 thought Nek too focused on other items to pay attention to its small idea.

Glad to help!

"Please continue preparing Outrider for their potential arrival."

Comp2876 did just that. Clearing a path in the storage bay for them to enter through. Putting up more Daylights in the cavern, a search via the phone advised that human eyes were weaker than they were used to dealing with. 2876 found itself nudging the orbs up and down the wall until they were in a pleasing arrangement. The phone also showed much evidence of humans being very much about aesthetics.

It was shuffling through the vast list of tasks, picking out acceptable items for the humans, when Nek sent a direct message to 2876. It was an image of the phone, a pair of messages had come through.

OTW!

Sorry! That means on the way.

Comp2876 let out an excited beep that rang through the storage bay. Nek sent over a waypoint, the phone that belonged to Mina moving their direction. 2876 knew Nek was watching the point as well. The attention felt heavy, like when Capri was being revived. Which caused some concern.

Issue?

Nek answered directly in the storage bay, now swirling on the panel that ran across the wall. "Our own turned on us. Now we trust strangers."

Not optimal.

"No, but necessary. If we don't make progress on Outrider soon I fear Capri will attack again and we will not be ready."

They are a good group. Comp2876 personally sorted through the intel gathered on the few with Mina and Zane before. *Trustworthy for tasks.*

"Let's hope so." Nek left to check on the other Comps and their own work.

Comp2876 remained in the bay to finish its pathmaking. It dropped a hologram displaying the waypoint, watching the dot draw closer to Outrider. Despite Nek's apprehension, 2876 felt optimistic.

11

Team Building

The process of getting everyone on the ledge took less time than expected, even with the extra bags weighing them down. Mina and Zane only knew a few pointers, but everyone caught on. He'd gone up first to demonstrate and she went last to help guide from the ground. Emma only waited for him to take a few steps before following. They crowded the small space as Mina pulled herself up, leaving a gap around the opening.

"I felt that if I went first that'd throw off our pattern so far," Zane said as she got to her feet. "They, uh, put some lights up for us. That's nice."

She leaned down and saw bright white balls pressed into the wall, making it easier to see the ship from out here. Mina made a mental note to make sure this was covered or that the lights were off come nightfall. "Is it wider?"

"Yeah! See, I thought so too." He crouched down on the other side of the opening.

"Ah yes," Sean said. "The eighth wonder of the world, the tunnel leading to the alien ship."

"Right, sorry." Mina, pushing away her desire to grab one of those lights to pull apart later, moved into the tunnel.

Behind her Zane said, "Okay, so this is the real last turn back moment. You can wait back at the car or hike over to the festival and call a ride. Also, totally understandable if you need to scream, or cry, or whatever once you see it."

"That's comforting," Steph said as she started in. "Remind me to handle your Independence Day speech if you ever need one."

Zane went next. Over the sounds of their shuffling Mina heard Sean and Emma bickering at the opening.

"So we agree that our moms would kill us if they found out we let the other go first," Sean said.

"Or do this at all. Death by aliens would be a mercy."

"Roshambo. On three."

They counted together, "One. Two. Th-"

"Hey!" Emma shouted as there were scuffling sounds by the tunnel entrance. Mina glanced back to see the edge of Sean diving in. Emma shouted as she recovered and moved in close behind him, "It's not honorable if you cheated!"

"Yes, but you'll be the one having to tell my mom that."

While the tunnel was larger, it felt cramped with all of them inside. She picked up her own pace for the sake of getting it over with. Mina crawled until she was out and able to move aside. The newly placed orbs around the interior of the cave gave a fresh view to the size of the ship. There was more dimension to the color, swirls and shades that were lost in the low light before, but the dark also concealed a fair portion of the damage done from its fall. Outrider came down hard. Still an intimidating view. Damaged or not, this was a big spaceship. Like big, big.

Very scientific, she thought.

Zane scuttled over to sit by her as the other three worked through different stages of putting their brains back together upon seeing the ship. Sean was somehow looking at only the top dome while taking pictures of the rest of the ship's body. Steph was humming a tune, as her eyes darted around the cavern. Emma was rolling her shoulders, inching toward the edge to look down. Mina noticed Zane watching Emma, he seemed satisfied with her reaction. Little hard to say Mina made all this herself.

She got up and leaned over the edge near Emma, disappointed to find no new lights down that direction. "Still can't see the whole bottom level."

"It really is the whole Hill." Emma stepped around her to look farther down the path. She

kicked a small rock off the side and they watched it ping off the ship a few times. When the sound fully faded, Emma muttered, "Sorry, about before."

"It's fine. This is all crazy." She caught Zane's eye, the smug look was not natural to his face. Her guardian best friend.

"There's miles of this thing," Steph said, still to the tune of whatever song she'd been making up.

"Do we have any idea how large these aliens are?" Sean asked.

Zane shook his head, refocusing on the ship. "The one we saw earlier was a bit taller than me, but relatively person sized."

"What?!" came from the rest.

Mina dropped her face into her palms. She'd left the attack out of the story, Zane had been too distracted with a muffin to notice at the time. "Was going to slow roll that out, Zane."

"None of this is slow roll," Emma waved toward the ship, her guard fully back in place. "What alien did you see?"

"Tall, trim. In a suit, we think," Mina rattled off. "Or they are the suit. The small robots chased it off. So someone they don't like."

"There is an evil alien running about The Park? Maybe the city by now? And your plan was to come see them at the cafe?"

Mina was pretty certain Emma's small apology was being rescinded. Before she could think of a defense, one of the flying robots zoomed up from below the ledge. It came to a halt a few feet above their heads. The white light of its scan waved over them, everyone squirmed. A second scan went over Emma. The robot's screen flickered and then a message of *Companion confirmed!* rolled across. The robot lowered to hover across from Mina. *Hello, Mina!*

"Oh, wow." She fought back watery eyes of excitement. Her name on this little screen. This little, alien screen. "Hello to you too!"

We are thankful for your help! It moved to Zane and repeated the statements, each of them receiving a personal greeting. *Please follow!* It moved down the pathway.

At the dropoff that stopped them earlier, the robot flew down to the next level and waited there. They could see the same *Please follow!* message shining up. With the extra light, Mina picked out the amount of damage the small robots created with their shots earlier. Silver lining of the shootout was that there were now holds to use, but not enough for the entire way down. She found a small crack in the rock about a foot back from the edge that they could get a spike into.

Mina tapped Zane to turn around, looking at the other three. "This is why we needed the rope." She leaned over and called down to the robot, "Give us one moment, we'll be down."

It hovered in place, she took that as understanding. Mina dug out the long rope, a spike, and a small hammer. "Anyone besides Zane have a good arm? We need this to hold."

Emma stepped up. "I can give it a swing."

Steph and Sean watched her set up the line. Mina turned back to the ship. Zane looked around to the other three, "Everyone feeling steady? It's a safe space, trust me."

"You're coming on a little hard about that," Mina said over her shoulder. "Are you going to be okay?"

Zane laughed, a little too hard, "Wha? Me? I have nerves of steel. Better even! Whatever this is made of." He waved at the ship.

"Raise your hand if you saw him nearly losing it at Restoration," Emma said and raised the hand that wasn't smacking in the stake. The rest followed, including Mina.

"Traitor!" He gave Mina's leg a nudge. "Okay, so my panic response may lead to puke. But I'm doing fine this time, in case anyone cares."

"Proud of you, buddy," Mina said as he tied off the rope. "And being so brave, you should go first. If you make it down fine, the rest of us should be golden."

"Is that a-"

"You are made of so much muscle and so little body fat, do not even start with me." She handed him the rope. "You also can demonstrate how to do it. And if it fails, you'd take the least amount of damage."

"Fine, use logic to make me sound good." Zane took the rope and showed everyone a quick and easy way to wrap themselves and how to release it as they went down. He backed over the edge, made sure everyone knew the best holds if needed, and slowly dropped to the level below. They saw the robot greet him as he untangled himself from the rope. "Yes, hello again."

The rest took their turns, Mina going last again. Each got a second greeting as they landed. Mina looked up at the ship from their new position. They were lower down on the center level, making her feel even smaller and further intimidated. Somehow, even though it was plenty intimidating to start. She spotted one of the glow sticks from earlier. It was crushed, the solution inside soaked into the ground. The alien must have stomped on it during its retreat.

The robot's screen changed back to *Please Follow!* It turned and moved farther down this lower path. They passed the blown out spot, the ship was dim beyond the torn paneling.

Steph leaned back toward Mina and asked, "Did the alien do that?"

"Yes," Mina answered, willfully not focusing on how nice she smelled. "But with weaponry. Not just bare hands or anything."

"Minor comfort, but I'll take it."

The robot stopped, aiming its screen toward them. *Capri.*

"What's Capri?" Mina asked.

It moved to line up with the hole. *Capri did this.*

"Their name is Capri?"

Correct! It pushed away from the ship and back down the path.

Mina stepped around the others to keep up with the robot, her long list of questions at the ready. "Do you have a name?"

Comp2876! Secondary.

She wasn't sure what Secondary meant in this context, but she did remember 2876 was the number the voice on the call mentioned. This was the device she'd fixed yesterday. "Hello, Comp2876! Good to see you again."

There was a single string of lights on stands that made a weak railing out onto a chunk of rock that got them closer to the ship, where an open loading bay door waited for them. There was a bit of a drop, but only about a foot to jump across. Four more robots hovered in the large room beyond. There wasn't much to see other than stacks of crates, which looked as dinged up as the ship, but there was a dimly lit path cleared away going further inside. The others tossed their bags over. Before any could land, the waiting robots rushed to catch them. They were pulled inside and opened, the items being scanned.

Mina jumped across still holding her bag, it held all her personal tools. A robot was unzipping it before she slipped the strap fully off her shoulder. "Please be careful. Some are expensive and I will be grounded for multiple lifetimes if anything happens to them."

Noted, appeared on the screen. It held up her soldering kit. *Define.*

"That's what I use to heat up metal for small parts. To reconnect them. I did it on," she looked around at the few robots, unable to now distinguish 2876 from the rest, "I lost them. Comp2876?"

2876 left from sorting Steph's bag to push over to her. *Mina fixed Comp2876!*

"Oh, by the way, is everything working okay? I didn't mess anything up, did I?"

All functional!

Thuds landed behind her as the others jumped across. The group milled about the front row of crates as they waited for their bags. Every box was thick walled, designed to withstand a lot, and gave no indication of what was inside. Or really, they said exactly what they stored, but printed in the same writing she'd failed to decipher before. She was maybe holding a grudge against the script and choosing to ignore it.

Steph came up beside Mina. "Comp2876 sure is excited. So many exclamation points."

Replicating speech diction from device! Filled the Comp's screen. *Incorrect?*

Mina laughed and nudged Zane. "Told you, you use exclamation points too much."

"It's not wrong to be excited or passionate about stuff," Zane defended himself. He looked at Comp2876, "You're doing great, buddy!"

Define. Another Comp raised two bags of chips.

"Snacks. Uh, food. Nutrition?" Zane answered. He caught a look from both Steph and Sean. "We may be here for a bit. Need snacks."

Emma leaned over the bag in question. "This whole bag is snacks. Did you clean out your kitchen?"

"We may be here awhile," he repeated. "And it's a bit of mine and a bit of Mina's."

"If you see my good cookies are in there," Mina called over. "No you don't." She went back to explaining all the tools she'd brought along to 2876.

Sean moved farther into the storage bay, looking at the symbols painted across their sides. "This kinda reminds me of Atlantean, but more pointy." He looked to a nearby Comp, "Can you tell us what's in here?"

"Supplies," the voice from the phone rang out around the room. "This room holds a range of goods, but their integrity has not been verified. Low priority for the time being."

Emma pointed to the dark panel that ran around the room above their heads. Colorful ribbons waved and swirled across it. "Are you Outrider?"

The lines spiked as the voice spoke, "No. The ship is Outrider. I am Nek. I am within Outrider."

"AI," Steph whispered.

"I believe you are referring to artificial intelligence." The waves shifted closer to Steph. "I am not artificial. Simply, different." Nek's waves dropped to low bumps for a moment. "I am sorry, it is difficult to explain and we do not have the proper time. There is much to do and our understanding of this planet is still a work in progress."

Mina zipped her bag back up. "Nek is right. We naturally all have a million questions for each other. But we came to help, let's see what they need first. Maybe play twenty questions along the way?"

"Please follow Comp2876. We have several tasks to delegate throughout Outrider."

As they moved farther in, the door behind them shuttered and began to rise. Once closed the door sealed well enough to look like a wall.

"No offense meant, but would it be possible to keep that open?" Zane asked.

They watched the lines move around the panel to settle closer to him. "Due to an ongoing threat, we must keep Outrider sealed."

"Capri," Sean threw out. "Whoever that is."

"Should we have notified anyone about that? Cops? Military?" Zane asked.

The waves ruffled with no sound. "I do not believe that will be the safest way forward. Once more repairs are completed, we will apprehend Capri ourselves."

"Let's maybe not get more involved than we need to," Emma said in a low voice to the group.

Comp2876 zoomed overhead and directed them to another door which opened into a hallway that stretched to both sides and another straight out behind the robot. Lights triggered down the middle hallway. Nek's waves appeared along the panel as they entered. "We are very grateful for the help you are giving us."

Mina wanted to run straight into the spaceship, memorize every inch she could while she had it all to herself. Somewhat to herself. She realized Zane was hanging back and forced herself to wait for him. He watched the doorway to the storage room slide closed, this one at least still looked like a door when it shut.

He rested an arm on her shoulder, speaking only to her, "This is the right thing to do, yeah?"

It was her turn to be the guardian. "If it feels wrong at any point, we'll go."

And as much as she knew the loss of this ship would hurt, she meant it.

12

Ain't That A…

How absurd. The idea of Comps detaining her. All their simplistic little efforts against her and they amounted to no more than a minor annoyance. The shots they landed were more a matter of odds than skill. Who ever called on them for combative reasons? How often were their defensive protocols used at all? Or practiced? Another result of the Collective gone timid.

But it'd been a distraction all the same, Nek taking the opportunity to block her Pak from the framework. Leaving Capri with no database to pull from for her surroundings. This was an unwelcome obstacle on top of her body still shaking off the effects of stasis. She'd managed to grab a couple Comps that fell within arms reach as they fought. Stashing them away in the extra containment pouch on her side made them nearly weightless, but she felt them tapping against her as she moved. She could potentially put together one useful Comp between their parts, clearing the directive to attack would be easy enough. Her Pak was in good standing, but she caught a fraction of latency as she sorted through available data. Fractions of seconds could cost her down the road. It was likely tied to the long disuse, along with the lag in her own body, and she expected this would clear up soon enough.

Capri kept running after the Comps were all destroyed, under the expectation that Nek would send a second wave or local reinforcements on standby. Though thinking back to the bit of Outrider she'd seen, them being prepared for her might not be the case. Most of the interior looked the same as she last remembered, slashes and punches through walls. Sections blown from the Comps sent to sacrifice themselves when Nek finally took Capri's stance seriously. Nek surprised her by choosing to take the ship down in order to stop her. Not only was none of her team willing to side with her, but Nek risked the entire ship and their own life to keep Capri from getting her way. An overreaction, if you asked her.

With a thought, she commanded the helmet to pull back into the neck of her suit as she finally stumbled to a stop. Fresh air felt better than the overly filtered version the suit circulated. There'd been a path not far outside the cavern hiding Outrider, but she'd taken a hazardous course directly into the plant life - after falling down the initial rockface - to give herself cover while taking out the last few Comps. Leaving her now in the middle of a large expanse of greenery, struggling more than she'd like to catch her breath.

"Best to get some bearings." She tapped her band to send up the one recon drone her Pak contained. Which returned the useful information of there being greenery directly around her, only greenery. There was the path behind her, not safe if Comps were still patrolling. Further down this incline was a clearing containing a small building. Capri's system made an estimation of the route needed to reach the structure.

It didn't take long to break from the treeline and step into the open space, though she didn't appreciate how her legs shook as she did so. A quick scan showed no other movement. It was only her, the building, and a scattering of tables arranged alongside it. Capri still approached cautiously, triggering her helmet back up, but nothing stirred as she closed in. An idea to lay across one of those tabletops and never get back up crossed her mind, but she pushed it away.

There was writing on the door, but her Pak's system held no reference point for translation. The lock was easy enough to bypass, setting off no alarm as she entered. Another scan from the recon showed nothing of immediate danger inside. Capri pulled back the helmet once she felt certain the place was clear. Thankful to avoid another fight so soon.

She figured this must be an outpost of sorts. The floor looked heavily scuffed, maybe a training center. Tables were folded up against one wall and chairs stacked in a corner. Given the surrounding view from the large windows, it was a lot nicer facility than several others she trained in. There was one workstation along the back wall. Small bits of paper with more writing she could not decipher were tucked into a rack along the front. She moved around and tapped the screen of the console, but nothing happened. Jabbing at the keypad beneath it did finally bring the screen to life. She figured out how to select programs with the smaller piece of hardware - an over cumbersome system, to be honest, but all was pointless until she could understand what it said.

Capri dropped the broken Comps from her pouch to the desktop. One's casing was split enough already that it only took some minor work to peel open a space big enough to access the decks and compressed tools inside. The tools expanded once released, becoming easier for her to use on the other Comp. In a few minutes' work, which only took so long due to the small shake in her hands, she was connected directly to the local device and sending data to her Pak. Given the less than desirable conditions, it expected a long wait in completing an update. She would be more concerned about the time were she not cut off from the framework. That meant Nek couldn't see what she was doing either, making her harder to locate. Especially if there were no more Comps to send. Nek would be alone for a while.

That thought alone made Capri itch to return to Outrider, but her vitals still read lower than she liked. The shake in her hands increased once she stopped distracting them with work. At some point she'd dropped into the chair behind the desk, the worn cushion giving little comfort but better than being on her feet. Not a surprise after the stress she'd been put under immediately upon waking. The thought wasn't exciting, but she needed to let herself recover more before taking another run at Outrider. Better to make that call now than before her body completely shut down on its own. Capri set a tripwire alarm on the only door, dropped the blinds over all the windows, and settled herself in on the floor behind the desk, out of sight of all of it.

Suppose there is rest for the wicked, whispered something pretending to be Rin. There were memories that tried to stir up with it, flashes from that last day. A look given through the pod's closing door.

No time for that, Capri pulled the sides of her helmet up and filled her ears with static. Scattering any thought that tried to form. Not long after her eyes closed, she was near dead to the world again.

13

It's a Spoke System After All

Comp2876 officially enjoyed having specially designated tasks. Possibly because 2876's only current job was assisting the humans as they worked around Outrider. It floated between their stations, checking to make sure they were not in need of anything or wandering off. So far this mostly entailed directing Emma through the halls, she had an issue following the layout between Fabrication and the docking ports where Mina and Steph were working. Currently, she was waiting for parts to complete and would need directed back soon, but 2876 needed to check on Sean and Zane.

Wait for you? It asked.

"I think I got it now."

Comp2876's estimations showed that as being untrue, it didn't move.

Emma sighed, "Let me try. Left. Right. Right. That gets me back to the center hallway. Two branches over. Straight on from there."

Close!

Emma scrunched up her nose. "Don't tell me! It's, um, only one branch over?"

Correct!

"And it only took four times to get it."

With that, 2876 left her to move the next batch of Comp parts alone. It pushed through the halls to Zane and Sean who were sorting debris from the stasis bay, due to the sheer amount needing moved. Comp2876 was

94

personally glad to avoid entering that room.

"I can skip the gym for a few days after this," Zane said as he pulled another broken piece of paneling away, letting it clatter onto the pile in the hall.

"I can continue never going to the gym," Sean said, dropping his own twisted chunk of frame in their somewhat organized piles. 2876 shuffled pieces to keep them separate. It gave them a quick rundown on the sorting needed when it left them here earlier. Nearly everything was recyclable, even if that meant melting down and starting over. Their goal was to find items ready for immediate reuse and save time on repairs. The results were poor so far, but they pressed on.

Zane leaned into the opening the Comps cleared earlier. "Looks like there are Comps in there. Should get those back to Mina and Steph."

Comp2876 watched them crouch down and go in. It hesitated, but followed through and regretted the framework automatically pinging the other Comps scattered about the floor. 2876 attempted to detach itself as it scanned and pointed out worthwhile pieces. They followed the trail back to the open pod. There was one small splatter of blood against the inside of the door. Records confirmed that a Comp landed one good shot on Capri when things kicked off. Unfortunately, it was only the one.

"So this was where that Capri person was," Sean said. "And fought their way out."

Correct. 2876 changed the punctuation at the last moment from its now normal exclamation, which felt wrong to use here.

"Yeah, we saw them blow out the side of the ship this morning," Zane said and rolled his shoulder, wincing slightly.

2876 recalled the signs of injuries in their hiding spot. It pushed around to him. *Injured?*

He dropped the shoulder. "Oh no, I'm good."

"It's kind of singed," Sean said.

"It's fine."

Detour for medical care? There wasn't any power going there yet, but 2876 was sure Nek would make a small exception to care for their helpful humans. As long as they wouldn't mind being around all of the Warden remains. That put a damper on the entire idea.

"No, really. All good. I swear." He shuffled his armful of components. "We should get these back to Mina."

Please follow! Comp2876 led them out of the bay, fine to let the task go. It pulled ahead as they went down the hallway, but picked up their low conversation.

Sean asked, "Are we sure we're on the right side of this?"

"I think doing them a favor will make sure we're at least on their good side."

"I suppose." Sean turned too early and took a couple steps toward the branch leading to the medbay. 2876 was about to go after him when he backed out on his own. "Think we can get a map of this place?"

"It's not that hard. You were only one early."

Correct! Comp2876 began digging through stored data for a map of the ship; no one onboard needed one in a long time.

Zane turned them into the correct hallway. "It's weird how quickly this becomes normal."

"True. Sci-fi is going to be weird to watch after this," Sean agreed.

The pair only made it a few steps in before they heard Emma call out behind them. She was holding two trays full of fresh Comp parts and sighed when she saw them. "I took a wrong turn again."

My apologies! 2876 should have remained with her, making sure she didn't accidentally go into a section they weren't needed. Nek never made the rest of Outrider officially off limits, but advised 2876 privately that it would be better to contain them to certain areas.

Emma shrugged as much as she could with the trays in hand. "Nah, all good. I wanted to test myself."

"And you failed," Sean muttered.

"Shut it." She gave him a nudge with one elbow, keeping the trays balanced.

"This does prove my point that we need maps though," Sean said.

"It's a hub and spoke system. If you're lost, you go toward the middle," Zane countered.

"Yeah, but some of these sections have some rather twisty internal halls,"

Emma said. "Before I heard you guys, I saw the few other Comps floating around in one of them. Working away on their own projects." She glanced toward 2876.

Comp2876 couldn't answer her on that. Well it could, notes for which Comp was working on which task was a basic enough search to do on the framework. But the ones Emma saw were working on the database repairs, somewhere Nek did not want the humans going. Luckily, it finally found the Outrider map. 2876 swung around to flash, *Map available!*

A hologram of Outrider in full projected out from 2876, showing the ship upright and all three levels slowly turning. The top and bottom sections disappeared as the middle cut in half to show a top down view. 2876 blurred the branches still unused, or out of bounds, for the time being. No need to over complicate things with directions to the living quarters, escape pods, holding cells, remaining storage, and other areas they wouldn't see. Comp2876 zoomed in to where they were, dotting out the short path remaining to the docking stations. The group continued forward with Comp2876 guiding them.

"Fabrication is larger than I expected," Emma said. "Comps are small, but there's some huge printers in there too."

"Maybe it makes replacement parts for the ship?" Sean offered.

Comp2876 beeped to get their attention. *Correct! Also repairs for Guardians. And specialized weapons and tools for Wardens.*

"Guardians?" Zane asked.

"Wardens?" Emma added.

Comp2876's screen went blank as it loaded relevant information, which quickly became overwhelming. It also realized this was information needing cleared with Nek before going forward. *Processing answer. Much information.*

"Maybe we can narrow it down?" Zane asked. "Is Capri a Warden?"

Was! Unfit for duty.

"So Guardians are different."

This hologram was easier to recover as Comps often checked over mechanisms after encounters. The map disappeared and a large mass replaced it. The hologram unfurled itself to fill the entire hallway. It took a couple swings with sharply clawed hands at an invisible target, 2876 felt this was the best way to illustrate there were several appendages on the form. There were long, spindly, tentacles coming off the lower jaw which snapped out toward the humans. 2876 did this because they sometimes twitched at passing Comps in error, which it did not enjoy. Zane dropped back a couple steps from the towering figure, looking it over top to bottom. Comp2876 turned the head to give them a better view. Sean drew back as well. Emma got closer, counting the eyes.

"That is some Cthulhu type thing." Sean looked down to the floor as if he might see through to the next level. "These are creatures you have here?"

Incorrect! The hologram halted midswing and shrunk down to a more relatable size. Several portions pulled apart. Emma was now standing in the mechanical workings of the legs, Comp2876 moved around to properly display the moving parts. It then shifted up to the large set of eyes, which were actually the thickly glassed windows of a control room. Comp2876 added a figure sitting inside. The tiny flickering form moved as if pushing levers and buttons, the larger figure around it adjusted accordingly.

"Guardians are giant robots that Wardens pilot," Emma put together first.

Approximately correct! It wanted to give her a win.

They weren't technically robots, as this planet understood them anyway, but that was as close as they'd get to defining it currently. They'd run into a few approximate answers while they'd been here already. Partially due to Outrider still updating to Earth languages and partially due to not having the available time to break down the highly complicated answers they were searching for.

"Does Capri have one of those?" Sean asked.

The hologram disappeared. *Capri is no longer a Warden. Guardian remains in Outrider.*

"That's comforting," Zane said as he got the group going again and completed the short trek back to the docking stations.

Comp2876 scanned over the long wall across from them, filled top to bottom with charging ports. It was good to see how many were filled. While it watched, a charging Comp powered on. The new Comp instantly picked a task off the priority repairs and ducked into one of the several tunnel pathways that connected to this room. 2876 checked in with all the Comps working here via the framework, glad to see their progress coming along. The group stepped around the temporary workstations, carts moved from Fabrication, to reach their friends working away at the back. Every surface was filled with Comps in various states of repair. The working Comps only paid attention to the humans if they needed to shift out of their way. The cousins paused at each station, mesmerized by the work being done, but Zane was unfazed.

Steph was against the back wall working on a small section of docking stations that were heavily damaged. It was more a job of ripping out the old and installing the newly completed parts, which Steph assured 2876 that she could handle with a little guidance from Mina. Who herself was hunched over a table, magnifying glasses on, and soldering away inside a Comp. Neither one even looked up as the group approached.

Zane came up to Mina and nudged her leg with his foot. "Where would you like these?"

"Also these?" Emma offered up her trays.

Her too wide eyes looked up at them through the glasses. "More Comps?"

Sean shifted around the load in his arms. "These may be more for parts than repair."

"Let's see what you got." She stood, stretched her back, and pushed the glasses up on her head. Mina looked over the broken Comp bits they'd retrieved. 2876 offered up its own breakdown of the parts, which she looked over and thanked it with a quick nod. "Yeah, these will need extensive work. More efficient to strip what we can. Put them on that far cart for now."

A row of stations flickered on behind them. Steph celebrated from her lying position, the top of her still inside the panel she'd been working on. "All docks are now online!"

Comp2876 beeped as loudly as it could. *Great job!*

Sean gave her a bit of applause after he dropped the broken Comps down. "Way to go!"

Mina, who'd been smiling widely at Steph until she stood from the floor, checked over the trays Emma carried and looked around the room at the other stations, trying to gauge where they were all at. "I think…yeah, step over here quick."

Comp2876 could have delegated for her, but held back. Interested in seeing how she'd solved the situation.

The two stood in the center of the room. Mina took one tray and stepped back. Emma looked nervous, "Are we going to chuck them or something?"

"No, but maybe stand extra still for a moment." She looked around to the working Comps. "New parts, fresh and hot. Check 'em out, see what you need."

Scans ran over the trays from several directions. Arms unfolded and parts were snatched away. 2876 watched as needs tick off several work tasks. Thankful beeps rang out as they went back to work, leaving the trays empty in under a minute. Emma stood with her eyes shut tight until she heard the Comps all settle back at their stations. Mina was sporting another large grin.

Zane took the tray from Mina. "I feel that you may be having a tad bit of fun in all this."

"Aren't you?" Her glasses fell back down onto her nose, wide eyes blinked at him.

"It's getting there. Still lots of questions." He looked to 2876. "Buddy here has been cool though."

Glad to help!

"I have a note going on my phone. Steph and I have been adding to it."

"Should we start a group chat?" Emma asked. "I have some questions too, but don't want to double up."

"Absolutely!" Mina stepped back to her station and pulled her phone out from under a sheet of casing. She jerked the phone away, pushed the glasses onto her head, and pulled it back closer to her. "Actually, better than that. I'll make a doc we can all edit, better for formatting than a group chat."

Comp2876 watched them trade information. It took so long, comparatively, that 2876 began idly shifting non-priority tasks around as distraction. How long would it be until a Comp found time to dust again anyway?

Mina finally sent out a document containing the few questions and answers they'd managed to put together so far, something 2876 saw because Nek tied Zane's phone to their private communication. The humans, besides Zane, pulled out their phones and instantly started typing. 2876 noticed Nek's attention shift to the questions as they loaded in.

Zane gave a little wave. "Would I be able to get my phone?"

Before 2876 could answer, Nek rolled into the room's panel. "Yes. My apologies. It was helpful for initial contact, but I believe we've reached a point of functionality where I can connect independently with local systems."

A Comp nearby accepted the task, its screen updated. *Retrieving device from deck.*

"Oh, you don't have to," Zane called out as it ducked into a tunnel. He looked back to Nek. "They're busy, I could come grab it."

"Thank you for the offer," Nek said. "The Comps tunnels are rather direct. This will get your phone to you faster."

2876 knew that him going to the deck required many safeguards being moved out of the way, something Nek wanted to avoid. It also knew the deck was currently focused on pulling research on Earth, gaining needed information about their new - really not so new - location. Outside of the one console tracking the humans directly, which they certainly didn't need to see.

"Oh, well, sounds good then. Thanks! You'll know where to find me." He shoved his hands into pockets, watching the other typing away.

Nek left the room, back to other work, but Comp2876 knew they were still watching the document.

Sean whispered, "Guess we're not allowed on the deck."

"Or we're simply not needed there." Mina sat back at her station. "Not everything is a thing."

Emma tucked her phone away and headed out. "Going back to Fabrication for the next batch. Comp2876, care to come with so I don't get lost again? I think one or two more times I'll have it down."

Gladly! Comp2876 headed into the hallway after her.

Zane pulled Sean out behind him. "And best we get back to our grind."

Sean groaned, "I deal with that enough at work."

14

Flirting in a Time of Robot Repair

Mina tipped back from her newly repaired Comp, cracking her back out of habit. She looked for an empty space on the wall, happy to see they were running low, and slid it in to charge.

With the back wall repaired, Steph was cleaning up scraps and organizing the tools Mina lent her across one end of a tabletop. Steph held out a gauge toward her. "So I noticed some of your tools have Property of Hephaestus Labs labeled on them."

"My parents work there. I have permission to use them. Some of them. Maybe not to the extent of being on an alien spaceship, but what they don't know…" Mina let it trail off as she scooped up a new Comp to work on, knowing full well her parents would be ecstatic about this ship. Their inquiries about Outrider would be the most they'd talked to her in forever. And didn't it feel a little good to keep that from them.

"Totally get it. I've raided my parent's homes for projects plenty of times." Steph set a few things back in the bag. "I can see why you like this stuff. Getting something working feels good."

"It does." Mina resisted the urge to look at the cute girl complimenting her tools and hobbies as she dropped back down at her workstation. She believed this fell into the 'play it cool' scenario Zane tried to explain once.

"I should learn how to do more of this kind of stuff. Seems like a bit of an investment though."

"You're welcome to borrow stuff from me. I even have some junky tech at home you can practice on." Mina worked very hard to not look up. Her grip on the soldering iron was feeling sweaty. "Text me anytime you want to try it out. I'm easy to get along with."

"You are," Steph replied quietly, then cleared her throat. "I don't want to sound like I'm taking advantage of you and your stuff."

"You're not! Really. I'm glad to give some pointers. Oh! You know what, you can take those Comps apart." She pointed to the remaining Comps beyond repair. "Knowing how something comes apart is part of learning how to fix it."

Steph moved to the cart with the Comp bits left by the guys. She sat on a stool and began picking at the casing of a Comp. "That would be great actually, you giving pointers, I mean. I should learn some real job skills before I end up at Restoration forever."

Mina felt her stomach tighten and regretted her offer. "Do you not like it there?"

"Oh no, it's great! I'll stay there through senior year for sure. Probably for a bit after that even. Mitch is great about my weird hours. Hard to find that. But, I mean, the goal is to one day not need any sort of day job. Ya know? But I'm being told I need a backup plan."

"Theater is pretty decent around here. Lots of film students need actors. You'll catch something. You're great." She was careful to not mention the run off to Hollywood option.

"You've seen me?"

Mina fumbled her solder, nearly burning herself. "There was the musical at the end of the year. And then Zane talks with the guy editing a short you're in. Gave him some stuff to practice on. We hang out and work on projects a lot. I caught some scenes. It was that slasher thing, you were all stuck in a mall."

"Mallrat Massacre." Steph pulled out one of the internal tracks.

Mina pretended to just now remember the name. "Right!"

"Was it actually good? It sounds weird, but I couldn't watch it. I'm a little jumpy when it comes to horror." She fidgeted with more hardware as she talked, freeing it from the track and dropping it on the tabletop. A Comp buzzed over and took the entire piece away immediately.

"I never saw the completed thing, but as far as local indie films go the scenes I saw were entertaining." She'd stopped watching when Steph's character died via a mob of mannequins come to life, but it'd honestly been a good kind of dumb fun up until then.

"Good to know. Maybe it won't haunt me too much down the road." Steph set to work on the next layer of hardware.

They both fell into their work, the room filled with quiet taps and buzzing. Repairs were completed and the few remaining spots filled up on the back wall. It actually seemed that the Comps were talking more than Mina and Steph. Beeps would go back and forth between them, but no message would appear on any of their screens. Mina assumed that they were also receiving private updates from Nek as more of the ship regained power.

From what Mina could put together, the Comps had a rather intricate dynamic. She'd witnessed them reacting to requests in a hive mind sort of manner, like with the trays; the set could all turn and shift in unison. Or switch tasks between each other without issue. They swapped stations a few times and barely paused as they began new work, like they'd internally optimized which in the group were best for which task. So they featured individual strengths used to make up the whole, but could also work completely outside the group when called on. Like Comp2876, which went around as a guide and gave help where it could. As well as keeping tabs on them, she suspected but didn't mind too much.

She knew that Nek created tasks, but never called out specific Comps outside of 2876. They divided the work out among themselves. So were they a hive mind functioning as one full 'entity' or individuals so committed to their directives that it only appeared a hive mind? Nek was a sentient being for sure, but Mina was still nailing down the Comps.

Mina realized she'd been staring at the Comp in front of her rather hard. She shook it off and added her new questions to the list, which had grown considerably with it being a group effort now. While her own entries were focused on how the tech worked, the others filled in queries of Capri, sections of the ship, Nek, and general first contact kind of questions. Her finger hovered over the **Do you come in peace?** and thought to delete it, but stopped herself. Maybe it wouldn't hurt being a little on the nose. There were also a few questions showing answers, or partial answers, the others were able to piece together so far. As well as a scattering of facts thrown on the sheet with tangent questions added on:

Fabrication is a whole bunch of 3D printer looking machines. Also huge, automated forges.

Capri was a Warden. Not anymore. Fought way out of ship.

It was a team of them. Others didn't make it? Capri killed them?

GIANT ROBOTS IN THE DUNGEON.

Robot dungeon is the bottom level of the ship.

Googled Outrider = escort or guard, syn for scout...first of other ships?

Mina added an asterisk to the last entry, **May not be a perfect translation. Meaning could be different for them?** She really didn't want these to be evil beings. That would be a rather big let down. Not to mention 'traitor to humanity' being a horrible epitaph to claim.

On the other side of the room, Steph spread out parts and stepped away from her table. She called out to the Comps, "If you can use anything here, come and get it."

Mina watched the same organized swarm occur around Steph, but unlike Emma she kept her eyes open; smiling as the robots cleared away what they could. If Mina wasn't dealing with a crush the size of Outrider before, she certainly was now.

15

You Wouldn't Download a Keyblade

Comp2876 ensured Zane and Sean reached the stasis pod bay before circling back to Fabrication, finding Emma hesitating at a crossroads that led either to the living quarters or the Fabrication stations. She spotted 2876 coming up the hall. "Don't tell me, I got this one."

You got this! Comp2876 repeated.

She pointed to the right. "This way?"

Correct! It pushed to the right ahead of her.

She celebrated as they went on. "Almost turned too early twice before this." She slowed again as they passed a set of scrawled directions on the wall. "Hey Comp2876, what does that say?"

It turned back and dropped a hologram overlay, changing the symbols to read Fabrication, Galley, and Quarters all with arrows pointing different directions. 2876 was concerned the additional information might get her turned around. Not to mention the other two remained out of bounds for the humans.

"Ah! Well, I'll know what symbols to look out for now." She pulled out her phone and snapped a picture. 2876 watched her write the new information over the image. Emma also dropped it into their document as they moved. Adding the note, **Here's what some of the Angry Atlantean means**.

Back in Fabrication, several machines were churning away on different projects. Completed pieces waited at the end of conveyor belts, which

107

Comp2876 instantly loaded onto trays. Internal cooling kicked in given the higher temperature here, it always got warm when the larger Fabs came on. Emma walked up to one of the larger forge's screen and tapped through the structural designs loading in, mostly wall paneling at the moment. 2876 kept the same queue running internally. With more Comps coming online, they could start on bigger repairs. Comp2876 was eager to have more tasks ticked off and its attention drifted to the long list. Deciding that the next four Comps online would install the panels over the hole Capri made.

Emma was still at the screen, swiping far enough to find Warden Caro's saber that autoloaded for replacement. Her eyes grew as she took in the weapon that, after a quick calculation, 2876 knew was slightly shorter than her arm. "Don't think that will fit on a tray."

She glanced at 2876, who remained shifting tasks, and walked around to the machines further in the room. There were more large forges, but they were inactive. Nothing more for her to discover back there, which is why 2876 stayed still. Comp2876 waited for her to ask about the saber, but nothing came. It looked back to the tasks, somehow managing to lose its place, and dropped a hologram against the wall for a better perspective.

"A lot needed to get Outrider working again," Emma said from behind it.

Comp2876 flipped to show her its screen, but the projection remained on the wall. *Correct!*

She'd pulled another cart from the back. They'd piled there during the crash, sorting them out was a very low priority. Emma looked over the dinging up cart, wheels shaking loudly as she pulled it along. "Seems you all came down pretty hard."

Capri did this. Comp2876 snapped the message to its screen, rather than roll it out like it did every other time.

Emma touched the pocket holding her phone, but left it there. "Capri got you stuck here on Earth?"

Too many system failures. No one left to repair. Outrider shut down to minimum output.

"No one came looking for you?"

That was an avenue of investigation Comp2876 knew Nek still needed to explore. It put together the best answer it could. *Distress beacon was activated, but no response. Outrider too far from Collective for assistance.*

"What's the Collective?"

Comp2876 felt a shift on the framework. Nek rolled into the room on the panel behind it. "Emma, may I have you join Zane and Sean with cleanup? Comps will be online soon to cover delivering parts where needed."

"Sure, no problem." Emma looked to 2876 as Nek rolled out, but it shifted back to sorting its list. Trying to pass off that it'd been stopped from answering. "Can you get me there?"

Gladly! It pushed out of the room.

Emma followed from a couple of paces behind. She pulled out her phone and opened

the document that 2876 watched in its private channel with Nek. There were new notes from Mina about the Comps' processing. Underneath those Emma typed in, **I think Comps have the potential for emotions. 2876 seems upset about Capri when they're mentioned.**

2876 almost added a message saying *Accurate!*, but caught it in time.

She also added:

Bigger parts are being made.

Wardens/Outrider are part of a Collective (?), but too far away to help.

Think Nek can listen even when waves are not in the room.

Steph was active in the document too, she typed in, **Possibly like Alexa? Always passively listening for when you say their name?**

Emma shook her head. She looked up to Comp2876, the nearest Nek panel, and then back to the phone. 2876 watched as she tipped the phone back toward her chest even further, not knowing that was a pointless gesture. **Asked 2876 about Collective, Nek rolled in and moved me to help Sean and Zane IMMEDIATELY.**

Mina became active. **Nek may be selective of what we can know at this point.**

Should we be selective back?

Their framework was horribly disorganized, 2876 itched to sort it out.

Comp2876 settled for a personal overlay, giving their entries a color coding to keep them straight.

Steph typed, **They've already gone through Zane's phone. Nek said they can connect independently now. Assuming that means the internet. So is there much they can't find out about humans/Earth already?**

I vote for moving carefully.

Same. Steph left the doc as they turned a corner. Emma spotted the Fabrication symbols on the wall and pointed to the one below. "Does that say Stasis?"

Correct!

Mina was still active. Her icon hovered under Emma's last note for a long moment, but all that came through was, **Fair.**

Emma closed the document and slipped her phone back into her pocket as they came around to the last turn leading to Zane and Sean. Another Comp appeared from a tunnel between them. It moved toward Zane, his phone secure beneath it. They watched it hand over the phone and duck back into another tunnel, already onto another task. Zane was swiping it open as they met up with them.

Comp2876 pushed closer to Zane. *My apologies!*

"For what? It didn't take long to get here."

2876 showed a replay of accidentally cracking the screen. *Repaired!*

He looked over the phone. "Oh! No worries. Honestly, I've broken like four myself in a lot dumber ways. And it's fully charged. Nice!" He opened the question document and scanned over the information they'd already gathered. Zane flicked a look at the panel, then over to Emma. "Doesn't surprise me."

Sean shoved a chunk of debris off to the side. "Happy, happy, joy, joy."

"Well, we're here. So best to tread lightly and do what we can." Emma grabbed a couple of pieces and moved them from the doorway. Dropping the twisted metal on the pile for reuse. Not that the distinction mattered much as their stacks were close to meshing together. "Comp2876, does the reuse pile go directly to Fabrication or somewhere else?"

They go to an offshoot of Fabrication. It scanned the different piles. Resisting the desire to fix the stacks. *Materials noted. Will be collected later.*

"We can take some now. Keep things moving."

Comp2876 knew the message to give but felt unsure about it all the same. *Unneeded. Comps online soon.*

She let out a sigh and shoved part of a pile with her foot. The three shared a look but went back to clearing the doorway.

16

Rage Against the Machine-Based Organism

Capri jolted awake, she was on her feet with a hand hovering over her Pak, ready to drop the blaster waiting inside. After a tense moment, she realized the alarm at the door sat untriggered. Pure paranoia was all that woke her.

Her armband announced the translation was finished and her system updated. It also informed her that she'd been sleeping far longer than anticipated, but nothing to do about that now. She pulled the full helmet on and tested the update on the device she'd plugged into. The information was all drivel, schedules for gatherings and minor area reports were all she found, but the important fact was she could read it now. Through the dismantled Comp's connection to her Pak she triggered a search for information on the immediate area. Satellite images made it easy to assess where Outrider crashed and became covered by resettled terrain. Capri dug a little deeper, finding that nearly five hundred years had passed since they'd arrived on this planet.

They'd been left by the Collective, and more specifically - annoyingly - she'd been left. Had they written her off as a failed mission? Her stung pride aside, not even trying to retrieve the investment that was Outrider felt irresponsible. It didn't sit well with her, being dismissed and left to rot. Being thought so little of, after how much her importance was insisted upon before. Capri toyed with the idea of having something impressive to shove back in their faces upon her return. Something the size of a single-handedly conquered planet.

Looking over a more current map tacked up on the wall, she'd not made it far in her run. Though seeing how she wasn't found in the excessive downtime led her to believe Nek was focusing on repairing Outrider. The crash must have damaged most systems, along with their long time spent in disuse. Getting back inside without detection was impossible, even with the ship in such a poor state. Especially with her now being locked out.

That could work in her favor though. Maybe she could manipulate the readout to register as something else completely. Visuals would give her away eventually, but if it bought her enough time to get through that tunnel and maybe close to the ship, it'd be worth the effort. Capri's hand hovered over the control pad for a few seconds before finally pulling off her Pak, the suit retracting with the motion. Leaving her in the more casual training gear she'd been wearing when everything went wrong on the ship.

It'd been foolish to assume the normally sheepish Caro would be the easiest to bring to her side first; that saber was a feat to break. No matter what Ali accused her of then, she didn't mean for the broken blade to end up in Caro's side. She didn't think she had anyway. As it turned out, the idea that any of them were able to be reasoned with was out of the question. Rin wouldn't even entertain the idea, which truly surprised her. But she'd made her point and stood by it. Death wasn't her intention, but they wouldn't stop and she would not fail. It took Nek dropping the ship to put her down and even that only lasted so long.

If only they were here to see the further evidence of her argument. This planet rolled on for centuries while she slept and what did they have to show for it? Under a Warden's command, it would've been a grand fortress of a planet by now. Primed with soldiers ready for the Collective's cause. Rather than helpless civilians in constant need of protection, like every other planet they once patrolled. Maybe it wasn't too late, if she could get what was hers from Outrider. Maybe a little more while she was at it, there were more Paks to be had.

Capri stretched and felt the sting of the one hit on her shoulder; on top of the last remaining sluggish effects from stasis clinging to her. There was a small medical kit tucked under the desk, she cracked it open and cleaned her shoulder. Other bruises spread across her body from the fight, but nothing bad enough to scar and join the scattering of others she already sported. Small favors.

She swiped the pad to pull up repair mode. The Pak expanded across the desk, making it easier to access hardware. Capri moved the deconstructed Comp from the computer to the Pak. Once inside the programming, it was regrettably easy to fully block her signal from all of Outrider. Another small tweak would allow her to make the readout register as a Comp, she built a small program that allowed her to turn that on once she was ready. No need to have Nek sending a search party for a rogue Comp now. Hindsight told her that having backup plans like this would've been useful the first time around.

"Pointless to fuss about it now." They'd all been dead for hundreds of years and she was still here. Her stomach tightened, she told herself it was because of the stasis.

With that small adjustment done, Capri smacked the Pak back on her side. Her suit shifted over her body, allowing her to breathe easier. She did a lap around the digital posters along the walls, pulling the helmet up to test the translations again.

Guidelines for Community Space
Book Your Next Event with The Park Today!
Exciting New Innovations from Hephaestus Labs!
Camping Regulations and Safety Tips

What a dull building she'd found refuge in. Capri stretched again and ran a check on her vitals. Things were looking better, but not yet at peak status. She thought it best to head back and make an attempt for her Guardian anyway. The longer she waited, the more Comps Nek would have online. The few before were simple enough, but a full swarm could be an annoyance. Or worse yet, Nek could have Outrider's actual defenses up and running again. There were a few tricks in those halls to stop any potential invasion,

Capri assumed she'd caught Nek enough off guard before that they never triggered any during her fight with the other Wardens. Outside of those exploding Comps.

Another small pinch in her stomach as a flurry of memories ran through her mind, how hard they'd fought against her. How they'd looked at her like a stranger once Caro was hurt. She'd found herself on the wrong side of that cold Rin stare, and almost surrendered right then knowing what wreckage that look brought on an enemy. But she stood her ground until Rin threw her into that pod, barely coughing out a final threat of how Capri would remain there until the Collective was informed of her actions. Her last thought was hoping Rin made it to a pod of her own, given how badly the gash Capri put in her side was bleeding.

She cursed all the intrusive thoughts away. No way to change what happened. Her only option was going forward. Given she held no saved schematics of Outrider in her personal system, Capri thought of her path from memory. If the impromptu exit she made was still open, that would be best. Even if they patched it up, it was a weak point in the hull. A con being that it was also close to the Comps' charging docks. If they'd been working on themselves in the hours since her departure, they'd be close at hand. It was dangerously optimistic to think she'd catch them all charging. Better to plan for the chance of a swarm and go from there.

What were the odds of making it to the deck? While taking her Guardian was priority, cutting Nek from Outrider completely and taking the entire ship for herself was an appealing thought. No matter the direction, the time spent in that elevator shaft was dangerous. Comps would have essentially a shooting gallery on her. Not to mention the blast doors Nek could shut going either way.

There were fewer doors toward the Guardians than toward the deck, given that Guardians would typically be activated and defending themselves by the time Outrider itself was in trouble. Capri only needed to get next to her Guardian and lock it to her new programming. One ally in this fight would make all the difference. But she'd thought that before too.

"Stop," she growled at herself. Unaware she'd punched through one of the posters, and the wall behind it, until her heads-up advised of the damage. Capri pulled her hand back, letting glass, wiring, and plaster fall to the floor.

With the Guardian she could cause major damage to Outrider, giving Nek more to deal with and split their attention. Making it even easier to then reach the deck and rip them out. Or she could make a quick exit out of the cavern, causing trouble for this city. Given they'd been here so long, clearly no Collective was coming. Nek would be forced to bargain due to their 'protective' disposition. A full swarm could do nothing against one Guardian and there were no other Wardens to activate the others. Can't allow a planet to be devastated, could they?

"No matter how drab a planet it may be," she said looking out one of the windows at the mass of trees around her. There were options, that much she knew, and given the sad state of Outrider she was willing to bet they weren't ready for anything she'd do. Capri pulled her alarm off the door, sliding it back into her Pak. Best get to it.

17

Qs & Qs & Qs & As

The imaginary version of Zane reminded Mina once again that constantly hunching was not healthy. She twisted around on the stool, getting only one small pop in response. Next time Zane came around she'd have him heft her up and do the rest.

Steph pulled away from the Comp she was deconstructing and leaned toward the hallway. "Do you think people will be able to hear the ship outside?"

While Mina'd grown accustomed to the sound, it had increased while they'd been inside Outrider. "Mmmm, that's a good question. Likely depends on how thick the rock walls are around this."

"You did blow a hole into the side with minor homemade explosives."

That was now the second person to remind her of that.

"Fair point. Hey, Nek," she spoke to the panel as their waves rolled in, "I'm not sure if you're already monitoring the area, or can yet, but we were thinking there is a chance people may pick up on the ship now that things are running."

"Thank you for the concern. I am monitoring a few feeds. I believe by the time any would become concerned, Outrider will be able to vacate the area."

"You're leaving?" Mina hoped she didn't sound too hurt.

"Outrider will be going into orbit. It is the safest option."

"And what about all the terrain you'll be moving?" Steph asked.

"I am working on a plan to keep damage at a minimum." Nek shifted through the panel. Was this their fidgeting?

"Guess we'll be getting a gorge back. Or would it be a canyon now? Just a big pit?" Steph waved as if wiping the words away in the air. "We'll see what it looks like once you're gone. Name it then."

The two watched the waves roll out, both reaching for their phones as they disappeared. Steph's fingers were faster. **Nek is taking Outrider to space.**

Emma was already active, adding something about a sword, but jumped down to the new note. **Do we get to leave first?**

I would assume. Mina wrote.

We can hope. Emma responded.

Sean became active. **Zane is heaving again. Should we leave now?**

Mina huffed at her phone and caught a concerned look from Steph. She apparently was the only one not leaning toward fleeing. **Everything is fine. We've done nothing but help them. We'll leave once they are set. I bet they won't even go until the festival is shut down for the day and the park is mostly clear.**

Her phone buzzed, Zane texted her directly. **I know you love this place. You and I being on an adventure is one thing. But there are three other people potentially risking their lives here. Are you sure about this?**

She knew this wasn't him doubting her, he didn't do that. But he did know, and was the one to make her aware, that she suffered from major project tunnel vision. Mina sat back, giving herself the once-over he'd do if here. Was she biased on this? Possibly. Was her reaction more based on wanting it to not be a dangerous situation rather than it actually being one? Also possibly. Nek was withholding, that was true. Even keeping 2876 from letting too much slip by. Emma's wandering confirmed they were being allowed only in certain areas. So while Nek appeared grateful, they were at a figurative arm's distance.

There was also the Capri matter and Nek's certainty she'd return. The longer the group stayed, the more likely it would happen while they were here. Mina wanted to stay on Outrider, but those moments hiding with

Zane earlier were tense. Unpleasant. In no way something she'd wish to put him through a second time. They'd been wholly unprepared and it was reckless to do so again. What were the options then, outside of straight-up leaving? She knew the Comps contained weaponry if things went sideways. They, at the minimum, held off Capri before. Wouldn't do much against the giant robots in the level below, if it came to that, but that was an issue for another time. Hopefully.

Across the room, Steph was pulling open the casing of a Comp. The interior expanded in the way they'd come to expect. Mina opened a blank note and typed a message. She gave a quick laugh and stepped over to Steph. "Look at this quick. I love these guys."

Try pulling the weapon out.

Steph gave a better fake laugh. "They are so good. You should see the one on the bikes."

Mina deleted the note and responded to Zane. **I am optimistic, but I won't be reckless with everyone here. I promise.**

I trust you. He replied.

She didn't want that to be for nothing. Mina settled back at her station and shuffled around hardware. A few minutes later her phone buzzed with a text from Steph. **I can get it out. Not sure on a trigger yet though.**

Nek rolled in, their waves tighter than she'd previously seen. "I must advise against this action."

Both girls jumped, phones smacking against the tables. Steph's hand stayed on the device. The working Comps stopped moving and all tilted toward Nek's panel.

The little blaster wasn't even out of the Comp yet and none of the active Comps were near enough to see her screen. There was only one way Nek could have known what she'd asked of Steph. Mina stood from her table. "You're in our phones."

"I needed to ensure you would not share our location with unapproved individuals. There was no danger in you talking amongst yourselves." The waves moved closer to Steph's side. "I would have removed myself once you left Outrider."

"So we do get to leave," Steph said, eyes on the Comp nearest her.

"Why would you believe otherwise?" The waves swirled, colorful tendrils sprawling across the panel. "In reviewing interactions, I see I owe you an apology. I have come across as more reserved than you deserve, given your generosity. My attention is strained, much is being repaired at once. Much needs completed for the safety of this ship and your planet."

"Why is the planet at risk?" Emma called from the hallway. Nek must have directed their group back this way once they saw what Mina and Steph were up to.

"Capri is a danger." Their voice now echoed from the hall too. "Her goals are not aligned with the Collective anymore. Much of the damage you have seen around the ship was due to her personally. In an attempt to stop her from leaving, I enacted an untested protocol that affected Outrider faster than I anticipated, and more severely than expected. If she would return now, obtain her Guardian or more of the Paks, many lives would be at stake."

So Nek was trying to leave before Capri could get back. That didn't bode well for Mina's idea of waiting for people to clear out first.

"What's a Pak?" Sean asked as the three came into the doorway. A few more Comps not far behind them.

Comp2876 pushed into the middle and dropped a hologram of a square device that was smaller, but thicker, than their phones. Basically an older cell phone. A figure appeared and placed it against their side, from it expanded a suit that Zane and Mina saw once before.

"Capri has her Pak," Zane said. "That's how she managed to get out."

Correct.

Mina noticed the lack of an exclamation point.

Nek expanded to every panel in the room, ribbons of different colors surrounding them. This must be their way of trying to press a point. "One Pak is powerful enough. If she were to obtain more of them, she could recruit a team of her own."

"Where are they?" Zane asked.

"Secured at the deck, with me. Sealed for the time being, as a precaution."

"That's why I couldn't come get my phone?"

"Correct."

"So those are safe," Emma said. "What happens if she gets to the Guardian?"

"While her recent behavior is erratic, my estimation is she would wreak havoc on the city. Force me into making a deal for the sake of the planet."

"What would she want?" Mina asked.

Comp2876 shifted to a new hologram. Showing them a tall, blue tinged figure, short hair with buzzed sides, and eyes that looked hard even in this recreation. She was gesturing widely, talking to people that weren't there. Audio came in as she said, "We were sent to sit and train and die. Wardens are meant for more than that!"

A different voice, from a person not projected, "We all agreed to this mission. Our job is to make a solid foundation for the Collective to build on."

"Foundation, yes. Build fighters out of this region, absolutely. But why wait generation upon generation for our enemies to find us? Why not strike first?"

"That is not proper Collective procedure," a faded Nek voice replied.

Capri stared up, almost properly aligned with the panel in their room, but stood frozen in place. Nek pulled away from that spot. Comp2876 turned off the hologram. *Relevant information complete.*

Sean flicked a scrap of casing across one of the workstations. "So the only alien to survive was the evil one. Hate to see it."

Mina worked to wrap her own head around all the information Nek was finally sharing with them. Not artificial, just different. They needed to remember that Nek wasn't a program they were dealing with, but yet another alien lifeform that was capable of being as stressed and reactive and able to make mistakes as they were. Mina moved closer to the panel nearest her. "I am sorry for what Capri did to your Wardens. I'm sure it was a tough call to risk Outrider like you did. And I understand you're under a lot of strain." She looked around to her odd group of best friend, crush, and classmates; made a call she hoped not to regret. "But this may be more to take on than we expected. I want to stay and keep helping, but I think if anyone else wants to leave they should be able to now."

"Absolutely," Nek said. "You have done much to help us on our way already. We are in your debt. Comp2876, please escort anyone who wishes to leave."

Please follow! 2876 moved out into the hall.

Mina remained in her spot, watching the others side-eye each other. She'd said she was staying and meant it. Zane crossed over to lean against her workstation. "You were kinda badass there," he looked back at the group, "I'm staying with her, by the way."

Steph took her hand off the disassembled Comp and leaned back against the wall. "I hate leaving things unfinished."

Sean looked to Emma. "It's both of us or neither of us. What say you?"

She cracked a few knuckles and glanced up at Nek. "If we can keep this more open communication going, I'd like to stay."

Nek shrunk back to one bundle of ribbons near Emma. "I am glad to do so. While we are still adapting to this planet some concepts may be challenging to explain at this time, but I am happy to work with you on that."

Sean clapped his hands together. "So we're staying! All good. Can we get a peak at those Guardians at some point? Before you leave Earth."

They all watched Nek's waves spike up and, for the first time, heard them laugh. "That can be arranged."

Mina watched everyone's shoulders relax. The Comps broke out of their rigid halt, drifting back to their jobs. Comp2876 came back into the room, the screen changing again. *Glad to have you!*

"Guess we should get back to sorting out the wreckage," Zane said. Sean looked less thrilled by the idea, but moved to follow.

Nek's waves expanded out again and flashed white around them. "Please move to the elevator. You will be guided."

Comp2876 snapped back to *Please follow!* It pushed out to the hallway, bobbing up and down. Mina believed that was the most nervous gesture she'd seen from a Comp yet.

"Did something just happen?" Emma asked as none of them moved.

"Proximity alert," Nek shrunk back to smaller waves that joined 2876 in the hall.

"The lights aren't only lights." Mina left her station and moved out of the bay. "Smart."

The rest followed after her. Comps surrounded them, their small weapons extended. Steph checked the direction, "Oh, I definitely would have shot myself."

"Good thing it didn't come to that."

"May we pick up the pace a little with an evil alien on site?" Zane picked up speed, gaining a few paces on the group and pulling Mina along with him.

A bang hit the side of Outrider somewhere behind them, close to where they'd come in. The few Comps around them, aside from 2876, peeled away toward the sound, joining a mass already heading that direction.

Please follow!!! Flashed in a few colors on Comp2876's screen.

They all ran up the main hallway toward the center. The metal cylinder that ran through the levels was pulling up from the floor to reveal a glass elevator shaft inside, it stopped a quarter of the way up. There was another bang and more groaning metal behind them.

Emma looked back at the sound. "I don't think all the paneling for that hole was finished."

Nek appeared nearby. "I dare not risk the time to open this completely. Please continue forward."

Sean and Emma were already rolling underneath. Steph and Zane crawled through next. Mina went last with Comp2876. A third hit came from far behind, this time she could hear the metal giving way. The same sounds from the morning followed, the Comps returning fire.

"Capri is within Outrider. Please continue forward." Nek's waves became a tight spiral.

"How did she get so close?" Mina asked. "The tunnel orbs should've been plenty of heads up."

"An issue that will be investigated." Nek didn't sound annoyed, but there was an extra tightness to them.

Mina caught Comp2876's screen flash red for a moment before returning to the now constant follow message. "Can the Comps hold her off?"

"Them and the doors should be enough," Nek said as the outer shield dropped back and the glass slid aside. The door snapped shut once they all packed in.

"Should?" Zane asked as they felt the floor beneath them rise.

"Contingencies are in place."

Mina wondered what exactly that meant. They couldn't drop the ship again. There were no Wardens to fight. So what could Nek do to keep her in place? The large amount of rubble outside the stasis pods came to mind. "Do you mean blowing up parts of the ship?"

"No, but Comps contain failsafes. I must see to Capri. This will put you on the deck." Nek disappeared without rolling off, apparently that was a choice they made.

"All that work we did," Mina sighed, imagining Comps blowing up in an attempt to stop Capri, wrecking more of Outrider than already damaged. She leaned against the wall, her arm squeaked against the glass as they moved, confirming it was only the floor moving them up.

Zane put a hand on her arm, the grip a little too tight, and pulled her away from the side. "If we live, we can do it again."

"Look on the brightside," Sean said as they heard doorways closing below them and saw another opening above. "There'll be even more to do."

"Might be hard to keep this secret after that though," Steph said. "If a lot blows, someone is going to hear it."

"Maybe the music will cover it." Mina felt her stomach tighten. "The music festival! It's on the other side, but if this goes bad those people are in immediate danger." She really put a lot of eggs in the 'Capri won't come back for awhile' basket.

"So are we. Right now." Zane paced the small space. "One thing at a time."

The elevator slowed as they came into the top level, they heard metal sliding shut below. There was no glass wall here, only the metal shield stood between them and the deck. A thud far below rang up the elevator shaft. Mina looked to Comp2876, "Is she trying to come this way?"

Shots fired at the first blast door. Minimum damage. Calculations have Capri moving lower in the ship.

"Going for the Guardian."

Correct projected destination!

They watched the shielding pull down painfully slow. Mina tapped against the wall of metal as it went. "How much is stopping her from getting to them?"

Four blast doors. Various protective protocols within Outrider. It showed the count of Comps active, but that number went down every couple seconds.

"Can you remote in to the other Guardians?" Steph asked. "Use them as a defense?"

Guardians only respond to a Warden's Pak.

"And the rest are here," Emma said as the shield finally lowered enough for them to step over. The floor sealed shut after they all cleared the space.

Mina allowed herself a small moment of enjoying the view as they officially stepped onto the deck. The elevator brought them into the center of a ring of consoles with thick glass screens. Straight across from them, the largest display stretched to the top of the dome and Nek swirled in the center. A rainbow of ribbons shifting around the screen, occasionally moving to another display in the room as they looked around. Each console featured feeds scrolling by, blending between English and their alien language. Internal shielding was coming down over the dome, making it so they couldn't look out into the cavern. She wanted to touch everything, but knew it wasn't the time. Instead, she moved to a set of pedestals pressed against the wall behind the elevator with the Paks suspended in the air above them, save for one that remained empty. Every few seconds a wave of energy ran in front of each, a shield.

"Capri will be contained," Nek assured them as Zane and Emma untangled a pile of chairs that crashed against one side of the deck.

Mina looked around at the different stations. "Is one of these capable of sending out messages?"

"No local forces would arrive in time."

"Not for here, for the festival. We should get people moving out of there, as a precaution."

Comp2876 pushed to the console on her right, items lighting up on the dash as it hovered there. Mina stepped over and saw it translating in real time so she could understand. There were a few options for local signals. She saw a couple active venues, two small ranger outposts, and several points from around the festival. Mina hit everything, "Hello? Hello, can anyone hear me?" There was nothing. "Is anyone able to respond?"

Again nothing but crackling air came back again. "People are in danger. Hello?"

"Who is this?" a voice finally responded. "This channel is for official use only."

"Oh! Hi! Yes. Sorry, but people need to leave the festival. Immediately."

"I suggest you clear off this channel before you are found," the ranger warned.

"They think you're a kid playing a prank," Sean said quietly from not far behind her.

She leaned into the console, unsure where the microphone was exactly. "I'm not making a false threat. The Hill…is going to explode."

Not much of a lie, to be fair. Only leaving out the 'because a spaceship is going to break out of it' part. Mina glanced at Comp2876 and saw the total Comp count drop again. She heard another explosion below.

"Clear off this channel kid, this is your last warning."

"Told you," Sean whispered.

Mina glared at the highlighted ranger outpost that was fighting back. "We are going to destroy The Hill. If you won't believe it, fine by me. All that blood is on you then. Get your asses moving."

She hit the channels, blocking any from giving another response. The Comp count dropped again. All she could do was hope that she'd sounded threatening enough to make them listen.

18

There's a Cool Song Playing Somewhere

Mina backed away from the console, bumping into Zane. He looked pale green as he asked, "Did you make us terrorists?"

"Eco-terrorists," Emma called over from the other side of the deck.

"They weren't listening!" Mina said. "I had to scare them into doing something."

Sean leaned over another console, tapped a few times. "Looks like they are calling the cops. Rangers are on the move. It may have worked."

"Point for eco-terroism?" Mina smiled at Zane, but knew she wasn't winning much ground there. Even Nek's waves, low and tight, felt like they were judging her. Or maybe they were focused elsewhere, she tried to convince herself it was that. There was still an attack going on below after all.

Sean leaned back. "Looks like they are now calling…everyone. They are calling everyone about a threat to blow up The Hill."

"They will arrive too late to reach us," Nek said - clearly still present in the room. "But projections show that if evacuation measures are taken immediately, the majority of people will clear The Park."

Comp2876 scrolled out a new message, *Good call, Mina!* If there was a confetti and toot horn function, Mina could imagine 2876 setting them off right now. As meager of a win as it felt.

"Where is Capri now?" Emma asked.

Part of Nek's large display switched to a camera feed of the main hallway around the elevator. Capri, suited up, took shots at the Comps around her. They dodged and weaved as they could in the small space, dropping into the tunnels to clear shots for others as needed. There were signs that one or two Comps used the self-destruct option as a means to stall her, but Capri appeared barely singed from the attempts.

"They're holding her in place," Zane said.

"They aim to buy as much time as possible," Nek said. They moved about the deck, consoles lit up behind them as systems triggered. On the screen, something that looked like a turret unfolded from the wall and aimed at Capri. Not the kind of failsafe Mina expected.

"I think I leaned on that panel once," Emma said.

Nek, still on the deck, also appeared in the hallway video feed. "Stand down."

They watched as Capri turned to the panel. "Give me what's mine and I'll go."

"Oh, I could have told you that voice was going evil one day," Zane whispered.

"How are we understanding her?" Steph whispered back.

With Nek and 2876 too distracted to answer, Mina took a crack at it. "Outrider systems are translating into English. The ship possibly has a replication of her voice saved? Like with the playback Nek showed us earlier. A sort of universal translator, useful for a task force that travels space protecting different planets who likely have their own languages."

Comp2876 managed a quick *Correct!* before scooting over to a console, tapping away at notices coming in from the ship.

Nek whirled on the main display and in the hallway panel, ignoring the teens. "Guardians are assigned to Wardens. You are no longer worthy of the position."

"Yet the Pak remains with me."

"What does that mean?" Emma asked.

Mina had no guess on that one. Comp2876 offered nothing either as it tapped away around the room.

"Stand down," Nek repeated.

Capri tilted her head toward the turret and laughed, "You're bluffing. That's not fully functional yet."

"Stand down or find out how wrong you are."

She gave a wave to the turret. "Fire."

The weapon spun, sounded like it was drawing power, and extended straight out to bash into Capri's chest; she fell into a branching hallway. Indeed a bluff.

"Nice hit, Nek!" Sean clapped. "Kick her…can we assume ass?"

Comp2876 pushed around to him. *Ass is an acceptable translation!*

"2876 said ass! This day is really turning around."

"Feel like there is still a bit to go before that can be true," Emma said.

The camera shifted to Capri's new location. Comps were in the process of pushing her farther down this hallway. Capri fought her way back to standing, continuing to back up as she did. They saw her glance toward another offshoot, away from Comps and the elevator shaft. She dashed into the hallway, the camera feed shifting again to follow along.

"She's not heading for the Guardians anymore," Zane sighed. "She's on the run."

"That's the way to Fabrication." Emma pointed to the batch of writing on the wall. "Nek there was a sword queued up on one of the machines."

"Why was a sword being made?" Steph asked.

Nek's swirl in the room jumped over to a panel by the Paks. "Diagnostics of Pak systems showed Warden Caro's saber was destroyed. They autoload into the system for production."

"It was set for after the paneling. Was it completed?" Emma asked, stepping up to the console Nek now hovered over. "Maybe we can halt it?"

Another box appeared on the main display. A picture of the saber and a status: **COMPLETE**. The camera feed showed Capri moving into the room, ducking behind the first set of machines before the Comps caught up. Their view jumped to another angle within the room, but they couldn't see Capri. The sword was in view, the metal still a dull red as it cooled.

"Maybe she won't notice?" Mina asked. "Too focused on Comps?"

A hand came from out of frame and Mina wanted to kick herself. They could see a small wisp of smoke from whatever the suit was made of contacting the hot metal. As Capri stepped further into frame, they watched the saber ripple and become black. She spun it a couple times and turned to the Comps entering the room. The angle gave Mina a better look at her suit, which appeared rather battered now, even spying a few small breaks showing bluish skin. The Comps' efforts weren't for nothing.

Emma moved closer to her cousin. "How's the day looking now, Sean?"

He rubbed his forehead. "This isn't great, but I still take expanding 2876's vocab as a win."

Capri advanced on the Comps. They continued taking shots, but the saber was able to deflect them. Sending bolts all over the room. A list of newly acquired damage within Fabrication started to build on a screen. In a free moment as one group of Comps fell and others closed in, Capri pressed her blaster against the hilt of the saber, another ripple went over both weapons. The blaster was absorbed into the saber, now sporting a thicker blade, leaving only a trigger behind on the hilt.

Mina wanted an instant replay of the two meshing together. How was that possible? And what kind of weapon does that result in? She didn't like the guess that came to mind. "Please say that won't-"

Capri took a swing toward the new line of Comps within the doorway. A large blue bolt ran up the blade and shot out, cutting them all with one blow.

"How many Comps are left?" Zane asked, white knuckling the edge of a display.

Comp2876 updated to show twelve Comps left, which matched the number now on screen with Capri. They learned from the first swipe, spreading out across the open space in the front of Fabrication. She was moving forward again, trying to force a few back into a bunch.

"Can that sword get through the doors?" Steph asked.

"Eventually," Nek answered. "But Outrider will make the move to orbit soon. Before she can reach the Guardians."

Sean leaned into his cousin, "Going to space is a win."

"Still under attack!" Emma smacked his head.

Mina looked away from Capri and to the growing list of damages. All their progress was negated and worse damage was being done right before them. If Nek made any of these final Comps explode, they'd have a hard road back with Fabrication destroyed. Not to mention what Capri would do if she wasn't stopped, to Outrider and Hurst. With them standing there watching it happen. It wasn't right. It wasn't fair. She stepped toward the Paks, watching as the one in the middle rose up. "What if you need more time?"

"Paks are very intricate. The selection process takes time. Not everyone can maintain one." Nek must have kept enough awareness in the room to know where she was looking. A list appeared on their main display, a checkoff for ignition. More sections on consoles lit up and the general hum of the ship grew louder.

Mina looked to the ever growing list of damages. Caught another notification pop in as more of her Comps were destroyed. She turned back to the Pak. The shield shifted, now glowing with a blue tint. "But could a person do it for long enough to get us off the planet? Get her cornered somewhere it'll do the least damage."

The screen flashed, Capri's latest saber bolt killed the current feed. The new angle included the spread of Comp pieces behind her. She rushed by the scattered few remaining Comps from Fabrication to another hallway, still not going back toward the elevator.

Comp2876 pushed closer to the screen. *Issue!*

"Projected target is the generators." Nek shifted toward 2876. "Outrider is barely above the power needed for take off. If she-"

The lights flickered once through the deck before cutting out. Leaving them in the glow of consoles. On the screen they saw Capri, lights flickering around her, standing in front of one of the large turning generators, saber still pulsing with bolt energy.

Comp2876's screen shined brightly. *No Comps remaining!*

Nek rolled through several of the displays around the group, forgetting them again. "Prioritizing systems needed for launch. We're near critical. We can't lose much more."

The camera feed dropped in quality, becoming grainy and the audio cut out. Making Capri's second swipe at the generators come across like a silent movie filtered through a potato. Sparks flew around her while new updates of failing systems appeared on the deck.

"You need help!" Mina shouted up to Nek. She wasn't about to lose any more of this ship. It already meant too much to her.

"Um, Mina. How'd you do that?" Zane took a few steps closer to her, but he wasn't looking at her, more off to her side.

She followed, seeing her hand through the shield and wrapped around the Pak. Her arm tingled with pins and needles. Mina stepped back from the pedestal, expecting the Pak to catch on the shield, but her fingers remained tight around the surprisingly heavy device as it slipped through. Something from inside the Pak burst out around her hand. A substance rolled up her arm in a series of interlocking hexagons, hardening as it went. The process was quick, and mesmerizing, enough that she barely found the time to react as it covered her upper body. The Pak slid across her arm and down her side, resting on her hip, before sending a trail of material rolling down her leg and another up toward her head. Even though they'd watched this exact thing happen in 2876's hologram, some innate survival tactic made her suck in a breath before her entire face was covered.

Zane dashed across the deck, stopping short of touching her. "Mina!"

She watched through the tinted helmet screen as the suit covered her legs, forming hardened boots that boosted her up a couple inches. As the material settled a teal band rolled out across her right arm and down the side of her leg. Her vision filled with a heads-up display, a lot of systems coming online and wanting attention. She let go of the breath she'd been holding. A tiny fan somehow situated within the helmet pushed cool air across her face, but Mina thought she'd feel better with the helmet off. Before she could move to find a latch, it receded into the neck of the suit. She sucked in another gulp of air from the surprise. "I'm good!"

"Oh, wow." Steph took a few steps closer. "You look awesome."

Nek rolled over. "This is…unanticipated. And it is too much for me to ask of you."

"I want to do it." Mina stretched her arms in the suit. It felt a little loose, like it was made for someone slightly bigger than her, but the difference didn't throw her off too badly. "Please, let me help."

This plan of action was only backed by the few self defense classes Zane insisted she try out, but Mina wasn't losing Outrider. Not without whatever small fight she could give.

Nek's waves darkened, Mina thought they might refuse. The seal above the elevator began to retract, they could hear the blast doors below doing the same. "The teleport would be faster, but that is still broken. I will bypass the safety lock on the elevator to get you back down quickly. I will assist you as best I can."

Mina looked back to her odd group, ending with Zane. She felt guilty pulling her best friend into this, and also that she couldn't imagine being here without him. "I'll be right back. You've already come far enough with me on this. I can't ask any more of you either."

Zane took a hard gulp and stepped up to another pedestal, a green wave ran over the shield. He watched the Pak come level with his hand and gave her a smile. "You don't have to."

The sincerity of his statement didn't stop the yelp that escaped as the suit expanded over him, a similar mint green band filling in as it finished. Steph, Sean, and Emma all lined up to the remaining Paks as Zane stepped back and dropped his helmet.

Sean elbowed his cousin as they both put hands on Paks. "This counts as a major win."

"Very unexpected," Nek said as the final three stood before the main display watching the suits cover themselves. The consoles flickered with another drop in power as their colored piping filled in; Emma in shimmering silver, Sean a rusty orange, and Steph a dark purple. Mina watched them stretch and shift, getting a feel for the new weight of the suits. Their Paks settled to a similar spot near their hips on the band, glowing the same colors.

Zane took a step away from the group. He leaned into a console, but pushed back a second later. "Thought I would…you know. But I got it. All good."

His helmet pulled over his head as they all stood around the elevator shaft. Capri's continued attack toward the reactors echoed back up.

"The barrier doors around the elevator are opening now," Nek advised. "I will need to reseal everything behind you."

"This is going to be so cool." Mina stepped onto the elevator floor, feeling it bounce as each of the others followed suit. The floor dropped so fast, Mina was sure they all hung in the air for half a second before falling after it. Nek whirled in the corner of her heads-up display for a flash and then their feet were sucked back down against the floor, magnetized in place. A small shout came from the others as they dropped, but Mina was too busy laughing.

19

Bit of a Mess

Capri left the generators, feeling she'd done enough damage for the time being. She needed Outrider partially functional, enough to let Nek beg as they were trapped within a crippled ship. Seeing as how no further Comps swarmed her way, she must have cut through the meager amount repaired in her absence. All good by her, the small pool of energy she'd gained from that rest was waning, not that she'd let on with Nek watching. She hated to admit that they'd gotten a remarkable amount done for the time. Almost a pity to tear it all back down, but also therapeutic to watch it crumble at the same time.

"Time for my prize." She moved toward the main hallway, hoping Nek was distracted with keeping Outrider online and not about to throw another turret at her. That had been crafty, Capri still felt the sting across her chest. The lights were no longer flickering, but settled at a dim glow. There were also telltale signs of a launch coming, another thing Nek was likely distracted by. Time was short.

She came around the final corner to the elevator and stopped, thinking she'd fallen back in time. The last several hours truly being a bad dream. Her team filled the hallway, making their way toward her. Had she only fantasized her confrontation with them going so poorly? The memory of Rin's stare hit her again; something she'd never willingly be on the receiving side of. Was Nek heartless enough to use projections of their fallen Wardens?

Looking over the group again, none of them gave off nearly the proper level of confidence. Capri realized the colors were all wrong too. Not a trick. Not her team. Strangers were carrying their Paks. Her anger spiked to a point that her vision blurred at the edges. A vitals alert went off in one of those fuzzed over corners.

"Whoever you are," she shouted to the imposters, "you don't deserve those."

"Weird. That's what we've heard about you too," Blue, standing in the center, replied.

The way they moved was awkward, none were used to the weight of the suit. One kept a hand on the wall for balance even. They independently changed pace as they couldn't figure out a proper formation in the hallway. None pulled a blaster to try for an early shot on her. They weren't trained. Insult to injury, Nek sending nobodies to face her. The Comps would be the best fight she encountered today. Capri set her footing, raised her saber, and waited for them to waste energy getting to her. This would be over quick.

There was only a faint buzz to her left as a warning before a Comp emerged from a tunnel and smashed into her helmet. It pushed back before hitting the other wall and fired a couple shots back at the same spot it struck her. All those hits resulted in a single crack across her visor. It ducked into another tunnel before she could take a swing.

With her attention on the tunnel, Capri missed the first punch coming in from Blue. It was weak, suit propulsion doing more for the hit than the being inside. Green came in behind with a better blow to her ribs. Capri steadied before Green's second attempt could land, deflecting them into Orange and ducking under another sloppy swing from Blue. She kept Silver and Purple back with a swipe of the saber. They tried to get around her, draw her away from the elevator, but they were timid. Unsure footing. Clearly no plan of attack, treating this like some brawl in the training yard. Messy.

Capri shouted toward the panel, "I'm going to kill these ones too, Nek."

She batted away Blue's third attempt. Orange grabbed her saber wielding arm and tried breaking her hold. They came close to loosening her grip, but Capri held fast and charged a bolt. They backed off before it finished, evidence that they didn't know what the suits could take. Good to know. Not to waste the bolt, she shoved Purple into the wall and aimed the swing out at the elevator barrier. Leaving a red slash against the metal. It would take a few to get through.

"Enough playing with children." Capri charged the saber again, catching yet another punch from Blue, throwing their momentum toward Green. She moved around the tangled pair to send another swipe at the door.

"That's rude," a voice said behind her. A set of arms came around her sides, silver band shining over one arm. Capri was pulled into the air and sent flying backward. Her upper back cracked against the floor, pain shooting across her shoulders and neck. The air knocked out of her, taking near the last of her reserved energy with it. She rolled out from the impact, thinking that maybe Silver contained a scrap of real fight in them.

"Where'd you learn that?" Purple asked Silver, who recovered back to standing already.

"Watched a lot of wrestling as a kid."

"Practiced plenty too," Orange added as they kicked at Capri's hand holding the saber before she was able to fully stand.

Her grip loosened in the fall, the saber spun into the air and was caught by Purple. They tossed the saber, letting it spin once in the air before catching it in their left hand. "Nice! Wanna see what I learned for a show?"

They swung wide and landed a partial slice across Capri's side, catching a section already scuffed and worn. The suit took most of it as there again wasn't much power behind the hit, but Capri noted a small cut making it through. She also noticed how the saber didn't attune to Purple. Another thing they didn't know how to do. Nek had truly thrown Paks at some random kids and sent them out. Shameful practice, but Capri wouldn't feel bad for them. They were in her way. She'd take it out on Nek later.

Purple moved to make another hit, overconfident after their first swing. Capri caught the blade with both hands, thinking it must look intimidating to the child, but Purple laughed. "Hey, do you know this choreography too?"

They kicked Capri in the stomach, pushing her back into the wall. Saber leveled to her chin a moment later. "I am Indigo Montoya."

Capri snapped out to grab their wrist, bending it backward in hopes to break a bone. "I don't care."

Green came in to break the hold, but Purple still dropped the saber and it clattered away from their group. They looked back to Purple, "Remind me to high five you for that pun later."

"Have to get to later first." Silver came in to grab Capri's other arm. They strained, but pinned her to the wall. "Also, indigo is technically more blue than purple."

"Such a pessimist." Orange flicked Silver's arm as they went after the lost saber.

"I prefer realists." Silver was trying to hook a foot behind Capri's to keep her off balance.

These children talked more than they fought. Orange picked up the saber, whirled it around once. Tossed it behind their back to catch in their other hand, yet never took control of the saber either. Capri twitched a couple fingers as she located the command within her system and made the blaster shoot while in her grappled position, catching Orange by surprise and sending them to the floor; saber falling free yet again.

Silver let go of Capri and went for Orange. "Oh God! Se-"

"No names!" shouted Blue, who'd moved around them all to act as a barrier to the elevator.

Green shifted to grab the freed arm, but Capri was faster. Copying Silver's intent, she hooked a foot on Green's leg to tip their balance and shove them to the ground. She moved toward the saber, but that troublesome Comp rushed from another tunnel and smashed into her helmet again. Turning the crack into a large web of splinters, her heads-up display wavered. She would taunt them about a Comp doing the most damage, but she was too personally insulted by the same fact.

"Outrider is nearly prepared for take off," Nek echoed through the halls.

Blue looked to the panel as they moved between Capri and the saber. "Did people get out of the festival?"

"Minimal damage should occur. We only need a bit longer."

Capri's stomach turned at this display of meager teamwork and then turned again from a wave of her stasis sickness coming back. She found it mildly humorous that Nek's last plan was to drop Outrider to the surface and the current plan was to now leave said planet. They all stopped to balance themselves as engines kicked on across the outside of Outrider. A series of thuds hit all around the level as portions of rock came loose and fell aside from the ship. Capri's display settled, but the visor was too damaged. She did away with the helmet. Using a boost, she hit Blue hard in the short distance. Sending them both down as Capri wrapped hands around their throat. Blue's head smacked into the floor, but they fought to break Capri's hold. She lifted them almost to sitting upright and smashed them back to the floor, hearing their head bounce around inside the helmet this time.

Capri leaned in close, putting effort into not sounding as winded as she felt. "You won't make it off your planet."

"Bad call on the helmet," Green called as a foot came into her peripheral.

She ducked and pulled the helmet sides back up, but their foot clipped her enough to knock her loose from Blue. Capri leaned into the roll and brought herself closer to the saber. Realizing as she came back to her feet how far they'd managed to move her back. Her one cut to the barrier looked like a poor result to the amount of effort already put in.

"Enough of this." She made the last leap for the saber and set another bolt to charge as she straightened. A whir came from beside her, a turret unfolding from the wall and pushing toward her face. The saber bolt was wasted cutting that away, the large mechanism now hanging loose on the wall. As she ducked underneath and set another charge, that Comp came through a tunnel and hit her square in the face. Her already spotted vision fully blurred as she fell to the ground.

20

Catch Your Breath

Mina groaned from her spot on the floor. She tipped enough to see the rest of her group clustered in the hallway, but didn't feel like getting up yet. Not until the pounding in her head died down a little first.

"Is she out?" Emma kicked Capri's foot, no reaction came.

Sean leaned over Capri's face, still holding his arm, and pulled the saber away. "Seems to be."

Nek appeared on the nearest panel. "Paks contain restraints. Access it on your display, then tap the Pak to release it."

"How do you-" Steph started to ask and then jolted back. "Oh, okay, you just think about it. Is this thing in my head?"

"Monitoring brainwaves," Nek explained. "An extension of the system that reports vitals. Used only for your quick time needs."

"Cool." Steph tapped the Pak on her hip, which turned brighter purple before a pair of thick cuffs dropped into her hand. "Very cool."

Zane crouched down next to Mina. "Hey there, the baddy is officially knocked out. Can you take your helmet down? Let me know you're not dead in there."

She sat up and did as requested, revealing her split eyebrow and embarrassed look. Mina gave the tender back of her head a soft touch, it pulsed with pain but her hand didn't come back bloody. That was a good sign at least. "Didn't do that great at leading a charge, did I?"

140

"I think you did rather well considering the lack of experience. We all did." He pulled her up to her feet, clearly making sure she could stand steady on her own.

"Speaking of," Steph turned the cuffs around. "Nek, how do you open these?"

Comp2876 pushed out of the tunnel it last disappeared into, moving slower than normal due to its splintered screen and damaged casing, a piece hanging on by a sliver of metal. One jet sputtered as it neared Steph. It extended an arm to hit a small button, opening a portion to slide around Capri's wrist.

"That's the real MVP there," Mina said as Zane let her go. She held her hands under 2876. "You deserve a little rest. Wanna lift?"

Thanks! flickered on the fractured screen before it dropped into her hands. The screen dimmed as a small diagnostic kicked on. Mina mentally made her own list of repairs.

Sean grabbed the saber and pointed back to Emma. "I think runner up goes to my cousin, The World Champ, right there."

Emma gave a little curtsy. "Who knew anger management issues as a child would pay off?"

Nek shifted through a couple panels along the wall. "I apologize for not assisting more. I should have advised on some basic functions."

"No worries." Mina gave 2876 a little rub on its casing. "You got the ship ready for take off. We ran distraction. Plan worked." On cue, another set of groans rolled through the halls as engines kicked up and more rock dislodged from around the ship.

"You all performed remarkably well," Nek said, "Though we are not finished yet. We need to remove that Pak and take Capri to a holding room."

Nobody commented on Outrider having holding rooms. Mina figured that if Wardens were meant to fight bad guys, they would need to keep a few locked up on occasion. They all snapped their helmets back into place. Emma and Zane each grabbed an arm and lifted Capri, putting her into a sitting position against the wall.

Mina stepped in and tapped the Pak on Capri's side, but nothing happened. She tried to outright pull it off, but the Pak didn't budge. "How do we take it off her?"

Nek's rolls tightened, moving up and down the wall panel. "The Pak should be rejecting her. I previously blocked her from our system and it seems she's further tampered with the Pak. We will need to access the programming directly and see what she's done. Best to contain her first."

Given the height difference, Capri's feet dragged as they went around the elevator to a new hallway for the group. Their suits translated the wall writing as they went, in addition to arrows on their displays to direct the way. She knew it was 2876 working from within the system due to the small *This way!* underneath each one. Still being helpful as it laid in her hands.

Another set of engines kicked up, the ship shook and they all shifted to keep their balance. Nek moved near Sean and Zane. "May I request a task from you two?"

"Sure thing." Zane handed his arm over to Steph.

Nek moved down a short hall that broke off from their current one. "Please follow. Our medbay is here."

While Emma and Steph stayed put, Mina followed a few steps behind. They came into a thin, long room. Beds lined the walls, five of them with blankets draped over what were clearly bodies. It caught Mina by surprise and she was sure the guys were too. She hadn't given much thought to where the Warden remains were being held this whole time. Mina wondered who's Pak she wore, who she might need to thank.

Nek moved through the panels over each bed. "Normally, Outrider can self-stabilize during launch. Given the current condition, would you remain here and watch over them? Make sure they don't..."

Not that falling would hurt, but they all understood the sentiment. Sean pulled back his helmet. "Absolutely, we'll take care of them."

Zane dropped his too and gave a quick nod to agree.

"Take off will commence shortly." This timed perfectly with the rumble from engines ramping up again. "Thank you."

The two took up spots in the middle of the room. Keeping them nearly the same distance from any given Warden bed. Nek moved back to the hall. Mina also measured the distance from Zane to the nearest potential receptacle. She caught her best friend's gaze, knowing the look of fading adrenaline in him. "You good here?"

Zane took a deep breath. "No yeah, I'm good. This, weirdly enough, I can handle."

21

The Final Frontier

Mina jogged back to the pair holding Capri; Nek leading them onward to the hold. Comp2876 flashed a short countdown from her hands. She started telling the others to brace themselves, but then Outrider launched - 2876's countdown was off. The hard jolt sent Mina into a wall first and then to the floor. The others fell straight down due to the extra weight of Capri, whose face once again hit the floor. Thrust kept them in place until their suits adjusted. Emma pulled herself up first, held out hands to the other two.

"Going up!" Steph cheered.

"Or a bigger version of the drop tower ride we took a few minutes ago," Emma said.

Mina laughed as she grabbed one of Capri's arms, Comp2876 tucked in the crook of her elbow. "Is that a realist perspective?"

"It is. Remember how this thing sat unused for hundreds of years covered by rock?" Outrider shook again, they paused until it steadied itself out. "And we still have to make it to space. Speaking of, where did Capri come in at? Won't that hole suck the air out of the ship?"

Nek rolled by them on a panel. "Her point of entry was in a smaller storage area near where you came in. It was sealed off to protect the ship as a whole. We'll lose some materials, but in the grand scale of options-"

"Not too shabby." Steph grabbed Capri's other arm and heaved her up with Mina. They all received the update on Outrider's position, another few seconds and they would be very, very, very far from home.

Mina readjusted her grip on Capri. "Nek, can you tell the damage left behind us yet?"

Nek fell behind them on a panel. "One moment. Stabilizing has proven difficult. Almost there."

"Oh, yeah, no worries."

They continued down the hall, 2876 directing inside their displays. Mina was starting to wish they'd done their fight a little closer to these holding rooms. She felt the arm pull against her and looked to see if Steph was struggling too, but instead met Capri's glare. Capri jammed both feet into the floor and pushed off Mina to smash Steph into the wall. Comp2876 pulled itself free to circle around, recovering faster than Mina did, but flew a bit wobbly with a jet still sputtering.

"Capri is a problem, again," Emma called, squaring up with the battered ex-Warden. Her swing connected with the side of Capri's helmet as she pulled it all the way back on. She took another swing toward the visor, aiming for the weak spot, but was deflected.

"Idiot children." Capri moved back from the group, twisting the cuffs still restraining her.

"Still rude." Mina kicked the back of her knee, bringing Capri down to kneeling.

Steph made a grab for the cuffs, trying to pull Capri all the way to the ground. "Seriously, I've done taxes like twice now."

Emma landed a kick on the damaged helmet. Fragments flew off Capri's visor as it finally broke away, one angry eye glared out at them. Outrider tilted, sending them sliding down the hall. Comp2876 was self-stabilized and took the opportunity of Capri passing to send off a couple small bolts, but its targeting was evidently damaged as only one clipped her.

As Outrider corrected itself, Capri was the first to her feet. "This is the most annoying day."

"Says a lot about you. Your yesterday included killing your team." Mina got back to her feet. Not a very smooth comeback, but she was new to this kind of banter.

"I gave them an offer, they chose to die." She looked over the trio, still twisting at the restraints. "I can give you the same offer."

"Says the one in cuffs." Better.

Capri stretched to her full height. "Nek will throw you into the fire, along with countless others who are not worthy of Warden. All to stop me."

Nek shifted to tight white waves. "Your goals are not aligned with-"

"You know nothing of the Collective's true desires. They sent us out to explore and strike new ground. Why not create something better with it?"

"You would consume the lives of this planet to wage war against-"

"Those that have already done worse!" She looked back at the trio. "Listen to me. They can't stop a full force of Wardens."

"Are we Wardens or are we children?" Mina asked. She felt like they were intruding, listening in on what was technically still a very fresh argument between the two.

Emma stepped up beside her. "You also literally just called us unworthy."

Steph tilted her head. "Hey, look at that, I found a new menu."

The cuffs glowed with a light purple and snapped to the wall. Capri strained, but they wouldn't budge with the newly activated magnetism in place. "You are picking the wrong side."

"Weird thing to say, seeing how this used to be your side." Mina watched her struggle for another moment, that pull was pretty strong. "Um, can we move her?"

"On it." From Steph's wrist sprang a small holographic display, originating from a smooth band on the suit, no bigger than a watch band. Mina glanced down and realized she had one too, as did Emma. Steph dragged a finger over the display. The cuffs pulled against the wall with a low scraping sound, dragging Capri along with it.

"So I take it that everything is okay?" Zane asked in their ears.

"On the move again," Mina answered. "You guys take the ride okay?"

"We're all secure here," Sean said. "Tell Capri the ghosts of her team said she sucks."

Emma passed along the message, adding on, "How's it feel knowing this bunch of worthless kids are going to be the ones given them the final respects they deserve?" She held Capri's one eye glare for a beat before continuing. "Do you think if they were here they'd be happy to have you in cuffs too? Or would they have just put you down for good?"

Mina was thankful that Vengeful Emma was on their side, she'd never handled mean girls very well, but she also thought it best not to let Emma get too carried away. "We'll be turning you over to wherever you came from. The Collective, I believe? I assume they have some kind of bylaws about team slaying."

Capri dropped her helmet again to stare down Mina, the grin she sported was alarming. "The Collective will welcome my return."

Steph tapped at the band display, jerking Capri further down the hall. "The cuffs say no."

Capri pulled at the restraints, causing a ripple of purple electricity to run over her hands. She grimaced, pressed a foot against the wall, and pulled again. More electricity sparked out, matched by black waves that came from Capri's own suit. Through gritted teeth she growled, "I took no joy in the fallout of my team. But you pests, you I'll gladly put in the ground."

Steph tapped around on the display, but nothing responded. The entire space filled with a warning about the spike in energy. "That probably won't hold much longer."

Mina watched the arcing electricity around Capri. "It's too unstable to get close."

Emma looked at Nek. "Got another turret to punch her with?"

Capri screamed, a mix of pain and rage, as the cuffs inched off the wall. Bits of the metal paneling coming off with her. The build up of energy burst outward, throwing the trio back down the hall. Mina shook her head to clear her vision, but regretted it as a flash of pain shot over her skull. Getting checked for a concussion would be smart, too many hits to the head today. They all pushed themselves up to see Capri standing, cuffs fallen at her feet.

Her suit was torn across the front, hanging loose in large batches, ribbons of blood rolling down her sides from where the electric burst cut through to skin. Or they were seeing older wounds being exposed, Mina couldn't be fully sure. New angry welts crossed her face, along with a few glittering pieces of the visor. She used one hand to hold the other arm in place, the shoulder sitting lower than it should. Capri looked behind her and stumbled toward another breakoff hallway. As she disappeared, Capri called back to them, "You won't believe me, but I do hope you come around to my thinking."

They all ran forward, turning the corner as a door slammed shut to the right. There was a small window built in, they watched Capri pull off her Pak, revealing how bloodied she'd become from her fights across the ship. Mina realized it was a testament to the strength of her anger, which must be the only thing keeping her upright at this point.

Capri leaned heavily on the dash inside and pressed the Pak into the control panel, it expanded to take over half the board. She looked back at them and smiled, giving a weak wave with the one good arm.

"Nek! You gotta get in there." Mina tried to pry at the door.

"Her Pak has pushed me out of the pod's system. I can't get back in." Nek paced through panels behind them. "I didn't anticipate her running."

Emma punched at the window. "Coward!"

Capri gave a wider, broken smile back. She dropped into a bench built into the wall. "We'll have more fun. Another time."

The console flashed behind her, another launch countdown. They stared each other down until the window snapped shut.

"She's really getting away in an escape pod." Steph leaned against the wall behind them.

Mina turned around to Nek, who was still pacing. "Any outside weapons to target her?"

"It took everything Outrider had left to launch. By the time they are online, that pod will be too far away." Nek's tight roll loosening into spiked waves.

"How is that pod working?" Emma banged against the door again.

"They have their own independent power units. For situations like this where Outrider's own power is compromised."

The door shook, they heard the hiss of the pod detaching from the other side.

"Can you predict her direction?" Mina hoped for one bit of good information.

Comp2876 dropped a diagram that flickered between the trio. It showed this side of Outrider and pointed arrows off in every direction. Nek rolled across from it. "This was an unanticipated move. The pod does not have unlimited power, but she can gain a decent distance from us before we have the proper systems back online. I expect she will head back to the planet, but can not estimate where she would land."

Emma dropped her helmet and leaned against the wall. "Downside of being in space, there's a lot of it out there."

"And we don't have the numbers to spread that far," Mina added, "Not until more Comps are active. Unless the Guardians are designed for space travel? We could take those out."

"Not advised. They are highly complicated and you have no training for such things. Your small amount of skills barely kept you alive this time. Capri wants her own Guardian, but we can not risk her gaining control of any of them. Best action is to regroup and begin repairs. Again." Nek disappeared from the panel.

Mina felt that went against Capri's 'throw you in the fire statement', but it was likely Nek didn't believe they could keep themselves alive out there for long. Which was probably fair. She looked at Comp2876. "Are they mad at us?"

Long day, flickered on the screen. Its one jet sputtered completely out.

Mina caught Comp2876 before it dropped far. "I agree."

22

Chaos in Mirrors Are Closer Than They Appear

Right after Mina made them eco-terrorists.

Restoration landed a great spot for the festival. They could see the main entertainment stage, but not close enough to be overpowered by music. The bombardment instead came from whatever product promotion was going on a row over inside a tent. Sam was pretty sure it was some kind of kitchenware demo with a musical number, basically lots of clanging. Guess that was how they kept on theme for the festival. Sam was grateful Dad decided to use their small canopied seating area as a screening room for music videos or music centered short films from local artists. They liked this set up. It was a lot easier than arranging the mobile art gallery and spending most of their day stopping people from getting their literal sticky fingers all over the pieces.

Megan leaned in over the coolers. "New Girl is heading over."

"Her name is Henrie." Sam spotted her coming up the row, but waited until Henrie made it to the edge of their canopy before calling over. "Henrie! You made it."

"I'm guessing Steph has a tracker on me," she laughed and stepped up to the register. She must have picked up on being snooped on during her talk

150

with their dad earlier.

"Actually, Dad said to keep an eye out for you. Whatcha think?" Sam waved around to the stand and then wider out to the festival as a whole. Faint pot banging in the distance.

"Bigger than I expected. The festival, that is."

"We love any excuse to set up booths around here." Sam dropped a big scoop of ice into a large plastic cup. "Sweet tea or something different?" There was a faint twitch in her eyebrow. Sam caught her hesitation and tried to redirect. "That was really weird. Me knowing your drink and all. Let me try again?"

"No, it's okay. Can I get the peach one this time?"

"I will update the spreadsheet." They watched her eyebrow fully arch up this time. "Bad joke. I'm not that obsessed. Or obsessed at all. No one is obsessed with you actually. Not that you aren't nice. Seem nice. Here is your drink." Sam shoved the cup into her hand and walked away from Henrie before she could respond. Before their mouth kept going of its own accord.

Megan was almost falling into the cooler from how hard she was laughing. She caught Sam's arm as they passed and held them in place. She straightened and turned back toward Henrie. "Sorry. Forgive them. Sam generally has themself completely together. Annoyingly so, at times. I think Mitch putting them fully in charge of the festival tent has them a little strung out."

Sam managed a small shrug, running the tent wasn't too bad. As long as people behaved. Beyond their embarrassment, Sam noticed the music coming from the main stage was gone. Must be a band switch going on, which meant they should get ready for another wave of people to come through. They tried to pull away to the snack case, but Megan held them in place.

"It's all good. Really, I'm used to being the new kid." Henrie took a long drink as she stepped back and watched the current video play. It was one of the more subjective pieces, something about a sentient kazoo. She looked back at the pair. "Do we have to understand the art?"

"Oh, not at all," Megan said.

"Don't directly insult anything in front of my dad though," Sam added. "You'll get a whole lecture and I can tell you from experience it's not great." Hours. He could go for hours.

A festival security guard, not much older than any of them, stepped around Henrie and leaned over the register. "We need you to shut down and send people toward the parking lot."

"Is there a problem?" Sam pulled away from Megan. Already running through a few of the exit strategies they'd thought of this morning during setup.

"Festival is being shut down early for the day."

"Why?"

The guy shrugged and started moving on to the next vendor booth. "We've just been informed to close things down."

"Wealth of information," Megan muttered as she went to pull the plug on the screen.

Sam stepped out to the edge of the canopy to look down the row, seeing a crowd coming toward them from the stage. There was a figure stepping up to the microphone, the faint echo reached them a second later, "Attention everyone, please head toward the parking area in an orderly fashion. We are unfortunately having to shut down early today. We will return tomorrow. Watch our socials for updates. Again, please head toward the parking area. Thank you."

"Still not any kind of explanation," Henrie said from beside Sam.

"Yeah, but best to get to it." Sam turned back to see Megan already waving people out of their seating area.

"Do you need help packing up?"

Extra hands would be great, but Sam wasn't about to make her work before she was officially on the job. "Oh, you don't need to do that. We have a sys-"

Sam was cut off by a park employee now coming down the row with a megaphone. "Please leave your booths as is. You may return once the issue is resolved."

"Nevermind."

A woman across the row stepped out to call after the worker, "We can't leave all our stuff for anyone to take."

The worker gave a hard sigh and dropped the megaphone so only the nearby booths could hear. "There is a security matter that needs addressed. To do that properly, the entire park needs cleared. Your items will be safe."

"I don't believe it. How can you possibly clear the entire park? I'm not leaving." She took a dramatic step back toward her booth.

"Ma'am, we need you to head toward the parking lot. If anything happens to your booth, you can make a claim with the festival." The park employee moved on before the woman could respond again, starting up their megaphone speech.

Sam watched the woman teeter for a moment, clearly upset that her fight ended so quickly. They caught her eye and mentally willed her to let it go. The woman went against her own statement and followed the worker down the row. "You can't expect us all..."

Sam lost the rest of it in the crowd going by. Their tent was clear, aside from people trying to step in for a final drink on their way out, but Megan and Henrie waved them off as Sam took the time to pull the drawer and mobile card reader. They joined the current batch moving out, certain they would find things ransacked to some degree tomorrow. Megan and Henrie stayed close. Not far along, Sam spotted the park worker and vendor woman arguing. He was taking the barrage with a fair amount of grace given that the woman was doing what he wanted anyway.

"Is it actually possible to clear this place?" Henrie asked.

"I mean, each entrance has a gate so they can track who comes in," Megan said. "So they know the number to get out."

"People out on the trails may be harder to find though," Sam mentioned.

"I'm sure Hephaestus has their spytech around to help."

Henrie looked completely confused.

Sam rolled their eyes as the urban legend and moved on from it. People love a good conspiracy. "A security issue sounds more like a festival problem. So with us gone, it probably solves most of their worries."

"But what makes them clear out a whole event?" Henrie asked. She was watching another batch of people being shooed out of the banging pots tent. "They aren't giving anyone much time. So what's the hurry?"

Their trio caught up to the arguing pair. The worker hit the end of his patience and pulled her aside to an empty tent. Henrie grabbed both their arms and made them hang back.

The man leaned in with an angry whisper, "There has been a threat of attack on The Hill. We need to evacuate people calmly, but efficiently, as we don't know if this is a legit threat or not. We are being overly cautious to not potentially risk everyone's lives. So please vacate and do not incite panic or we will have a mass of injured people no matter what. And that will be on you."

The worker stomped back into the festival, raising the megaphone to start their spiel again. Their group made awkward eye contact with the woman as she finally did as requested and moved out toward the parking lot, quicker than the average person around her.

It was Sam's turn to grab their arms and pull them along, liking the idea of following orders. "Guess we got an answer."

Sam looked back once they reached the first row of the parking lot, caught a few rocks tumbling off a high ledge of The Hill. Even the rocks were getting out, but there were a fair amount of people behind them. They stalled out. "What if someone was missed back there? Or still refusing to leave? Or hiding?"

Henrie pulled on them as a Jeep of park employees rolled by. "Actual authorities are on this."

They turned back to Henrie. "Where's your car at?"

She laughed, "I actually took a Lyft here. Didn't want to mess with the parking."

Megan nodded. "Normally a smart move."

"You'll come with us then." Sam headed for the Restoration van. They didn't have far to go since they'd gotten here early to set up, but it did mean they were blocked by other cars and people moving farther into the rows.

Sam hopped into the driver's side, dropping the cash box and card reader into a box behind their seat, and Megan took the passenger side. Henrie crawled into the back, moving empty catering crates out of her way to take a seat right behind them on the floor. While waiting for a break in the line of people, Sam noticed a buildup at the exit from the mass exodus. A park employee started waving cars to split into another route being opened; it must have been closed off to ensure attendees stuck to one path, but explosively desperate times called for desperate measures. That brought a flow back to the traffic, Sam felt their shoulders ease a fraction.

Henrie scuttled across the van to look out the back window. "There's helicopters out now. They may be looking for people."

"Or like, a giant stick of dynamite sticking out of The Hill." Megan gave an overly hard, single laugh to her own joke.

"If any of this is legit." Sam forced themself to not think about the rocks falling moments ago. It was a struggle to think of a best case scenario here. If it was a hoax, that still meant there was someone willing to make that kind of threat toward hundreds of innocent strangers. They caught a break in the line and inched their way into the exiting row of vehicles.

Henrie bounced against one of the van walls. "Ow."

Sam looked back through the rearview mirror. "Sorry, I should have mentioned it'll be a rough ride."

"It's better than trying to hoof it. Or staying here." Henrie scooted back up and pulled one of the containers up behind her back for good measure.

As they rolled forward, Sam saw a security guard stop mid-stride toward another waiting car and look back at The Hill. They leaned closer to the window to glance back. The sun had dropped, covering The Hill partially in shadow, but Sam noticed there was now a sort of cloud blurring the edges. Sam's nose twitched as they realized they were looking at dust. The Hill was shaking. The windows started to rattle as they pressed back into the seat. Not a hoax.

Megan leaned out too, she looked considerably more pale. "Too long. We waited too long. Go. Please go."

"We got this." Sam was unsure if that was true, but knew she needed the encouragement and gave her arm a pat for good measure.

The problem being that there wasn't much room to go anywhere. Honks rang out and several attempted to pick up speed as the rattling increased. Only resulting in them all jamming in closer along the two paths out. They muttered how people needed to behave.

Sam spotted another two cars come up on their side and slowed to let them in. Megan gave a groan. They reached over and gave her arm a small squeeze again. "They would have shoved in somewhere else and possibly hurt somebody. We'll be okay."

A notice board, usually used for weather alerts, flashed at them.

NO INCOMING TRAFFIC

USE BOTH LANES TO EXIT

Sam stayed in place, letting others fill up the left lane. There was a small tightness in their chest, but they focused on the road. Their responsibility was getting themselves and their friends out safely. They noticed Henrie doing some kind of meditation breathing in the back.

She let out a long exhale and pushed up to see out the front window. Cars kept moving at a steady pace, which was good for them. The rattle persisted but didn't worsen, Sam put that under a different sort of good. A carved sign on their right read *Thanks For Coming!*

"The pleasure is all yours, believe me." Megan took a stab at the meditation breathing.

They kept rolling forward, the exit coming closer. Flashing lights farther up the road were blocking outside traffic to let everyone vacate The Park. Hopefully the highway would be far enough away from whatever was happening behind them.

Henrie shifted toward the back window. "I mean, it's still there. That's a good thing."

People, being so close to the end, were starting to become impatient. Sam noticed several drivers ride up close to the bumpers in front of them. Things bottled up a little as people turned out onto the highway, but they never stopped moving. This was good and fine and no reason to panic.

Henrie settled back down and pulled out her phone. "Oh good, my mom is freaking out."

"So it's on the news?" Megan asked.

"Not sure. She works at the hospital. I bet they got an alert too. Totally going to lie and say I left a while ago."

Sam wasn't sure why she'd do that, but decided now wasn't a great time to press the point.

A Jeep of park employees rolled by on the gravel shoulder on Megan's side. A few cars rumbled after them, opting to be done with the line. A helicopter buzzed over a second later. Megan let out a shaky breath, "If they're going, everyone must be clear right?"

Henrie glanced backward again. "Um, The Hill is, uh, glowing?"

Sam took the chance to look back. No more spotlights were on The Hill, it was making enough light of its own. The rock was red and crumbling, a large chunk crashing down the side. Creating a trail of fire behind itself as it tumbled through the trees.

Sam focused back on the exit, the best way to keep their sanity. Megan was still looking back. Henrie was up on her knees behind their seats so she could look out the back window. They could sense people were edging close to full-on panic, honks and shouts were heard all around. More cars cut around on the shoulder. In the rearview they noticed the glow shift from red to orange. The car behind bumped them.

"That isn't going to make anything better." Sam let out a long breath, their fingers wrapped tighter around the steering wheel.

Henrie reached forward to take Megan's hand. "We're almost out. Look at the lights ahead."

Megan pulled herself away from the now yellow and vibrating mountain. They weren't far off from the flashing emergency lights that hopefully meant safety. The tiniest fraction of tension left her shoulders, but she held tight to Henrie's hand.

Another small bump came from behind. Sam went to scowl via the side mirror, but the reflection flashed fully white and half a second later their vision did too.

23

Go, Go Ground Team?

Henrie pulled her eyes open, the right faster than the left, and found everything was still white. And smelled like coffee? She realized her head was inside a catering crate. There was a pinch in her side as she slowly pushed the container off. Glass and debris clattered to the floor of the van. The pinch went away, she cautiously looked down and saw it'd been her phone pressed into her side. It was shattered, but luckily for her the glass screen had been facing down. Looking out the back doors, they were both hanging loose on their hinges, she put together that they'd been pushed off the road and were now aimed at the trees. Which all looked flatter than before.

Groans and sounds of more falling glass came from behind her. She turned to see Sam and Megan shaking themselves off. Both wore a scattering of minor cuts like her, along with small burns from the airbags going off, but they weren't in horrible shape. Henrie's arm also felt rubbed raw, she must have slid across the floor on it. She carefully moved toward their seats, avoiding the glass and metal bits scattered around. "Might I request installing a handlebar back here?"

"I'll run it by Dad for the next van." Sam shrugged off their seatbelt and pushed open the door, it protested loudly and hung off balance. Megan did the same. It took both of them tugging on the side door to get Henrie out. The air was thick and warm, it hung on them as they stepped back on the road.

Other people were in the middle of a similar process. A few with working phones were taking pictures and videos, most performing self assessments or documenting the damage. Which, if she was honest, wasn't as bad as expected given that her last thoughts were of being vaporized. The cars left on the road were blown around, but people were getting out of them, for the most part. Henrie watched one man fall out of his car, one that chanced it on the shoulder and as a result was pushed hard into the treeline, and he stayed down. She reconsidered her 'not so bad' thought. Someone closer helped him back up. There were still flashing lights and movement out on the highway, several new sirens were going off.

"It's kind of a silver lining that he'll finally have to let this thing go," Megan said looking back at the van.

"I wouldn't put it past my dad to fix it up anyway." Sam was also watching the pair picking up the fallen man.

"Maybe he'll make it an art installation." Henrie pulled their arm, keeping them moving toward the exit.

"She is a fast learner," Megan gave a weak laugh. "You'll fit in great at the cafe."

Henrie was thrown by the thought of starting a new job on Monday after this. She turned back to The Park, expecting a red-hot mass bubbling behind her but there was nothing. No fire shooting into the sky. No burning chunks of rock about to fall down on them. Only an open skyline. No mountain. Period. Apparently that was the only thing vaporized. If she focused through the dim light, she could pick up that the air was wavy. Heat lines coming off the spot like a road in summer. That explained the wall of air they felt now. She could follow the trail for a while before a cloud bank blocked part of her view. It looked like the ones she'd seen when jets broke the sound barrier at demonstrations. But the center hole was massive and pointed straight up.

What happened here?

Sam worked their jaw a few times. They shook their head and must have popped their ears, now realizing how much noise was going on around them. "Oh, yep, that was throwing me off."

Across the road a woman was pounding against her passenger door from the inside. She was blinking rapidly from the head wound bleeding into her eyes and becoming more agitated with each hit. The man in the driver seat was attempting to calm her down, but not having any better luck with his door. Their windows were broken, but large jagged bits kept them from crawling out.

Sam shook their limbs, more glass fell. They called out to the other car. "Hang on, we'll come help."

Henrie, not totally thrilled at being volunteered, watched as Sam still checked both ways before crossing the street. Her and Megan jogged across after them. Megan pulled on the woman's door handle, but the shell came off in her hand. The woman, who was trying not to cry, said, "That was actually a problem before."

"Our passenger side mirror has been broken for months. We won't tell the insurance people if you won't," Megan said.

Henrie looked over the door and saw part of the frame bent severely in. "I'm not sure this will open. Let's try the other side."

Henrie saw the guy had managed to create a little give in the door. Again part of the top frame was bent and holding it shut, but less than the woman's side. "Lean back for me." She knocked the larger chunks of glass away with her elbow and used the bottom of her shirt to wipe away the remaining bits. "You push, I'll pull. On three. One. Two. Three!"

She placed a foot against the side as she pulled, but eventually it groaned and came loose. Henrie caught herself after a step, her hands ached from straining for so long. The guy nearly fell out of the car, but immediately turned to help the woman across. They shook themselves off and looked around.

The woman gave up on not crying. "Oh god."

The guy shook Henrie's hand. "Thank you. Is there anything we can do for you?"

She shook his hand quickly, her own stinging from the pressure. Henrie expected that despite her efforts there was some glass in them. "No problem.

I don't need-oh! Actually, are either of your phones working?"

He felt his pockets and pulled out his phone. The screen was cracked, but it turned on and he handed it over. "The towers may be pretty jammed right now."

Henrie pulled her mom's number out of the dregs of memory, tapping out a dumb rhyme they'd taught her when she was seven. She hoped her mom would answer the strange number.

After two rings, she did indeed answer with a concerned, "Hello?"

"Mom! Hey! It's Henrie. So, I might've been lying when I said I'd already left for home when you texted earlier." A poorly calculated risk.

"Henrietta! Where are you now? Are you okay? Where is your phone?" She only stopped asking questions because she ran out of breath.

"I'm on the exit road, I was almost out when things…exploded?" She gave a questioning look to the couple, they shrugged back. "Or whatever it did. I'm okay. Maybe a few little cuts and bruises, but fine. My phone broke."

"They will have an area designated for injuries. Get there and wait for me. Call again if you can. I'm leaving to get you now."

"Alright, will do. I have to give this phone back now. Love you."

"Love you too. Be safe!" Her mom was already hollering after someone before she ended the call.

"Thanks for that. Do you mind if my friends could make a call too?" Henrie turned, but saw Megan and Sam already moving on to another person trapped in their car farther up the road. Sam was helping guide the man through the window. She handed the phone back to the guy. "Nevermind."

"Why are those emergency vehicles not coming?" the woman asked as she looked out toward the highway.

"Aftershocks. Fallout. Radiation," Henrie rambled off, but stopped when the man gave a short heave. "That's as close as they'll get for now. Probably not sure if the area is safe for first responders yet. Not wanting to risk even more lives." Henrie started toward the other two, but made sure the couple was following her. A few helicopters circled around at the far edge of The Park. "More will show up over the next hour. I expect they're working to shut down any movement around the whole city already. They'll push in once they're confident it's safe enough."

The woman looked back at the space that used to contain The Hill. "What do you think happened?"

"It was red, like hot red," the guy said.

"It was fully white right before the," Henrie gestured an explosion. "And then…went up? I think." She pointed to the cloud bank, but the wind had already smudged the large circle there.

They caught up with Sam, Megan, and their rescued guy. Sam was ripping a sleeve off to wrap around a new cut on their hand.

Megan tucked her cracked phone away in a pocket. "Think the towers are too busy now. Can't get anything out anymore."

"I managed to get a call out to my mom," Henrie said as they kept moving forward. Caught herself before she added *so I'm sure my dad will be along soon to save us.* Great, now she had slivers in her palms and was sad.

On their way out the group helped a few more people break open jammed doors. Twice they approached a vehicle to realize the person wasn't unconscious, but dead. When they found another in the treeline with a person hanging out of the passenger side, they stopped going toward any car that someone wasn't actively calling out from. She fully reversed her call on this being 'not so bad'. Henrie knew for certain that there were more bits of glass in her hands by the time they reached the merge to the highway.

Police cars lined the shoulder of the ramp, their windows were cracked. A mass of flashing first response vehicles filled the road behind that. All other traffic was currently at a standstill, people pressed against the median to see what was going on. A police officer came toward their group, looking them over quickly and directing them to different spots to wait for medical care. Henrie, Megan, and Sam asked to stay together but the officer insisted Sam needed stitches for their hand and none of their makeshift stations were big enough for all three.

Megan gave Henrie a little guilty look. "You okay if I go with Sam? You said your mom was on the way. Sam may need my phone once things clear up."

Her stomach twisted at the thought of leaving these people she'd only known for about forty minutes, a weird sensation to get her head around. "No, that makes sense. I'm good! Once I'm home and can get to my laptop, I'll message you."

"You better." Megan gave her a quick hug. "This was a weird first meeting, but I'm glad you were here. Well I mean…you know…"

"I know what you mean. You two be safe."

Megan made a point to take a long, controlled breath. "See you later."

Henrie watched the two walk away as she was directed to sit on the back of a firetruck. A firefighter came over and asked questions to test her mental capacities. He shined a light in her eyes, it thankfully didn't hurt. She let him know that her biggest discomfort was the slivers in her palms.

"Let me grab our kit. See what I can do for you." He opened a side box and grabbed a bag, dug around until he found the tweezers. He clipped his flashlight to his collar as he came back to her. "Lay your hands out flat on your knees, please."

She let him start poking at her left hand without saying anything, but it got awkward fast. Also she needed a distraction from the ebbing pain in her palms. "Do you have any idea what happened?"

"There's nothing official yet. There was a threat made about blowing up The Hill. They decided to be cautious and clear out everyone. We were called as backup for crowd control."

Her hand twitched from one of the pokes. "Good thing they decided to be careful."

"No yeah, but they only really took it seriously because somehow they managed to broadcast to every available signal in the area all at once. One of the park employees was going on about it before they got carted off. Only one station managed to get back to them, but lots of ears heard it. Then reports came in around the same time of seismic activity. They were low, but unheard of for our area. The police chopper came by and their thermals saw The Hill heat up. Said it looked like it cooked from the inside out."

She wondered if he should be telling her all of this, but forgot the thought as he wiped her palm down with rubbing alcohol. Henrie sucked in a breath. "How'd they blow it up from the inside?"

"No one knows." He paused and glanced back toward The Park. "We watched it change color out here. Was odd you couldn't really feel the heat though, given how big it is. Was."

"And then the boom."

He turned back to poke at her right hand. "And then the boom. We were all knocked over. Signals were lost, just getting some of those back. Hill was gone. People braced for impact from fallout, but nothing came. Whole thing poofed away. No one's allowed close yet. But my buddy works in one of the taller buildings right on the other side," he nodded behind them toward the edge of downtown Hurst that pressed against the highway, "and he managed to send out a picture he got from the roof. It's blurry, but seems to be quite the crater in there now. Also said some buildings over there caught the edge of that shockwave too."

Yeah, he was definitely talking too much. She got the feeling he was still personally processing the entire event, it was a lot to wrap your head around. But Henrie appreciated having someone else talk this out for her. "So whoever they were did what they promised."

"But also gave a warning. Park was mostly cleared. Casualties could've been a lot higher. Property damage is through the roof, I'm sure. But Hephaestus can afford it. This all could've been way worse."

"All's well that ends…does this count as well?" She flinched as he wiped down this palm with the rubbing alcohol.

"I think this counts as the best option out of a lot of bad endings." He shined his light around on her palms. "I think I got all I can. They may get you lined up with a ride to the hospital to have that confirmed. Think things are still getting sorted. Sit tight for me."

She did just that, leaning against the side of the firetruck and zoning out. The tilted trees across from her became a blurred mass. More helicopters were circling, but kept their distance. Henrie refocused on one she used to see on base as they buzzed by, but there was some kind of company logo on the side. The sound behind her was becoming less voices and more doors opening and closing, the crowd on the other side of the median thinning out. Likely they were being officially ordered to leave as traffic started up again.

"Henrie! Where are you?!" came from the other side of the firetruck. Somehow in all this, mere moments after a not-so-natural disaster, her mom zeroed in on her amidst all these people. It was a superpower Henrie was familiar with, but would never understand.

She ran around the front of the firetruck. There her mom was, in her office attire, climbing over the median. Another fireman was asking her to not do that. "Mom!"

"That's her. Help me over," she barked at the fireman. Who in his stunned state held out a hand for her. Her mother had dealt with a career military husband for nearly eighteen years, she knew when someone behaved better if given direct orders.

Henrie met her halfway and slammed into her for a hug. Squeezing her even though her hands were still red and irritated. "I'm sorry for lying. I didn't want you to panic. I thought I could get out in time."

"It's fine. You're okay." She pulled back to look Henrie over, giving a light touch to her swollen brow. "Are you okay?"

"Yeah! A fireman already looked me over, but said I may need a second pass for more glass in my hands."

Her mom pushed back further and pulled her hands close to her eyes. "Henrietta, you-"

"Only little slivers. I pulled a few doors open for people. There was a lot of glass everywhere."

After taking a deep breath, her mom gave her cheek a rub. "You did good. Your dad would be proud. I can look over your hands at home. Let's get out of here."

"I think I'm supposed to get cleared by someone," she protested as her mom pulled her back to the median.

Her mother looked at the fireman, who was now holding off a few other stragglers from climbing over. "Excuse me, sir."

He looked back nervously, "Uh, yes, ma'am."

"Please tell whoever you report to that I am taking my daughter home now." She rattled off their names and her phone number, after not so patiently waiting for him to pull out a phone to write it all down.

Henrie mouthed an apology as her mother climbed over the median. He nodded and went back to holding off other people. They weaved through the small patch of cars to her mother's sedan parked on the opposite shoulder. There was a reporter power walking in their direction, a cameraman not far behind.

"Do you have a moment?" the reporter shouted over.

Her mom ignored them as she pulled open the driver door. "Henrie, get in the back for now." Not wanting her to waste time walking around with the reporter closing in.

She followed the order and slid into the backseat. The reporter was coming up to the back window as her mom hit the gas and drove along the shoulder. Henrie sank low as they pulled away, avoiding looks from onlookers they passed.

"Buckle up, Henrie." Her mom gave a look via the rearview mirror. She pulled the car back onto the highway once space opened up.

Henrie sat back up and did so. She felt silly being in the back. Like she was ten again and on the way home from some tournament. Henrie took a shot at an old go to. "Hey, since I did good today, can we stop for McDonalds?"

24

Text Home…Oh God, They're Calling

The trio found the guys waiting in the main hallway. With their helmets all down, Mina realized how tired they'd become in such a short time. She was certain that several previously unused muscles in all of them, besides maybe Zane and Emma, would be angry come morning. They all needed to think of an excuse for the bruises.

Zane looked around at the group, weary but smiling, "Anyone else have this on their bingo card? I didn't see it on mine."

"Thank you for coming with me." Mina gave his hand a squeeze. "To the ship. And doing," she waved at their suits, "all this. I know it was insane, but it was fun too." Her head throbbed, but she knew she wasn't lying.

Sean tilted his head. "You know, I'd have to agree."

"I've had much worse days at rehearsals," Steph added.

They all looked at Emma, who was staring at the floor. She looked down the hall, up to the empty Nek panel, and finally at them. "I mean, we aren't dead. So there's that."

Zane clapped. "Emma's on board, look at that."

"This isn't a win though," she pointed to the Comp parts scattered around. "Other than being in space now, we're practically back to square one."

"And with an enemy who has advanced training, a likely unstable mental state, and a desire to take over the planet," Steph rattled off. Emma nodded with each item.

"Don't help her," Sean said. "She gets smug."

"We should get back to the deck." Mina moved toward the elevator. "See what the new task list is."

She caught one sigh behind her, but heard them following. Zane was used to her 'always doing something' mentality. The others would catch on.

Much to do. Comp2876 scrolled out from her hands.

She gave the screen a tap. "I'll get you fixed up first."

When they entered the deck, every display was lit up. Nek moved about the room, checking on systems. The main display board filled with the list of damages and priority tasks, which was reorganized as they found new issues around the ship. Nek tagged their names to certain tasks, creating sublists that suited each of them.

Mina stepped toward the center display but turned to follow Nek as they moved. "Nek? Do we need to keep the suits on while in space?"

"Outrider is properly pressurized, you will be safe without the suits activated." Nek continued to bounce around consoles.

With the direct danger gone, they could return to the more mundane tasks of cleanup and repairs. They'd needed the Paks to stop Capri and that was done. Nek said the actual process for Wardens took a long time, they would need to start looking soon. Mina didn't want to give this up. The suit started to fit better as they moved about the ship, it felt good. It felt right. But she couldn't ask everyone to stick with this dangerous path. They'd go back to normal and Mina would…audition later on her own, she guessed.

"Sounds good. We'll get started putting Comps back together." Mina tapped the Pak, the suit retreated and the Pak dropped into her hand. She wanted to appear nonchalant for the others, but hesitated as she held it out over the pedestal.

Nek rolled over to her. "Why are you returning the Pak?"

"You said we don't need them to get around. Capri is gone. You need these back, right?" She felt her fingers tighten even as she said it, daring to hope she was wrong.

"Paks are," their waves bounced quietly for a moment, "intricate devices. They have a heavily encrypted code set into them. Making it so only those deemed worthy can fully access their capabilities."

Steph ran a hand over her Pak, the purple glowing brighter. "Yeah, you mentioned there is a long process for determining who uses them."

Nek shifted side to side, their version of shaking their head. "The Collective designed a rigorous training program to put together teams, but the Paks have the final say on who is a Warden."

"How does Capri still use hers then?"

"I fear her tampering may have affected the Pak's processing. But these," Nek moved back to the main display, "are in good standing and have assessed you all capable and fit for duty."

"We were kind of a mess." Emma's hand hovered over her own Pak. "And she got away."

All the shuffling and sorting of information came to a stop. Their waves were the same mass of colorful lines, but Mina could feel Nek solely looking at them for likely the first time. "Capri's escape is as much on me. She continually makes moves I do not anticipate. For this, I require assistance. I would be honored to have you all decide to stay on with us, but I know that is a larger commitment than originally asked of you. You are free to return the Pak now or whenever you choose."

Mina pulled hers back, feeling the warmth in her palm. She placed it against her side and tapped the pad, releasing the suit again. Never so happy to be wrong, but hoping her excitement wasn't too obvious. She didn't want to influence the others if they wanted to be done. "I'm happy to help, for as long as you need me, but I won't make that call for everyone."

Nek rolled closer to the others. "I know you still have many questions about where we came from and all that has already happened. I am happy to provide that to you as we go along. Capri's comments have given me concern about the Collective we left behind. It seems not every intention for sending our team here was with the greater good in mind. I...I have decided this is not a Collective expedition anymore. With Capri at large, this is a fight for the safety of your planet. But again, you are free to be done if you wish. I will expedite the teleport repairs to return anyone home who wishes to leave."

Zane looked at the others, no one wavered. Emma's hand dropped back to her side. He smiled at Mina. "We're with her. Tell us what you need done first."

Another list appeared on a screen behind them, various training regiments rolled out and became nearly as daunting as the repairs list. Nek did a big spin in place, that had to be their happy face. "Wonderful! We will have much to do, but I welcome you all. Wardens of Earth."

Mina wished again for the confetti and horns feature. She'd investigate that possibility for future Comps. Zane and Steph performed their postponed high five, then followed it with three more high fives in quick succession. Emma and Sean were doing some handshake they must have created long ago. Mina held in a happy squeal but hugged Comp2876 to her tighter.

Glad to have you, Warden Mina!

Nek shifted over to the console behind her, pulling up feeds from back on Earth. "There is news from our departure."

"How bad did it end up?" Mina scanned over the information.

"They did nearly clear out the area in time. Some injuries, only a few critical. There were a handful of casualties, I am afraid." They pulled up the few images gathered of the crater that now resided in The Park. "Our footprint is rather visible, but they have not tracked us."

"Can they track us?" Emma asked, coming up behind Mina.

A diagram popped up showing the path they'd taken upon leaving Earth, Outrider now resided on the dark side of the Moon. "I have set Outrider to move at pace with this moon."

"Something will eventually find us. There are always robots on the Moon and satellites flying about," Sean said. "And they keep putting more things on Mars."

Tasks shifted on the board. "I will have cloaking up as soon as possible. And once more systems are reliably operational, we can look to relocate."

Emma kept looking at the news feeds scrolling by. "How long till the teleport is going? I may have to head for the day. Parents have to be freaking out."

There was a flash on another console, Nek shifted over to the new information. "My first test run has failed. The teleport suffered more damage than expected. I will need Comps for repairs and further testing before I feel confident sending any of you through."

"I'm glad to hang out and not get stranded in space," Zane said.

Mina looked over their to-do list, which filled the majority of the main display. If they had the time, they might as well work. She picked out the few with her name and organized them on her armband. It reminded her of when she'd write reminders on her arms in middle school because she was always losing her planner and her parents, weirdly, wouldn't get her a phone yet. Less ink stains this way.

Her weekend was free and she was ready to dive right in, but she remembered she was now a leader of a team. Maybe? Kind of. Sort of. Zane's 'we're with her' announcement threw her off. Whatever she was, she had to think of the group now. "Who needs to check in with people back home? How bad would it be for anyone if we were stuck here for the night? And beyond that, expecting that the world might shut down over a missing mountain, how does your weekend look? I imagine we could get a decent amount done even if it's only a few hours each."

Sean smacked where his pocket would be, but the suit stopped him. He dropped it and pulled out the phone. "Yeah, this is going to be a rough call to my mom."

Emma did the same, talking to her mom before it even reached her ear. "Hey! I'm good. I swear. Mom, you gotta slow down. Take a breath."

Steph and Zane started swiping through their messages from family and friends. Mina confirmed all of social media was going crazy. Not to mention how quickly a disappearing mountain found its way to national news, rightly so. She looked up to Nek, "We may need a few minutes."

"Also, how?" Steph asked, gesturing to her phone. "I can barely get a signal in parts of The Park and have full bars here."

"Signal boost from the ship?" Zane asked and looked up to Nek, clearly hoping to catch an easy one before Mina.

"Correct," Nek said.

Zane celebrated with a quick fist bump to the air and went back to checking a family group chat. She knew he was putting off calling his parents, afraid to hear the sultry music in the background of wherever they were.

Steph rolled her eyes and called over to Sean. "Carter is going nonstop in the work chat."

He made a gagging gesture before going back to saying, "No, I don't want to look at new schools for next year. This was a freak accident kind of thing. It's fine!"

Emma was having the near same conversation. "If it's end times here, it's end times everywhere."

They all drifted to different spots on the deck. Bits of the same 'yeah, it's crazy' and 'no, I didn't see that video yet' repeated over and over. Mina was actually the one to inform her parents of the event, as they were neck-deep on a project several states away and hadn't looked up from their work in hours. Which made it surprising her texts got such a quick response, must have caught them on a food break. She spun in her chair, realizing she'd wrapped up contacting people well before the rest. Made sense, sadly. If this Warden thing stuck, it would be the biggest group of friends she'd ever held at one time. The thought made her a little sad, which surprised her, but the feeling was there all the same. Mina moved over to the console Zane was leaning against as he sat on the floor. She slid down and laid her head against his shoulder, this made her not sad.

He reached over and scratched the top of her head. Zane was insisting their house survived perfectly well before their conversation shifted to her. "Yes, Mina is good too. I've got the food and entertainment. She's got the equipment to keep everything running if the power were to go out. We're the dream team of apocalypse survival." He listened, sighed, and passed the phone. "Tell my mom you're okay."

Mina grabbed it. "Hi, Mrs..uh, Donna. I am alive and well. Promise."

"You two stick together while this gets sorted," said the soft voice of Zane's mom. Mina always felt she talked even softer to her than she did with most people.

"Nowhere else I'd be." Mina could tell Zane's mom felt guilty for being out of town the one weekend in Hurst's entire existence that something horrible happened. But it wasn't like anyone could have predicted this kind of thing. She hadn't and she was inside the ship.

"Were your parents in town? Do they know you're okay?"

"They know. They're in Oregon following some leads on a project."

"Flights may be shut down for a couple of days, but I bet Hephaestus will fly them in. Do they know when they can get back yet?"

Look at her, thinking of easy solutions her parents wouldn't offer.

"Oh. No. They're, um, staying in Oregon. Lots to do." They'd mentioned that Hephaestus would send them any readings that needed their attention. She was annoyed they were barely interested in The Hill disappearing.

Mina caught the faint 'these people' whispered only slightly away from the phone. Donna's chipper voice came back, "Probably safer anyway. Wait till things calm down. Now tell me, how's his stomach? Any upchucks?"

Mina leaned a little away from Zane and whispered, "Only like twice. Couple dry heaves, but he's done pretty well."

Zane twisted around. "Excuse you. I am a champ."

His mom laughed on her end. "Always so defensive. Anyway, brats on the grill sound good for Monday? That's the soonest we're hearing we can get back."

"Yes ma'am," Mina wiped away the little tear trying to sneak past her. It bothered her the random reactions she'd have to being cared for sometimes, but she didn't know what to do about them yet. "Will do. Here's Zane again." She passed the phone back and leaned harder into his side.

He did another series of yes ma'am, will do, and yeps before finally being allowed to end the call. "She's embarrassing."

"She's fine," Mina said through one small hiccup.

He shifted them enough to get an arm around her. "Are your folks really not trying to get back? Even for research stuff?"

"Lots of results coming in on their new project. Gotta stay on the leads. I'm sure Hephaestus has a team looking into it already. They'll catch up."

He sighed and gave her a nudge. "Forget them. We have a team now."

She looked at the other three. Steph was trying to end her call, insisting she couldn't do a video chat right now, but not being released yet. Emma and Sean were swapping phones, they appeared to be in the same conversation. Mina smiled but faltered. "You think we'll be good at this? I want to be good at this."

"You are good at literally everything I've seen you do. With one," he glanced at Steph, "slight exception. As for us as a team, we're wobbly, but we'll get there."

Mina tilted Comp2876 to look at its damage, but also glanced at Steph. "That should probably get back burnered for now anyway."

"Do not."

"This is a lot to take on! And to try adding in…ya know, it's too much." She fidgeted with a piece of loose casing.

"I swear to-"

"It's too much to ask of a person." Not to mention Mina was also fighting against her internal list of tasks and questions to chase after. Her parents would play catch up, but Mina was here now. She wanted to know everything before they did. It wasn't the most noble of intentions, but she was self-aware enough to know it was a notable percentage of her motive.

Zane gave her a hard look. "You get a month. No matter how long this takes. We come back to this in a month."

"Damn you, knowing my love for deadlines."

"Aye," Steph let out from across the deck, "I would take another fight with Capri over doing that again."

Emma and Sean wrapped up their calls soon after. They reconvened at the main display, checking over the list of tasks Nek continued to prioritize while they talked. Sean leaned against the console in front of them, "Lots to do."

"Everyone got cover stories for the weekend?" Mina asked. "Or do we need to do shifts or something?"

Sean gave a so-so gesture. "We're lucky our parents left this morning for a vineyard thing a couple of hours away and are now stuck there. We have a pre-established network of 'if anyone asks I'm sleeping at your place' with the other cousins, but we'll need to check in tomorrow morning when they get back to town."

"Speaking of which," Emma said, "Where do you think Robbie is at? He used it too."

"Probably that Velasquez girl. The one his mom hates."

"That's more dangerous than what we're doing."

Steph's eyes grew round. "I need to hear all about that later. As for the weekend, I'm good. Perk of divorced parents who don't talk unless it's through a lawyer. I'll just need to check in with at least one of them tomorrow too."

Nek spun on the display. "I can aid in that. I put together a quick interface for your phones on the armband. You will no longer need to fully retract the suit to use them."

They reactivated their suits and tested the new function. Steph tapped out a text, laughing as she scrolled through gifs across the armband. "You just threw this together?"

"Your calls lasted longer than I expected. I found myself with some time. As you use it, I will work out any issues."

"You are so cool."

There was a drop in conversation, Mina realized they were all looking at her. Even Nek was waiting. She panicked for a second, feeling the weight of Comp2876 in her hands. "We need more help. I think Steph and I will go back to the charging dock and get repairs going. Emma, are you good to take up delivering parts again?"

"Absolutely." She looked excited to get back to Fabrication. "Nek, do you have other pieces being made too? I can deliver them around so everything is ready for Comps when they are back online."

"That will be excellent." A small camera view of Fabrication appeared on their screen, showing all the machines churning away. "I've also started production on new Comps. You'll find their assembly line on the far right wall in Fabrication. They'll need delivered to the charging docks once completed."

"Emma's Delivery Service is here to help!" She was the first to head toward the elevator.

"Are you going to print yourself a flying broom?" Zane called after her.

"That would be irresponsible," she looked back to Nek, "unless you have something that is flying broomish that is a valid tool for us to have."

Nek's waves stretched back out. "No design template is on file. I will look into it."

Steph stepped onto the elevator pad. "I don't think Nek's gotten to that part of human

culture yet."

Emma stepped back toward the main display. "Forget about it. Really. It's nothing. Dumb joke. I'm going to Fabrication."

Mina turned to the guys. "I think I'll have you two on cleanup again. Grab us any Comp that might be salvageable. We also have blindspots from Capri attacking cameras. Can you get us reports on those areas?" She pointed to Zane. "I will let you borrow one of my kits. See if there is anything you can do a quick fix on. Remember to turn the power off before you touch anything. Please don't electrocute yourself. Again."

"It's only happened like four times," he scoffed.

She caught him twitch from clearly remembering each of those times.

They took the elevator down together, the barrier was now fully retracted from the center level. Sean and Zane heading off right away as the doors opened. Emma hesitated but stepped out after consulting the translated symbols on the wall. Leaving Steph and Mina alone in the main hallway. Mina gestured for her to go first, "After you."

As the two headed toward the docking bay, Mina remained very aware of how close their hands were.

25

I Feel Like (Space) Trash

"I have to kill them all." Capri pulled the Pak off the console and pressed it against her side. Her suit rolled over her, providing a small amount of relief to the wounds across her body. Caro always took issue with the slight numbing, but she never was short of nonsense to worry over. "They can never get the chance to tell the Collective about this embarrassing day."

Her Pak fully integrated with the pod's system, she was proud of her efficient programming given the meager means she'd worked with. Nek would be off her back long enough to determine a landing spot back on that planet. A bonus, control of two fresh Comps packed away within the pod. They didn't possess all the functions of full Comps, but they'd do for now. She set them on making one fully functional Comp from the pieces she'd picked up on the run. Capri activated the radar, wanting a feel for where she was floating through; there hadn't been a lot of time to familiarize herself with the area before. The scan caught nothing interesting, so she decided to keep straight on for the time being. No harm in floating a bit further out while she tended to herself.

Capri opened the medpack set into the wall, glaring at all the basic supplies. She allowed herself a fleeting moment to miss the automated medbay of Outrider, where one would simply lay down and have their damage addressed. Now she pressed a medicated pad against the cut on her face where the angry Green one kicked her. A hiss from the sudden spike of pain escaped her.

"This should've been simple." She kicked the wall, the thud was satisfying. "They're idiots. Untrained. Flailing. Babies."

Her armband updated with diagnostic results, the Pak needed to repair itself after that last unfortunate fight; something done faster while not on her. Capri was reluctant to have it off again but tapped the pad, re-exposing her injuries to the cool air. She kicked the wall until a warning flashed on the dash about damage.

Capri sank to the floor, more due to exhaustion than anything. She lifted her injured arm and slowly pulled until her shoulder snapped back into place. The kit didn't contain a sling, she settled for holding it against her body until the pain ebbed. With her one good hand, she continued cleaning her other wounds. By the end there was an upsetting amount of red-soaked swabs on the floor and every inch of available gauze wrapped around her. At least it was the blast she'd caused that did the most damage, rather than those brats or the horrible Comp. Once bandaged, she checked on the Pak - itching to have it back on - but it needed more time. No use going back without that active. She called for one of the Comps.

It pushed over to her. *Directive?*

"Keep us going in this direction until the Pak's repair is complete. Then circle back to Earth. Land us as far away from wherever Outrider originally was."

Understood.

"I'm passing out again, in hopes that this awful day was a nightmare. Or a premonition. Perhaps I can kill those imposters the second time around." The Comp couldn't do anything with that information, but she liked knowing her frustrated intentions were heard in some fashion.

Sleep well.

Capri released the small cot, barely long enough for her, but she'd used worse. Countless training exercises on hostile planets with horrible conditions. Cold ground and lulled to sleep by assurances that whoever was on watch would raise an alarm before whatever that noise was could eat you. The small sounds of the Comps and pod humming did well to put her mind at, somewhat, ease. With her eyes closed, this felt familiar.

Which lasted maybe all of ten minutes.

A long tone broke the calm and jolted her upright. She almost hit the Comp floating over her, the screen flashing, *Enemy detected.*

"How? Where?" She crossed the small distance to the window. Her programming designated Outrider as blocked, but not an enemy, so it wasn't them already on her tail. The radar showed the ship's last marked location behind her, but there was another ping coming from ahead and drawing closer. Capri checked the tag, known enemies of the Collective had designations set in the system. "Lenian."

Not ideal, but there were worse types to bump heads with. Knowing their style this was only a scout, manned by a low-level moron she could overtake. Capri thought back to that fateful talk with her team, in another life, of how long it would be before anyone else reached this far in the galaxy. She hated to admit, Nek was rather spot on in their estimations. They'd even guessed Lenians being one of the first to venture this far after them. But if they were still in the early days of their occupation, and if any power out there was still on her side, this would go back to a small base. Something meant for recon and surveillance, Lenians liked long observations before attacks. Stamp the flag down and claim it for Lenia before anyone else tries and without actually doing much. Something she could easily overrun on her own.

Remember how confident you were on Outrider a few moments ago? asked the imitation Rin.

"Shut up." She shook it off. They took her down only because of luck and their complete non-plan being difficult to defend against. And that Comp menace. And her own body still recovering. This was different, she knew Lenian grunts and their Pawns. Even five hundred years later, some things couldn't change. Lenians could be planned for. Even if the base was bigger than she hoped, and harder to overthrow alone, there was always intel she could bargain with.

Yes, they'll fall at your feet for centuries-old information.

"Enough." Capri glared at the console. Besides, she did have current

Outrider intel and was offended that this voice ignored that. Especially given that it was inside her head.

The Comp came around in front of her. *Evasive actions are needed.*

"No, keep steady. If they grab us, let them, and shut down our power. We'll take the free ride. Get that Comp up and running."

The screen flickered, challenging orders could short the little things. But it turned around and went back to repairing the Comp.

Capri sat back on the cot and kept watch out the window. She eventually caught sight of the speck that was growing larger. "That's fine, come and get me."

She barely blinked until it was in close enough range to grab a full scan. Like she expected, a simple scouting ship. Automated even, no direct pilot to deal with. It latched onto her pod, and pulled hard and fast in the other direction - it expected a fight. When her pod remained still, the scout slowed. The Comp drifted over to the console and shut down most of the power. Capri felt stiffness settling into her muscles. "Wake me when there is a visual of the base."

The Comp flipped and flashed the message, *Directive confirmed.*

She looked forward to facing an enemy she knew. Capri closed her eyes and allowed the small whir of the working Comps to lull her back to sleep.

26

Sleepover on a Spaceship

The bad news, the teleport was still on the fritz after a few more rounds of testing. Mina watched the last attempt, which did not go well for the empty crate. The good news, none of the others saw. She wasn't sure how they'd get Zane back home if he had. That left the team for sure staying on the ship for the night.

After a few more hours of cleanup, repairs, and randomly stopping to test new features on the suit as they found them, Nek appeared on their armbands to say they'd done more than enough for one day. There was a cluster of Comps back in the framework now, and more almost out of Fabrication. They could take over tasks while the Wardens rested. This announcement did also come after Sean attempted another trick with the saber. It'd been some kind of spin move, but he miscalculated the number of spins and would have cut himself if Emma didn't pull him back. No one else pointed that out, so she left it alone. Mina almost insisted on staying up for a bit longer, but caught a look from Zane that read 'you are exhausted, stop'.

"These suits are great." Emma shoved the Pak into her pocket as they were led to the sleeping quarters by the newly repaired Comp2876. "But I'm absolutely beat from all the running around today."

"My arms feel like they weigh a ton," Zane added, "2876, are there showers in the rooms?"

"More importantly, are there baths for those that no longer wish to stand?" Steph asked.

Warden quarters have private bathrooms! It dropped a hologram of the layout. Individual Warden quarters were only one room and a bathroom, but she figured it was more space than any of them had to themselves at home. Well, outside of herself - usually having a whole house at her disposal. She caught Steph's eyes zero in on the large tub shining in the hologram.

"I'm going to soak for like two hours." Steph reached out to give the image a caress.

Comp2876 came to a stop at a row of doors. *You can select any room! All layouts are the same!*

Mina took the first door in the line and looked over at the others. "Should we say, nine-ish to start again tomorrow?"

Everyone nodded in agreement and stepped toward different doors. Comp2876 let out a loud beep and flew in front of the row to push them all back. *Wait!*

Sean stepped back until he hit the other wall. "Are these trapped or something?"

Comp2876 pushed up and down the hall, but nothing updated to its screen. It came to a stop in front of the empty Nek panel and waited as they rolled in. "My apologies, everyone. I once again have overlooked this event."

Emma also stepped back from her door. "Event?"

"The rooms were used by our previous Warden team. These rooms have been untouched since…"

"So they're still full of their stuff," Mina realized.

"And likely tossed around from the crash," Zane added.

Emma shook her head and moved farther from her door. "No disrespect, but I don't know if I can mentally handle cleaning that up right now."

"And I would not ask you to." Nek paced the hall. "I will have Comps take care of these while you rest elsewhere." Earlier, they'd also designated taking care of the previous Warden's remains as a Comps' only task. The group was happy to help, but Mina was secretly happy not to intrude on something so personal. Especially if Nek wasn't ready for it. "Comp2876 will take you to our bunk quarters for tonight."

Comp2876 turned back to them. *No baths. Sorry, Warden Steph!*

Her shoulders slumped at losing those hours of soaking, but Steph waved it off. "Oh, don't worry about me. A shower will do just as good."

They weaved through another set of halls, not far from the private quarters they came to a pair of doors that Comp2876 triggered to open. The group walked into the large room, bunks were built into the walls on either side. The far end held another door that led to what must be a communal bathroom. Most of the bunk pads were tossed from their frames, and a couple of tables and their chairs pressed against one wall. They made quick work of sorting the room.

Sean visibly counted the bunks and leaned into Emma, "There's like twenty in here. There weren't this many people on the ship."

Nek rolled into the room's panel. "All Warden ships have quarters in the case of transporting civilians. Or support crew when they are required. Outrider was sent out with only an exploratory team. Our mission was to travel to this sector, farther than any Collective expedition had ever gone, and establish a base at which to train the local population. Then begin fostering potential Warden teams, who could also reside here."

"Which is kinda the same as Capri's plan, to start at least." Emma shuffled from foot to foot, not looking directly at the panel. "Weird how thin that line gets."

Nek's waves got a bit tighter. "Involvement would be voluntary, I assure you. Capri wishes to force the entire population into becoming an army under her command. To strike out against whoever she deems her enemy."

"We believe you!" Mina gave Emma a pleading look. "It's a lot of new information to process. And a little bit being overtired."

Emma pushed a chair around as a personal distraction to not look directly at Nek. "I may be a little hangry. Sorry, Nek."

Their waves lowered down, "Your reaction is understandable. I know there are still so many questions for us to address. Again, thank you for your work today. Please, get some rest. We will start again tomorrow."

Zane dropped one of the duffle bags onto the table now set in the middle of the room. "Who's laughing at all the snacks now? This spaceship restoration is sponsored by overly processed food."

Steph looked over the options. "If the teleport is working by morning, we should make a food run. Get some things with actual nutritional value."

Zane tried to scoff but choked on his mouthful of chips.

"That would be smart," Mina gave him a hard pat on the back. She'd make sure a few crates made it through the trip first. "Kind of excited to see how teleporting feels."

Zane held up his bag of chips as a toast. "To flying through hundreds of miles of space with only a suit we barely understand to protect us."

"Thousands," Mina corrected before she could stop herself. "Hundreds of thousands." She wanted to slap herself.

He set the chips down. "Can I get a minute in the bathroom alone? For no reason."

Sean held in a laugh as Zane disappeared around the corner. "He does know no one is judging him for that right?"

"He judges himself." Mina gave a sad look toward the bathroom doorway. "You gotta let him pretend to cover it and check in on him later in a roundabout way."

They all fell silent and caught one hard cough from the bathroom, but nothing followed. There was a bit of shuffling, him waiting to see if anything was going to happen. They'd all picked out bunks by the time he came back out. Sean and Emma took one stack, with Sean on the top. Mina took the top of the next stack over, Zane dropped his phone on the bunk below and went back to the food bag. Steph dropped into the bottom bunk next over from them.

Zane leaned against the table, chips again in hand but not eating. "Sinks are in an open area. Showers are all enclosed with doors and hangers inside for towels. But we can still do shifts if people are more comfortable that way."

"You and Sean can go first," Mina offered up. The other two girls nodded.

"Sounds good." Zane stepped back into the bathroom, almost forgetting to leave the chips behind.

Sean followed after dropping his Pak on his bunk. The trio left behind settled into their different preferred apps. After a few minutes, Emma leaned out to look at the other two. "Hey, are your phones charged up?"

Steph laughed, "Oh yeah, full charge. How is that? I've definitely been on this all day."

"Probably the suit." Mina pushed out from her bunk. "If Nek could get them to interface, I bet they can wirelessly charge as well. The Paks are a kind of power source all on their own." She pressed her phone against the back of the Pak and saw her battery symbol change to charging. "Yeah, look at that."

"Never have a dead battery again," Emma rolled back into her bunk. "Not a bad perk."

The doors slid open, Comp2876 pushed in along with a few others. Their extended arms each carried a vacuum-sealed silver package and gray, folded fabric. Comp2876 came over to Mina, *Supplies verified good for use!*

She took the bag and soft fabric offered, realizing the latter was a shirt and pants set. Mina pulled the tab on the bag and it filled with air. From inside rolled out bottles of toiletries, 2876 translated the labels to show what everything was. As well as highlighting that the clothes featured Outrider printed along the sleeve and pant leg in the angry alien Atlantean script. "Oh, this is great actually!"

Steph shook out her own. "Yeah, I was not excited to sleep in this after a shower. The suit helped, but this outfit is a bit sticky."

"Thanks, Comps." Emma held up the shirt to herself, it looked like a good fit.

Welcome! Flashed across all screens. Two Comps pushed into the bathroom with supplies for the guys. They heard knocks and both guys nervously gave out a response. Adding warmer, extra thanks a moment later. The Comps left, but 2876 gave them each one more *Good night!* before leaving.

The trio settled back into their phone scrolling. All was quiet until Steph rolled out of her bunk and went over to the snack table. She looked between it and their bunks. After some internal debate, she pulled the chairs away, spacing them out in a circle around the table, then pulled the blankets off the bunks across the room.

Emma rolled out, pulling her bunk pad behind her. "We should put the food under the table. And get the pads down first, to know how far out we need to make the walls."

Steph dropped the blankets on a chair. "Smart."

Mina watched as they moved the food and lined up their pads, making it so their heads would be underneath and feet facing out. She was embarrassed at how long it took to realize they were making a blanket fort. In her defense, she'd never done one before. Her brain instantly began engineering a possible solution. "I think we need a chair on top of the table, to give us more height. And, if it's not cheating, I have duct tape. That'll keep everything in place."

Emma nodded as she pulled a chair from the circle. "This is why you're the boss."

In only twenty minutes of work, the three girls finished the fort. Mina carefully laid out duct tape along the edges to secure the blankets together and make sure nothing caved in on them during the night. Often with her pressing from one side as Steph did from the other. Emma smoothed out the door flap so it sat neatly open. The guys came out to see them admiring their work, both unfazed by the change of sleeping arrangements.

Zane patted Mina on the back. "Which is my spot?"

"The pad with those gross dill chips you like sitting on top," Mina said.

"The lady who doesn't like her food to touch, coming for my preferences." Zane huffed and crawled into the fort. "The nerve."

Sean tugged the hem of his shirt as he kneeled to follow Zane in. "Is it weird that they found a set that fit?"

Emma grabbed her things and headed to the showers. "Are we pretending that they didn't learn all our measurements as soon as those suits came on?"

"That is true. Fair point." He disappeared into the fort.

Steph and Mina grabbed their items and followed Emma. Zane called out, "Hey, did you notice your battery is-"

"Pak does it," Steph called back.

"Ah, makes sense. That's probably going to be a catchall answer, huh?"

Sean participated in the conversation by being so far asleep already that he was snoring.

"Yes, yes it is," Zane said to himself as Mina left the room.

The showers were thickly walled off from each other, but they kept at least one stall between them anyway. No need to be weird and shower side by side. Mina turned the water up hot, steaming up her cube rather quickly. The process of scrubbing down her overworked body was all the energy she had left. By the end, her arms were heavy and she was leaning into the wall, letting the spray run over her back. Her mind stuck on the fact of how this absurdity of day was ending with a blanket fort on a spaceship.

A spaceship that was hers now, kind of. Theirs, she corrected as one of the other showers cut off. She was part of a team. A group of friends, she dared to think. Some of those new friends were robots and an alien lifeform she didn't fully understand.

She could hear Steph out by the sinks, humming the same tune from when they first saw Outrider. Mina thought it sounded a lot happier now. Maybe there was one, potentially, more than a friend here.

Because of the steam and water still pouring over her, Mina didn't realize at first that she was crying again. Not like with Zane's mom, a reaction that came from a larger internal uncertainty of parental figures no matter how lovely they were. These were pure happy tears. For this brief moment where she was alone, Mina let herself be wrapped up in the joy of how she was about to go to sleep between her best friend and her crush in a blanket fort on a spaceship. After they'd all agreed to become superheroes together. Even with the bruises and Capri threat considered, it was a good day.

When her eyes started to droop shut while standing, she figured it was time to get out. She discovered she was the last to leave, different sinks around the room held the scattering of toiletries they'd been given. Mina scrunched her hair up in a damp bun, resigning to deal with those consequences tomorrow, and went out to join the rest.

They were again scrolling away on their phones, aside from Sean who was still softly snoring. She dropped her Pak at the top of her pad, the others had done the same. The dim glow reflected off her duct tape seams in an unexpectedly pleasing way.

Mina started her own search through the pile of reactions and discoveries Hurst, and the world, put together while they'd been working. She caught a heavy-lidded look and smile from Zane, who was fighting to stay awake. He'd waited for her to come back. "Go to sleep, you doof."

Already halfway there, Zane lifted a heavy hand to run against one of the blankets. "Can you imagine if we'd met as kids," he yawned, "and got to do this before?"

"No could-of-beens," she chided, it was something she used to tell herself a lot more when they first met. How different things may have been if she'd found this one real friend sooner. She rolled over to face him and pulled up her blanket. "Only exciting tomorrows for us now."

He gave her a weak thumbs up, which thudded against the pad as sleep fully took him.

Mina reopened her phone under her blanket, not wanting the light to wake him again, and checked for any updates on the damage done. She needed to know before her brain would let her drift off.

For the first time in the city's existence, from what Mina knew, Hurst was getting global coverage. People were calling today The Big Shake 2.0. Every news channel and website was running a story on Hurst. They were all using the same few clips people filmed of the event, she hoped they were getting a nice payday. The entire park was locked down once the last few survivors were cleared out. Granted, it was impossible to keep people from seeing the aftermath given that the site was a literal giant crater. A few satellite images were floating about, an interesting before and after. Every story was filled with the same handful of distance shots taken from as close as the local news helicopter was willing to get. Mina spotted Sam, Megan, and that new girl in a few pictures from The Park clearing out. Maybe she could get Steph and Sean to find out from them how rough that'd all gone.

Experts, Mina wasn't sure how they found experts on this, were called in to talk about what happened at, in, and around The Hill. Basically, a bunch of people with different doctorates making educated guesses. A few from

Hephaestus Labs kept popping up, which made sense given that it was their park. She recognized her parents' colleges by name, not faces. Though she did spot that brown-nosing intern hanging around in the background of one researcher's shot from within Hephaestus Labs. Mel, staging herself to look deep in thought over some workstation covered in papers (probably blank) was a pain who would never be allowed on her spaceship. She'd start a Board of Shame. There was a sort of petty glee that filled her, knowing she could keep Mel from Outrider.

Kiss up to my parents all you want, she thought, *None of you will ever have this.*

The most current revelation was about how The Hill heated up the way it did, melting all the earth and rock, which then pooled down into the once gorge below. Which was why they didn't see massive fallout or damage beyond The Park itself. One of the Hephaestus people started to explain the actual science, but she couldn't finish the clip because Mel slid into the shot halfway through. She must've been watching broadcasts and going to whoever was on air. Gross.

Mina switched to a different report on The Park's damage. While it did happen fast, the area's sudden rise in temperature caught the surrounding trees on fire, but was put out rather quickly given the number of first responders already on site. Not to mention Outrider's departure pulled all the oxygen with it and snuffed out most of the flames. This left an additional black ring around what was now being called Hurst Crater. There'd been an RV parking area caught in the ring. Officials tried to clear it out, but a few families weren't quick enough. Mina was avoiding the list of confirmed dead or still missing, not ready for that tonight. The festival area was in shambles, everything knocked over and blown around. She caught sight of Restoration's brightly painted canopy top in one of the sweeping helicopter videos. Given that this shot featured no people laying about, she reminded herself that it could've been a lot worse.

She jumped over to another site running interviews they'd gotten with survivors from the exit road. A couple was giving their recount of the whole event, she turned on the captioning to avoid bothering the others. The woman was getting wispy as she spoke, "It was honestly kind of surreal. Something you only see in disaster movies and never think you'll go through. We were all just out to help each other. There was a set of teens who got us out of our car," she looked at the guy, "did we get their names? Oh god, we didn't."

He leaned in toward her, but the camera still picked up, "We got a number."

Steph sighed to her left, "My boss is so sweet."

Mina peeled back her blanket and rolled over. "What's Mitch doing?"

Steph tipped her phone toward Mina to show the message, **Hey there everyone! Wanted to touch base and make sure everyone is okay after today. We were very lucky that Sam, Megan, and Henrie made it out without any serious injuries! Though our trusty van will be on to greener pastures. Restoration Cafe will be closed for the weekend, but if things are more or less settled by Monday I will be going in. People may need some routine by then. Or at least some coffee. If anyone wishes to stay home, I absolutely understand, just let me know.**

"That is considerate." How many others were getting messages of 'we expect you in bright and early tomorrow' right now? People were already responding that they'd be in for their next shift if nothing else happened. Steph added her version of the same. Clearly, he'd built a sense of loyalty with the rest of them. Mina could learn from him.

She saw a message from the new girl, Henrie, come in. **I'll be there Monday. Excited to start!**

Mina swiped back to the photo she'd found earlier. "She was at The Park. Surprised her family didn't already pack back up and leave."

"I think they're used to tense living situations. Army brat."

A message from Sam popped up asking if anyone had talked to Sean, as he hadn't answered yet.

He's probably asleep, Steph answered right away. **I was hanging out with him and Emma when things went down. Clearly, he's adjusting just fine.**

Steph scrunched her nose after hitting send. "Is it bad they knew we were together? Maybe I messed up."

Mina waved it off. "People saw us leave the cafe together. And everyone had to be somewhere right? We're good."

Tell him it was aliens doing magic. He'll pull an all-nighter and figure this out, Sam texted to a different group chat that Mina noticed was labeled 'Non-Boss Chat'.

They both chuckled at how nearly on the mark it was. Steph focused on sending off more teasing about Sean to the chat. Mina decided it best to not creep and shifted back on her pad. She thought to look over a couple more reports but found her eyes unable to focus on the screen. After a couple of heavy blinks, she let the phone drop to her side and drifted off.

27

Knight Shift

Comp2876 quietly pushed by the bunk quarters, checking the status of their new Wardens yet again. Their connections to the Paks gave automatic updates to the framework, but 2876 liked the personal verification. They all were asleep, so 2876 dimmed the lights and shut the doors. It considered calling a couple Comps to stand guard, thinking of Capri returning, but calculations put that as a rather low turn of events and let the task go.

It weaved through the halls toward the private quarters. A Comp in each room was packing, quickly but carefully, away the belongings of their original team. Time would be made later to properly store their keepsakes, but as their task list remained substantial, Nek settled for simply putting it away for the time being.

2876 watched a set of photos go into a crate and proposed the task of sending mementos back to Warden families. Nek immediately turned it down, noting their time lost to stasis. They had no way of knowing if there were even any descendants of their team left. Who would they contact even? Trustworthy or not, the Collective left them to disappear in this unfamiliar sector.

There was rustling on the framework as the thought filtered through, the unease was shared. 2876 shifted to the private channel with Nek. Their attention was elsewhere, leaving it as alone as Comp2876 would ever be again. A sensation that was unnerving hours before, but welcomed now. It connected to the database, taking another attempt to restore full access to the older information, back to before they left on their expedition. Back to when someone reached Capri's ear and put that virus of world domination in her. Comp2876 could not reconcile the calculating and fiercely loyal Warden who'd walked these halls with the bloodied and manic person it faced off with today. She could not have turned like this on her own. Yes, she'd always been the most heavy-handed of their Wardens, but this?

2876 registered Nek's attention, watched as their waves slipped into the panel it idled by. *Unknown point of corruption.*

"Yes, it is upsetting. Given time, we may uncover who spoke with her on this horrid ideology before our departure. But I believe that will take time."

What could convince her to do this? The images of the Warden's stand against Capri filtered by again. They grew worse with each viewing as 2876 registered new horrible details. Caro looked so scared at the end, alone in the medbay that failed to heal her as the ship began to fail. Capri appeared scared too, in fleeting moments.

"She could be…quick to anger. Her passion kept her focused. Someone twisted that."

2876 hesitated, replaying Emma's comment from before and Capri's statement of being welcomed back. *Issue within the Collective?*

Nek swirled silently for a moment. "We are far from being able to answer those questions now. But I fear the answer is yes."

No longer a Collective sanctioned mission, Nek said so before. They were on their own on this strange planet, with a new team to protect. *How do we go forward?*

"One task at a time." Nek drifted back down the hall toward the bunk quarters. "Against mounting circumstances, I feel optimistic for them."

Good Wardens!

"I believe they will be, yes."

An alert popped onto the framework, the rooms were cleared. Crates were being moved to storage for the time being. Nek rolled in place until another alert pulled their attention. "We are needed in Fabrication."

2876 watched the new priority task appear on the framework. Given its

Secondary designation, it also caught the variations Nek shifted through in their channel. Memorial. Eulogy. Vigil. All options felt so formal for the Wardens they'd cared for. Nek settled on Farewell.

They kept pace with 2876 through the halls even though they didn't need to. Along the way other Comps joined. The framework quieted, still few in number but heavy all the same.

Passing by the main Fabrication room, the group came to the larger machines usually designated for Guardian repairs. The remains of their original team laid, still covered, on the conveyor belts. Nek paused by each on the panel overhead, saying nothing outright, but the Comps could see images on the framework. Bizarrely young versions, painfully alive, of their Wardens. Training. Tested. Triumphant. Honored to be chosen for this expedition. Celebrating within Outrider. Capri was featured in many of the pictures, a different sort of loss.

The belts began moving toward the warmed forges, the sheets catching first in proximity to the heat. Watching this, Comp2876 came to a strange realization. It felt - double-checked the wording - yes, felt angry.

Not at Capri directly, not as the young and wide-eyed version of her went by again. Not even mad at whatever unnamed force lay beyond her. No, 2876 was angry at this situation as a whole. Comps weren't meant to handle these rites alone. Warden burials should be grander affairs. Celebrations of their lives and achievements within the Collective. Mourned by those that knew them or fought alongside them, and used as examples for future Wardens to aspire to. Nek and the Comps would always remember the trials this team went through, but they deserved more. Deserved better. Deserved not to die by one of their own for a reason none of them fully understood.

Comp2876 felt Nek in their private chat and knew they'd witnessed this stirring of thoughts. *Wrong. Error. Unfair. Apologies.*

No, I agree, Nek answered quietly. They rolled back and forth over the machines as the remains burned. Turned to ash and truly left them.

2876 thought of the sleeping group of teens, themselves young and wide-eyed. As eager to take up this mission as the original team. Comp2876 constructed a harsh overlay of them on these belts. The image of their new

Wardens passing into the fire agitated the cluster of Comps.

Good.

2876 spoke this time to the framework, *Never again.*

Never again, answered back the rest. Repeated it over and over until the final pieces of their original Wardens crumbled and were consumed by the flames.

28

Staring Contest With the Void

The team, Mina was yet to come down from the excitement of having 'a team', stepped onto the deck together the next morning. They were finishing their snack breakfast and still sporting their sleepwear, no one was eager to put their previous day's outfit back on. Their Paks attached to their sides, a fascinating discovery that it could adhere itself to the fabric. While waking up in a blanket fort was an experience in itself that Tiny Mina cherished, the fact - once again - that this happened on an alien ship floating in space kept her laying still for a few extra minutes trying not to shed more happy tears. Processing the previous day caught up with her and was almost too much, for many reasons. Her body ached, and dark bruises spread on her brow and torso. She could see the others were the same, but as they munched through their small reserves, everyone appeared still up for the Warden plan.

Nek moved about the room, checking different systems and notifications. "Hello, Wardens! We have a pleasant amount of updates for you," their waves were high and their voice sounded lighter, the night of recovery had done them well too, "Outrider looks well on the mend. Comp2876 will give you an update on all the completed repairs from the night."

Their go-to Comp came forward and projected a full list of everything finished. More Comps were repaired, a full swarm (a term noted on the list) was back on the framework. Mina wasn't sure what the exact number a swarm was, but it expedited the amount of work completed. They'd even patched up the hole in storage, allowing that room to be used again as they sorted the rest of the ship, and moved on to the other damage on the outside hull. It was a relief to see progress made after the rather big setback of Capri's attack.

Nek moved around to a console closer to Mina. "I have an updated prioritized list of tasks for the day. I will leave it to you, Warden Mina, to delegate out as they best suit your team."

Your team. Her stomach did a little flip. Mina popped up on her toes for a second. "Awesome! Thank you, I will do that. First off, actually, I was thinking maybe we could do a quick run back to Earth for food. Since the teleport is up and running." She'd zeroed in on that fact on the list of repairs.

"And additional clothing," Steph added.

"And lots of coffee," Sean said, looking at Emma.

"And check in so we don't get murdered by our parents instead of Capri," Emma threw out.

"Yes! All those things too," Mina hoped she sounded convincing. She'd honestly spaced on the others needing to check in with family.

Nek rolled without responding, Mina thought maybe the waves got a fraction tighter. "I forgot to delegate Comps to the food stores, my apologies."

Mina stepped closer to the console they occupied. "No worries! We can go one at a time. That way the others can keep getting things done up here."

Nek smoothed out again. "Yes, that will work nicely. I'm finding myself constantly adjusting to this new situation. Many unexpected occurrences."

"I hope we're not throwing things too far off."

"No, no. Everything will be fine. Understandably, you need to return and grab personal effects. See your families so they know you are well. That is a new arrangement for us. It's…well, I suppose technically it's been a while since we had new Wardens."

"And it's also technically only the second day you've been without your old ones," Zane stepped forward and set a hand on the console. "Did you work with other teams before the ones here?"

"Briefly, we have our own sort of training courses before being assigned a ship on our own. This was the first team I was paired with since their formation. We did many missions together. The voyage here was meant to be the biggest yet." Nek stayed on the console, their waves dropped in height.

"Is there anything you need us to do?" Zane asked.

"We've collected their things from the private quarters. We held a…they were cared for last night. But thank you."

Mina stepped up. "We're here to do whatever you need."

"Thank you. Give me a few moments to determine coordinates for your landings."

"You can drop me by my-" Mina stopped herself short. Remembering the black ring of charred earth and wreckage she'd seen pictures of last night. "Oh god, my car."

Sean laughed, "Yeah, that does not exist anymore."

"I just paid that thing off too," she looked over to Nek, "See, we're all finding unexpected things."

"I'll watch for any mention of car remnants being found at the site. Though I do agree with Warden Sean, it's likely beyond recognition."

"What was the full fallout?" Emma asked. "Have they got a better idea yet?"

Several feeds came up around them. The news channels were on mute but captions ran along the bottom. They all were repeating nearly the same facts as the night before. Hurst Crater naturally caused a lot of buzz, but gave no full answers. The group stood silent as the names of confirmed casualties rolled by, a much lower number than it could have been but regretful to watch all the same. Injuries were up there, though in a strange bit of luck, anyone critical last night made a turn for the better by this morning. Property damage was mostly contained to The Park, a few downtown buildings, and a few hundred cars. Though it would take several years to recover the damage done to the plant life, the rest was estimated to only need a couple of months to fully repair. Mina found herself rather content with the outcome this morning.

"Doesn't seem that anyone is talking about the person who threatened to blow up The Hill." Zane scrolled through more feeds on another console. "Is that good?"

"It appears that information was not released to the general public," Nek answered. "There's not been much communication over open channels."

"And anything not so open?" Mina asked as a news channel cut to a set of military vehicles pulling into one of the roads to The Park.

"I'm trying not to be invasive. This tends to break trust with local populations. Take our situation with the phones yesterday. If events become dire, I can break their encryptions, but I hope we can establish friendly conversation before that becomes needed."

"That makes sense. Don't want to step on toes."

"I have set parameters for if any of you are mentioned in relation to the event. A top priority is to keep you all safe as we establish ourselves. Wardens are, well, in how we were trained Wardens were public figures. Though it's my assumption you'd all like to keep this quiet for the time being."

"Capri would have to get in line behind my mom to kill me, if she ever found out," Sean said. Emma and Steph nodded in agreement.

Zane gave a so-so gesture. "Depends on the mood I caught her in."

Mina didn't need to keep this from her parents for her, or their, safety. More for Outrider and Nek's safety from them. But she went along with the group. "Yeah, mine would get weird."

Comp2876 swung around the group. *Teleport online! Locations noted.*

Mina held a hand out to the others. "Let me take the first run. I only need to grab stuff

and pop right back." She caught a raised eyebrow from Zane. "And I want to know what it feels like. But mostly so that you all can have a heads up." No one argued against that. Zane dropped the eyebrow and looked extra thankful. She turned to 2876, "Lead the way!"

Error!

"Oh, sorry. Is it not ready?"

Teleport ready!

"So I need to go somewhere." They'd zapped the crates from a different room yesterday, but Mina only watched a feed and wasn't sure where it was.

Location noted. Comp2876 dropped a map, showing her house. Her room even. Giving the impression that she could be teleported right inside.

"Yes, but do I go somewhere here first?"

Nek laughed from the console in front of them. "Another apology on my part. Coming in is restricted to the landing pad," they showed the room Mina'd seen yesterday, "but you can leave from wherever you need. The suit isn't required, but I do recommend wearing them until you're more comfortable with the sensation."

Mina took a couple of steps away from the group and tapped the Pak, letting the suit expand over her. She tried to stop herself from wiggling around, but she was excited. She was happy they couldn't see her stupidly big grin. Comp2876 pushed in front of her and flashed a short countdown, as zero ticked over she became weightless. She floated and fell at the same time. Her visor blurred before quickly becoming all black, only her heads-up display remained for her to focus on. A small ringing started in her ears and as she began feeling a little warmth come through the suit, her feet smacked into solid ground. Which was followed by her knees buckling and her falling back into a wall.

She didn't feel any pain but hit the armband to check on herself anyway. No broken bones were reported, only a sloppy landing. Mina tapped out a text. **Everything good. Tip: don't lock your knees.**

Mina pushed off the floor and glanced behind her, eyeing the small dent her stumble left behind her. That would be easy enough to fix. It was far from the first time something in her place went wild and broke a wall. Zane once pitched that she turn her drywall skills into a hush-hush side job for anyone needing to cover up damage from a party or whatnot, but she'd passed on that business venture.

She dropped the suit to change her clothes and threw another couple pieces into her backpack. Downstairs she grabbed the few snacks left in her cupboards and three of the frozen pizzas stashed away. Outrider must have a kitchen area somewhere. Or maybe the Comps contained a tool that could heat them, she hoped for that option. She'd love to see a set of them rotating around, cooking her pizza like little robo-chefs.

Mina picked up on mumbling voices from the front of the house and peeked out the front window to get a glimpse at who it was. A good amount of people were milling about the block this morning, probably comparing what they'd consumed over the night. There was a slight urge to find out what rumors were going around, but she backed away and let the curtain fall. More important things to do. No matter how fun hearing their theories would be.

She double-checked everything in her bag as the suit released from the Pak. With a thought, she opened a channel back to Nek. "I'm all good here. You can bring me back now."

"We'll have you locked on in five…" Nek started to countdown.

Mina bent her knees and this time caught a tingle in her limbs. She even noticed a faint blue tint around her as the countdown finished. Another weightless moment, another blur, and a much better landing as she dropped onto the landing pad. Comp2876 and Zane were waiting in the doorway for her.

Welcome back!

"Everything good down there?" Zane asked.

"They're congregating in the street to chat, but all seems fine. Any idea where an oven is here?" She held up the pizzas.

"I will personally find it and make sure we have these ready to go for lunch," he took them from her, clearly excited for more calories. She generally did the grocery shopping for her house and always got the stuffed crust he preferred, but his mother hated. Zane tipped back in the doorway, "You guys decide who's next. 2876, you got directions for a kitchen?"

She dropped the suit as she came out of the landing pad and looked up the hall, this wasn't far off the main elevator hallway in the section that led to the escape pods. Mina caught the flash of Emma leaving next, a silver fuzz in her wake. Zane and Comp2876 were a few steps ahead of her, until they split off to another hallway and she kept on to the bunks. Mina tossed the bag into her empty bunk space. They'd left the fort in place for the time being, she expected they would use it again tonight. Even if the private quarters were cleared out, it felt odd to take up someone else's room. Maybe she'd get them a bit more shaped up as a team, make them feel like they'd earned the space. Mina headed back toward the elevator, wanting to pop up to the deck on her own. Steph and Sean met her halfway there.

"Hey, so the Comps have themselves pretty well repaired," Steph said. "Do you want me to help with the last of the cleanup or something else?"

"Let me think." Mina tried to remember the full list Nek put together without pulling out the suit again. Her memory was good, but the list was rather comprehensive.

Sean tapped her shoulder. "We actually figured something out while you were gone."

Steph looked excited. "Yeah! Tap the Pak like this," she demonstrated a series of spots on the pad.

Mina did as instructed. The suit didn't release, but she felt a current run over her left arm. Mina watched the black band wrap around her wrist, it wasn't a part of the suit like she'd thought. A darker version of the hologram display ran over her arm. "Can you see this?"

"We can. Anyone can, actually. Nek says we should avoid using it in public if we want to stay anonymous."

"They also said there is an incognito mode, but it takes some adjustment," Sean added. "Something to do with our eyes and brain waves again."

Mina's parents could rattle off exactly what brain mechanism would be triggered for that. They'd go nuts over this. Probably have her running tests twenty-four/seven. Fighting the urge to put her on a table and pick her apart in the chance exposure was affecting her internally. While Mel took grubby little notes. The mean part of her was once again glad to keep this away from all of them. She twisted her arm and watched the overlay move with her, she tapped through to their to-do list. "Looking at what we have going on, I'd say focus on moving parts around the ship. Keep the Comps on repairs."

"Aye, aye," Steph gave her a nod. She and Sean headed down the Fabrication hallway.

Before they got too far away, Sean turned back. "Whenever we break for lunch, can we go see those Guardians? Picnic with giants."

"I think that should be doable," Mina called back to him. That was still a big unknown on their personal list. She pulled that up on the armband next. Her momentum stalled out while she updated everything that they'd learned over the previous night and morning. Others had added in a few answers and questions already. While this list, the repairs list, and the training they now required was a hefty pile to work through, Mina didn't feel nervous as she took the elevator up to the deck. None of them were seriously hurt in their encounter with Capri or gone insane from the concept of being in space. That must be a good omen for their abilities to come, right? She looked to the main console as she came up, finding Nek there as she now expected. "Hey, Nek, is it safe to look out of the dome?"

"Yes, I can open one of the shields for you."

The plating nearest her slid upwards. Mina kept her eyes everywhere but the opening window, once again saving the view until it was fully ready. Her attention landed on the consoles that were all flickering with work, Nek's personal unending to-do list, but they were still surrounded by news channels.

"You should be careful," Mina warned, "Most of those are bad for your brain."

"Objectivity filters are being applied as needed," Nek said. "Many other intelligent species also carry the flaw of finding sensationalism profitable."

"Oh, we're not the worst you've seen?" Mina laughed a little.

"Far from it. The shield is open for you." Nek moved closer to the window as the metal finished pulling away. "Outrider does spin to aid in generating a stable internal gravity. This spot will come back around to the Moon in a moment."

"Oh, I wasn't after that." Mina stepped between two consoles and leaned in as far as she could. Her eyes adjusted to the odd lighting, as well as focusing through the thick curved glass, and then her brain needed to adjust as she watched the Moon slide into view. Okay, maybe that was kind of cool. She racked her brain to see if she knew the names of any craters slowly moving by, but nothing came up. Something to look up later. Their view continued to glide along and filled with stars, a few satellites were farther out. "Did they pick up on us?"

"I spent the first part of the night blocking signals coming from any devices in the region. Cloaking was fully functional early this morning. We'll be in the clear unless they run into us."

"Awesome. That's really awesome." Mina noticed Nek sounded less formal. She wanted to think it was from being comfortable with her there. Given that she was, kind of, sort of, acting leader for the group. But it was likely due to having slightly less on their own plate to deal with.

More stars came into view as they turned. Stars and black. Hurst wasn't a complete washout with light pollution, but she'd never seen this many before outside of pictures. "Do you know any planets with intelligent life that we can see from here?"

"This region was uncharted when we arrived. Earth was the first we found with any intelligent life, but that might have changed by now."

"So you don't know any of these stars?"

"Some vaguely. As reference points." They displayed a copy of Mina's view on a console and marked a few. "I've learned more from Earth databases."

"Exactly how far from home are you?" Mina watched their waves curl tightly and turn white. "Sorry, I don't mean to pry."

The rolls relaxed, the color fading back in. "You're fine. It's a reasonable question. It's the answer that is upsetting. We knew when we were given this mission we'd be farther from any planet we'd ever known. But our team would be together, that's what mattered. And now…"

"Your Wardens are gone. Capri is on the run. And you gained a whole new pile of headache with us around," after a pause she added, "The constant questioning doesn't help either."

"It's a natural reaction. For the record, I'd hate for any of you to stop questioning. I can relate to how frustrating the unknown can be."

The window was still full of stars, void looking back and all. She snapped a couple of pictures on her phone. They looked crappy, smudges on black, but it was more about helping her remember the moment. "I've always taken the unknown as more of a challenge, but I'm odd." Mina took a risk with another question, "Do you think, when you're ready of course, you could tell us about the previous team?"

"Certainly, they were wonderful examples of Wardens. Until the very end. They'll be useful for training." Nek reappeared on the display nearest the window. "And might I say, being odd brought you here. Led you to finding otherworldly technology and not only repair it, but agree to protect it. And your planet. That drive is why the others are so ready to follow you into this new venture. Many of our best Wardens could be classified as odd."

"I don't know if I can promise you being one of the best. But I'll do all I can to be good."

"That's all I would ask of any of you. May I ask why you wanted to look out?"

Mina tossed the question around in her head, trying to pin down the exact answer herself. The Moon was coming back into view, blocking the really neat stuff. "One of those unknown things. Didn't know if it would scare me."

"And your findings?"

"Looks big." Mina pushed off the window, satisfied with the view for now. "Can't wait to see more, but it's back to work."

29

Is it a Coup if No One Cares?

Capri was nudged awake by a Comp, its small alert beep not enough to rouse her. She pushed it away and sat up on the cot. Her chest protested, the bandages pulled tight against the angry wounds, but she'd managed with worse before. The scouting vessel was beginning its descent to the surface of the next planet over, the base no more than a square far in the distance.

She checked her armband, a notice there letting her know that internal repairs were finished on the Pak. Capri put her suit back on and looked to the Comp that woke her. "Get me whatever kind of readings this has available before we land. I want as much intel as possible."

Directive confirmed. It pushed over to the dash and tapped away. Small lights triggered as parts of the pod powered up again.

She didn't imagine they'd pull much information, but better to have crumbs than nothing at all. The pod shook slightly as their escort pulled back on the speed, a landing pad off to the side of the base lit up. Capri watched the structure grow closer, the initial square she spotted from afar was the wide base of a rather tall building. Small wings came off two sides of the main tower. Off the opposite sides sat the landing pad and a section completely encased with yellowed glass. This stretched up the entire tower and held cranes and supports inside, likely where they constructed their larger creations. There was a faint shimmer in the air from the cloaking covering the entire area. Her pod's connection to the scout must have bypassed it. The Lenians would be spotted in a minute if that ever failed. The entire building was constructed in the gaudy, patchwork, jewel-colored assortment of metals they loved so much. Making them stand out rather harshly against the planet's red color.

It reminded her of the colors those impostor Wardens chose for themselves, idiotically attention-grabbing. Her own team wasn't innocent of it either. She thought of how garish Caro, Ali, and Camden made theirs, while they thought her strange for keeping it all black.

Always in a mood, echoed in her ear.

She shook it off, refocused on the landing pad closing in. There were no signs of movement below, no one coming to meet their new captive. The scout dropped speed again and pulled up to bring them in for the final landing.

Capri looked to the one fully functionally Comp, completed just in time though the seams were messy, "You stay on me. Provide cover if anything attacks," she looked to the other two, "You acquire as much of the layout as possible before they blow you up."

There was a delay, but each eventually flashed, *Directive confirmed.*

It was so annoying when they got picky, which happened if you singled them out from the framework for too long. They started getting personal opinions. If by chance they survived she'd reset them, tighten up her programming, and avoid any potential pushback on further orders.

The scout swung around to put itself between the pod and the door leading into the base. They hovered as the loading doors pulled off to the sides. Comps fed her information with their limited capabilities. Lights flickered on as they came to a halt in the middle of the bay, no one there waiting for her. Capri could see doors on each side of the dock, but no one entered. Behind her pod, the doors closed, loud and slow. The scout vessel sent back a force command to drop any landing gear, it did the same and detached. She watched it shut itself down and settle. Several minutes passed with nothing else triggering in the room. No one to interrogate her. Or stop her from turning the pod back on and attempting an escape. What game were these Lenians playing? Were they observing her from elsewhere?

"Shut down everything in here," she commanded. The Comp at the dash tapped around, everything went dark, the only light coming from outside the window. "Black out the window too, don't let them see in."

A filter lowered, darkening the pod even further, but allowed them to look out. Capri pressed into the wall. Standing ready as she watched out the front, while the Comps kept an eye on the door in case anything forcefully pulled it open. She unloaded her blaster from the Pak, fully recharged for use. They stood waiting for so long the motion lights shut off, leaving them in full darkness.

"Since waking up, I have suffered nothing but insult after insult," she huffed. "Open the door."

The Comp tapped in the command, then pushed to her side as the door rolled open. Her small recon drone buzzed out first, doing a quick pass on the room. The one Comp with an actual blaster moved out next, reconfirming all was clear. The remaining two moved in time with her, pausing as the lights kicked back on. No alarm activated, no warning came through the intercom she spotted on the wall. Capri commanded a Comp to hit the scout vessel as they passed, it was fully shut down and didn't trigger any defenses.

Her recon drone pulled back and reloaded into the Pak, she liked it better and preferred to lose a Comp to it. Capri raised her blaster as they neared the door to the left, expecting someone waiting on the other side. She nodded for one of the Comps to trigger the door. The metal squealed and dragged against the tracks, shuttered to a stop a third of the way open. It was unusual for Lenians to let anything fall to such horrible standards. Capri realized that some of what she'd taken as decorative design along the walls was actually rust. Stranger still, no shiny Lenian was looking back at her through the gap.

She angled herself to see the other door, nodded to one Comp, "Go try that one."

Out of habit, she stepped closer to the scout, looking for partial cover. That door groaned, shook, and failed to open. Capri rolled her eyes. "All of you in the hall, see what's waiting there."

It must be an ambush then. Neglected base or not, you don't bring in an enemy and leave them to traipse about on their own. They'd let her get good and comfortable. More of a mental game than the Lenian type typically used, maybe they were actually capable of a smidge of change. Comps filed out and fed back their findings to her heads-up display, a map forming from their paths. As far as movement went, it was still only their points filling the space. Nothing. No one.

The space in the door was wide enough for her to slide through without issue. She moved down the hall. After being kept out by two doors fully rusted shut, she dropped her helmet. Put her blaster away after a few more. Capri found herself not checking corners. Soon she was banging into doors and shoving them aside as they otherwise slowly opened. In one instance pulling it completely off the rail when it stuck halfway. Without any degree of caution, she cleared the first floor without a single encounter. No uptight security system even chirped as she'd gone through. She should be thankful for an easy entry, but this was infuriating.

In her rage-fueled search, she'd found that the tower was centered around a curved staircase. Tucked inside the spiral was a small elevator. There were no solid sides to the elevator car, only curled and decorated bits of iron. Walkways stretched out from the staircase to connect to each floor. Even with seeing no one so far, her instincts wouldn't let her get in that lift. The stairs looked relatively worn with use. She abandoned the rest of her caution to stomp up the first flight. Comps came up behind her, taking points all around to scan this new floor. Nothing showed signs of hearing her noisy movement.

"This is rather bullshit." She shoved two Comps back into the open space through the middle. "Find me something to punch."

Her armband updated with their intel from the higher floors. There were workstations throughout the building fully stocked, but unused. Quarters covered in dust, save for two. One Comp jumped to the top but was blocked after the tenth floor. The lift went into that next level, but the hatch was sealed. The other circled back down to check the wings. These were open spaces for forming pieces for bigger creations, a large lump of something pushed into one corner, and their generators. Of which, only two were active.

"Find where the power is going," she commanded through the band.

Directive confirmed, popped back. One generator's power was all going toward whatever was above the tenth floor. The other was split between two workshops farther up. The Comp attempting to open the hatch dropped down to the eighth level to confirm what exactly was drawing power. Her main Comp displayed a live feed of the other's camera. Something was making noise inside one of the workshops, tapping and grinding sounds echoed into the hallway.

"Go in low and slow, I'll be up," she ordered. Capri snapped her helmet up, pulling the feed to a corner of her heads-up display. She took the staircase, stepping hard in hopes to eke out every groan or squeak possible in the metal. On the feed, the noise grew louder as the Comp entered the room. There was some kind of chain being dragged and a smaller bit of tapping happening further in.

The Comp dropped under a bench along the wall. It pushed forward in time with her reaching each new level. Capri was rounding to the fifth floor before it finally spotted a set of feet. All of them halted. She tilted her head, the Comp looked up to match. A shimmering green figure was slumped over a table. The dragging chain was this Lenian creep snoring.

Capri fought the urge to stomp her foot like a child. "The insults continue!"

The Comp moved from under the bench, a bold choice if not for the loud noise as cover. At the end of this long work table was a small automated machine working away on a thin sheet of metal. The tapping.

"What are they making?" She climbed to the sixth floor. Capri wondered if Lenian creations changed much in 500 years. At the least, they always provided an entertaining fight.

Without moving, the Comp zoomed in on the sheet, the shape of a wing was etched into it. The Comp pulled back and looked at the materials scattered out in front of the Lenian. Diagrams of some small creature. No dangerous additions or hidden weapons appeared on any schematics.

"Fearsome monsters indeed." Capri twisted and broke a bar of metal from the railing in frustration. "Pull back to the doorway. I'll be there soon."

Acknowledged.

Her other Comp rushed up from the lower wing and met them as she reached the eighth floor. Capri cut the feed from the Comp and thought to drop her blaster again, but a loud snore cutting through the room ripped apart any remaining patience. She came up right behind the sleeping Lenian and boosted her voice from the helmet. "Do not resist. The Collective will reward your compliance."

Capri's stomach knotted up, it was a rather knee-jerk thing to say and felt wrong. But the figure didn't flinch, didn't even stirred at her speaking. They let out another roar of a snore as their machine tapped filigree into the metal. She stepped around and grabbed the small tapping arm in the machine, it didn't take much to rip out. The mechanism continued for a few beats before shorting out. The figure didn't stir.

Her helmet snapped back. "Are you kidding me?!"

The Comps backed up of their own accord. She grabbed the back of the figure's neck and pulled their head a few inches off the table before slamming it back down. This finally got their attention.

They shouted and sputtered, reeling back into Capri. Looking up at her as they blinked past the pain of their newly dented nose. "Wha..what's happening?"

"My patience ending." She pushed them off the stool to the floor.

They pulled down papers and bits of metalwork with them. "I don't understand."

"I've been in this joke of a base for nearly an hour and you're the first thing I've found to take some aggression out on." She threw the stool behind her, crashing into the opposite wall. There were sounds of more things falling over, but she didn't look to see the full damage. Probably only more useless creations.

The Lenian backed away on the floor. "I can take you to someone else if all you're after is a punching bag."

Too simple. Lenian minions did tend to be wimps if they weren't over-encumbered in their advancements, but this was rather pathetic. Yet her training insisted on not passing up intel, "Who else is in this sad little base of yours?"

"There's another engineer across the floor. Two, agh, ow," they tentatively touched their nose, assessing the damage done, "two Maintenance Crew should be milling about. That's all."

"Your maintenance people are not worth the pay. This place is-"

"A shithole. I know," they pressed their back into the leg of another table and held their bent nose. "They dropped us here to keep an eye on the abandoned Collective ship. Said work and wait, we'll come to you soon. It's been too many years and nothing. We are rotting away out here."

This was a more honest answer than she expected so quickly, not to mention one that hit a little close to home. "Not a lot of loyalty within Lenians anymore, it seems."

"There was. I was. Then, as I mentioned, they dumped us on this rock. That planet's inhabitants are infantile. A bore to watch. And no one else has ever come after that ship, must have really cared about it."

She wondered how much this Lenian truly knew of the Collective, given that it didn't instantly recognize the suit standing before them. It was one thing for her to down-talk them, but a known enemy talking poorly of the Collective had Capri barely holding off the need to punch again. But she understood the frustration of being abandoned, at least she'd gotten to sleep through it. "You do know the ship came back online, yes? And that one of your scouts pulled my pod here?"

They gave a small, oily smile. "It wasn't my day to watch."

"So what are your plans of attack against the ship?" She leaned in toward the Lenian.

They pulled up their legs, curling their arms around their knees. "Send the scout. Get intel. Report back. They should get the message and send further aid in a month or so."

"You'd wait months?" She could barely wait hours.

"I once again point out this being a shithole with limited resources."

"Should I break off parts of your body for additional resources, Lenian?"

They flinched and pulled into a slightly tighter ball. "My name is Gregory.

And…wait…are you a Warden?" They found courage in this realization, straightening up slightly. "Shouldn't it be on you to strike us down first? You've got the working ship."

Unfit for duty, rang in her ears. "Loyalty is strained within the Wardens as well. I actually did you a favor," she crouched down in front of Gregory, "I already killed the others. So what can you do for me?"

"I can suggest some psychiatric help."

Capri pulled her blaster from the Pak, pressed it tight to their chin. "How about we get the rest of your crew, see if they have a better answer."

Gregory swallowed hard."Not much for humor in the old Collective, is there?"

"Not as of late. Move." Her Comp dropped in close and pulled its small blaster as she stood. The others circled with messages of *Please Comply* flashing.

Gregory stood slowly with their hands up, looking over the Comps. "Such an old design. Would love to pull one apart."

The Comps pushed back a few inches. She tilted her head as the helmet snapped up. "Bold request, given that I'm trying not to pull you apart myself."

"You can just say no." Gregory turned and headed out of the workshop with the Comps not far behind.

Capri kept a few steps back. Letting them lead her to the workshop on the other side of this level. She kept her head on a swivel, back on alert with confirmed other lifeforms around. "No chance of your Maintenance Crew sneaking up on us, is there?"

"Quite honestly, no. They are likely lazing about somewhere." Gregory gave a glance up to the blocked-off top floor.

"Because you were so hard at work yourself."

Gregory gave a sharp look back. "The process for my work takes time and a lot more mental capacity than your basic skills of punching people and making threats."

She let off a bolt close enough to buzz their hair, which was only very fine threads of metal, leaving a small section noticeably shorter than the rest. "You'd be surprised how much mental capacity it takes to let you keep talking to me like that."

They gave a brief touch to their burnt hair and turned to the next workshop's doorway. "Maxwell, I have a new friend for you."

"Nobody needs another of your damned birds, Gregory," called back a voice. "The ones roosted in the dining room are maddening enough."

"No really, this one's for you. I don't want them." Gregory moved in and off to the side, giving her a clear view of the second engineer.

They turned, as trim and pointy as Gregory, but a bit more rubbed and worn on the yellowed metal. This one didn't opt for decorative hair. Maxwell took in Capri, seemed unimpressed. "Who is this?"

"A Warden of yore. An evil Warden," Gregory pointed to the nose and hair. "After that, I don't know. It was your day on watch, sir."

She didn't know what the 'of yore' was about, other than referring to how long it'd been since they'd personally seen a Warden around.

Maxwell glanced at a screen behind him, filled with bright red alerts from the scout. "Ah, well. Are we done then? I don't mind being done."

Capri dropped her blaster to her side. "Is there no fight left in either of you?"

"That would be assuming there was a fight in us to begin with," Maxwell answered.

"Another reason we were tasked with this drivel of an assignment," Gregory added.

A Comp pushed to Capri's eye line. *Contact Outrider for captives?*

How did that slip through her programming? That couldn't be allowed. She grabbed the Comp and smashed it into the doorframe. Capri heard the other two Comps give small protests, but they didn't move to help. Once she saw the screen flicker off, she tossed it to Gregory. "Have fun. Back to your workshop. Neither of you leaves without my say-so."

Maxwell gave a salute from his seat and turned back around. Still unfazed by her arrival at their base. Gregory edged past her, the broken Comp pressed tight to their chest, and quickly made their way back to the other workshop. Her Comps took up positions in the two doorways. The missing crew members needed to be located. Capri thought to jump over the railing and take the quick route back to the first level, but given the state of this place she'd likely break the foundation and bring the whole thing down.

She called over toward Maxwell, "Are you any more helpful than Gregory in knowing where your Maintenance Crew is hiding?"

"Best odds are the Councilor's Suite up top. It's the only place they keep in actual good standing," Maxwell tipped toward the doorway and picked up his volume, "He should have been able to tell you that, but he does encounter a troublesome bit of faulty memory."

"He's trying to kiss ass," Gregory shouted from his side. "Only the lift goes up there. It was passcode protected, but we bypassed that ages ago."

Capri ran scenarios for the actual necessity of keeping those two alive as she waited for the car to come up from the main floor. Unfortunately, the odds were in their favor until she better understood the base's full capabilities. If anything, they were needed long enough to get back to an actual usable standard. It didn't seem wise to hope the two above were of any better use.

The lift was rather ornate compared to the state of the base around it, but if this was one of the few items looked after it made sense they bothered to keep it clean as well. Inside she found the control panel more on par with her current expectations, pulled open and wires strewn about. Sections of wire were stripped and reconnected to bypass the coded entry. Capri flipped the switch and rose toward the locked hatch. She braced as the car lifted, thinking the two would spring an attack, more a reaction from training than actual concern for her safety. The Comps still paced in their doorways, she heard the sounds of tinkering from each side. The hatch pulled back, allowing the lift into the suite, and she fell into a fit of laughter as the door popped open and she stepped into the massive room.

Plush fabrics were draped over the walls and thick rugs covered the floor, her boots sunk a full inch down. They'd aimed to conceal as much of the metal structure as possible, while still holding to the darker-toned color scheme. Overstuffed furniture appeared dropped at random around this wide entry room, which felt even vaster given the high ceiling. The staircase up the far side featured a soft wrapping around the railing and thick carpeting over the steps. Whoever once intended to live here and command the base held a different sense of design than the normal Lenian kind.

Laying passed out across two of the velvet couches were the Maintenance Crew. They were smaller than the engineers downstairs, she knew it was so that they may reach the tighter locations needing care. Their royal blue metal gleamed brightly, she didn't know if that was to ensure they didn't stain anything here or a sign of how long they'd gone without actually working.

Capri made no effort of being quiet as she approached. If her laughter didn't wake the pair, it would take another broken nose to do it. Given their smaller size, she elected to pick one up and slam them down onto the other. Her first victim didn't even make a sound until they were being flung down onto the second. Both bounced and sprawled out on the floor, looking at her with confusion.

"Not Councilor," one said.

"Who?" the other asked.

"Warden," she answered. That seemed to clear up their minds, bringing the appropriate fear into their eyes. Finally, something that made her smile. "You've not been keeping up on your duties."

"Engineers don't care," the first said, ready to pass the blame back.

"Only care for their own work," the second added.

"Leave us to whatever." The pair remained piled together, making no move to sort themselves out.

She leaned over, letting her blaster release from the Pak again. "I'm here now. I would like this base to be...let's aim for clean first. If you do not comply, you will be released from duty."

They scrambled away, metal grating on metal, repeating several times that they would comply. She nodded for them to enter the lift. The two pressed into different corners as she stepped in and flipped the switch back down. Capri watched them shake all the way to the eighth floor, where she made it stop.

She stepped out and slammed the door as they tried to leave. "Bottom to top. To work. Now."

One pulled the lever down with a trembling hand. With a thought, she pulled the fully functional Comp from Gregory's doorway and set it to watch the crew. So much easier than having to hunt them down later and bark out orders. Cleaning this place was pointless, she only needed it until she might retrieve Outrider or won the planet, but scaring them into action was fun. She'd needed that.

Capri took up position in the now empty doorway and saw Gregory hunched over the Comp she'd given him. "Thankful for your new toy?"

"I've gotten my hands on Comps before, but it's been a while. And never one this old. It's more so to finally have something different to work on."

She balanced her blaster on a couple of fingers. "So I've given you information, aid, and entertainment. And yet all I've gotten in return is sass and a headache. There must be something of actual use here."

Gregory stopped digging into the Comp and turned back to her. "That depends on what you want to do."

"I want my ho…the Collective ship back. Outrider. There are impostors pretending to be Wardens in there now. They've had time to fortify and wrongfully claim Paks. Getting back in will be near impossible. But if you have anything to pull them out, I can beat them on the ground."

"Personal vendetta. Bit dramatic," he flinched as the blaster aimed at him. Gregory leaned toward the worktable behind him. He swiped a few times until he found what he was looking for, pulling the image up from the table to show her the blueprint of a creation. "This can be put together rather quickly. It's simple in function, more of a show model. But if those imposters are not up to snuff as you say, it should do."

Capri took in the Lenian monster. They loved to base them off local creatures on the planets they attacked, a strange psychological part of their warfare she never looked much into. She wasn't familiar with whatever this originally was, but she liked how many sharp points it sported. Imagining those aggravating children impaled on a few gave her a spike of joy. "How long until you could have one ready?"

He looked longingly at the Comp only partly disassembled in front of him. "With Maxwell and I together, it should take a day. Maybe a bit more. Maxwell works slowly."

Maxwell was clearly listening in, as from across the hall came, "I can out-produce you any day!"

"Bicker all you want, gentlemen. Just get it done." Capri left the doorway and set her remaining Comp to float between the two. She felt they would keep themselves busy enough to not be any trouble. In the meantime, she'd take stock of a couple more floors before finding the Maintenance Crew and giving them another scare. With luck, this Lenian base might turn out to be worth her time.

30

Choose Your Fighter

"I'm telling you, it doesn't matter if the boots can stick to a wall." Mina watched Sean walk toward the top of the dome. "Unless gravity also changes orientation with you the blood still rushes to your head."

"I mean, we should at least test it," Sean spoke around his mouthful of pizza and hopped the last couple of steps to get himself over the elevator shaft. Nek sealed the floor once he'd started to climb.

"Nek, is this advised?" Steph asked from a seat at one of the consoles.

Nek moved as high as possible toward Sean. "It's not. I can provide the potential outcomes of this scenario for you."

"Let him learn," Emma called from her spot against the wall near the Pak pedestals, a large thermos of hot coffee steaming in her hands. "Honestly, it's the path of least resistance."

Zane took a bite of his slice of pizza. "Do a flip on the way down."

"Avoid all the consoles," Mina added. "We don't need to give anyone more work."

Sean bent his knees and jumped, but was pulled back toward the dome top. He stumbled a couple of steps. "The hold from the boots is stronger than I thought."

A small icon of swirls appeared on Mina's armband. Nek spoke quietly to her, "I have Comps outside, they can provide additional magnetization and keep him in place."

Mina barely caught the laugh before it escaped. She covered the best she could with a cough and a long drink of her pop. Pretending to use her sleeve as a napkin, she spoke quickly to Nek, "I think Emma is right, he'll just keep trying if this isn't memorable."

Sean tested his feet individually. He pulled one up several inches and let it fall back hard to the dome. "Gonna need a big jump."

"Do the Paks have any sort of crash pad they can deploy?" Steph pushed her chair away from the console. She was closest to where his landing/crashing spot would be.

"The suit should protect him," Nek answered. "Unless he were to land on his head, currently."

Sean shoved the last large bite of pizza into his mouth, took a few seconds to chew, and popped his helmet. He crouched low and pushed off the dome. Everyone tensed as he crossed the halfway point and was still pointed head first toward the floor. Mina stood up, ready to dive for him, but at the same moment she thought it was too late he flipped himself around. Landing in another crouched pose on the floor.

"Feel cool?" Zane asked.

Sean didn't move. "So cool."

"I've done that landing on mats." Emma, who hadn't budged, took a long drink of her coffee. "Super suit or not, that stung."

"Maybe. A bit." Sean tipped backward to sit and dropped the helmet. "You guys gotta try it."

Nek moved to a closer display. "Before more of the floor is dented, perhaps I can offer another task."

Sean shifted his feet to see the slight divots he'd left. "My bad."

"What do you need?" Steph jumped up from her chair.

"Something you all previously requested as well," Nek answered. "Would you like to see your Guardians?"

Sean scrambled to his feet and jumped on the panel still covering the elevator. "Yes, please!"

Nek shifted closer to him. "Would you like to take the fastest way down?"

"Yes! Let's do this." Sean hopped from foot to foot, clearly expecting the magnetization to kick in again, allowing him to drop straight to the bottom level. A second later he fuzzed over with an orange light and was gone.

Emma laughed, "He's going to complain that teleporting isn't very dramatic."

"He'd rather drop far enough to break his entire body?" Mina asked.

"I'm gonna spend a lot of time explaining him, aren't I?"

"Did you not already?" Steph asked.

Emma raised her thermos toward Steph, "Fair."

Sean came across their team channel. "Last one here gets the smallest, giant robot!"

Mina shot an arm into the air. "Nek, send me now!"

Nek did just that. Emma and Steph appeared beside her a second later. Outside the glass, they were once again surrounded by the thick metal cylinder that cut the elevator off from the level.

Sean leaned against it, looking smug. "Doesn't feel great to get tricked, huh?"

They heard Zane, still on the deck, over their group channel. He was chewing his last bite of pizza. Knowing him, he was holding up a hand to have Nek wait until he was done swallowing. "Does it work like that, the robots being up for grabs?"

"It doesn't," Nek laughed, "Warden Mina's reaction was unexpected."

"Lady loves her robots. If you hadn't guessed that already."

"Best to catch up to your team, Warden Zane."

"Come on!" Mina shouted over the channel, too distracted by the desire to see huge robots to spare much thought about Zane and Nek discussing her so openly. Sean was also bouncing from foot to foot again. Zane and 2876 dropped in and Nek appeared on their armbands.

"I should explain some aspects of Guardians before we head in." They sounded pleased at keeping them in further suspense.

"Heads up, they are kinda freaky looking," Emma said, "2876 gave us a hologram preview."

"Actually, they won't look like that anymore. These Guardians are made of the same material that forms the Pak, meaning they are rather adaptable.

And given the close connection Wardens have to their Pak, they emulate what the Warden envisions for their Guardian."

Comp2876 projected the image Mina assumed it'd shown before. A large beast that sported too many arms, eyes, and tendrils. Claws pretended to swipe out at them, the figure was only a foot tall as it hung in the air, but she caught Zane flinching anyway.

"What kind of creatures were the last Wardens trying to recreate?" Steph backed away from the hologram.

"These were relatively new. Our team selected new forms in honor of the voyage. We were traveling to unknown regions, they looked to creatures of legend. Tales brought back from explorers of what lurks beyond the farthest stars."

"Here there be monsters," Zane said. "Makes sense for going off the map."

"But they'll change now that we have the Paks?" Mina asked.

"Yes. They've already begun the process with your proximity here. Given the time they spent dormant, I was worried, but monitoring their systems over the last few hours shows they are in proper shape to acquaint you with them now."

"Good," Sean looked away from the image. "Cause I don't think I could face Cthulhu today."

As the cylinder pulled up, the group heard the groaning of metal coming from all around the vast room they now stood in the middle of. Mina ducked under the rising wall to step out first, drawn toward the sound of pieces snapping into place in front of her. The noise echoed up, given that this bottom level was so much larger than the other two and completely open. The Guardians needed the room. They were spread out in a circle, each pulsed with a faint glow as bands of material shifted around each other. She didn't miss that the glow matched their suits. The others didn't either as they split off toward their respective colors.

"We choose what they take the shape of?" Mina asked as she came up to the mass giving off her teal hue.

Nek was still on her armband. "Yes, whatever you desire."

"What do you guys think of keeping with the creatures of legend kind of vibe?" she asked back to the group. Thanks to the comms, she didn't have to shout overly loud to be heard.

"Sounds cool," Steph called back.

"I gotta do some googling," Sean said.

Not Mina, she'd known before the wall opened. She looked back to her Guardian and watched a plate of metal stretch from one side of the mass. Jagged and rough, a first attempt at a wing. The blue energy rippling over it looked appropriately like lightning. Mina thought about how she used to be terrified of storms, they'd send her crashing into whatever room the nearest adult was sleeping to curl in tight and wait out the noise. Her parents were always annoyed, turning her back around to her room. Her grandmother, when Mina stayed with her, was the one to finally talk her down. Against Mina's begging one storming night, Grandma piled blankets in her bay window and squished the two of them in. She leaned in close to Mina's ear and whispered about how storms were exciting because it meant one of them was close.

What's close? little Mina asked from under the blankets, terrified that the storm may be reaching out directly to her.

There it goes! was all she heard back.

She peaked out, trying to catch a glimpse of whatever Grandma was pointing at in the clouds.

Did you see it? her grandmother asked, giving her a little squeeze. After a couple of times, Mina was certain she did. The next morning Grandma told her all she knew about the creature living in the clouds, which was sadly far less than little Mina was hungry to consume. Storms weren't scary after that. For the next couple of years, she ran to the window, trying to catch a glimpse again.

Another length pushed out from the other side of the mass, more refined. You could see lines forming more distinct feathers. Mina thought of the little figure she'd crafted after her grandmother passed a little over a year ago. They'd come back from the funeral and she spent two days nonstop working, because the parts were so tiny and light. They'd break and she'd cry and then she'd try again, over and over until it was done. Zane begged her to stop, or eat, or sleep, or talk. Not her parents, but Zane. It was him barging in with a stack of food from his parents, demanding she take care of herself, that finally shook her loose from the shock of it all. The figurine floated over a plastic base, hidden magnets keeping it in the air, and when nudged the wings bobbed up and down. She'd blended T-Rex and Godzilla sounds to create a fierce little roar, while the base would rumble out little thunderclaps.

Mina watched the legs take shape, talons extending toward her and scraping against the floor. She took a few steps closer as part of the mass shifted forward, a beak formed in time to meet her hand. "Hey there, Thunderbird. You're a bit bigger than the one I have at home."

"That's awesome!" Zane shouted from the next spot over. "What do you think of mine?"

She looked over, seeing large thumping feet slap down. Antlers sprouted from a head that was still stretching to form a snout. "Is that a-"

"Jackalope! Yeah. Love those things."

"You're going to fight evil in a jackalope?" She was struck by the certainty, as she often was, that her best friend might actually be one of the best people in all of existence.

"A giant jackalope." He gave a scratch to the still rough-edged ear that flopped down next to him.

"The antlers do look intimidating."

"They are!" Zane turned back to his Guardian, still scratching the ear that was now showing flecks of green. "You like that? You like that, huh? Who's the best jackalope around?"

She wanted to contest that it was technically the only jackalope around, but she let it go. Mina looked at her armband, the swirling symbol of Nek was still there. "Are Guardians sentient?"

"That's a complicated answer. The Pak's programming is heavily inlaid within its structure. As mentioned, the Pak determines that those wearing them are worthy of their full abilities. Guardians only respond to those accepted by a Pak. In the past, they've shown reactive tendencies where the safety of their Warden is involved. Many have argued over the years if that qualifies as a form of sentients or not."

"Not artificial, just different," Mina recalled from when they first arrived, in that forever ago time of yesterday. The day before that she'd blown up private property with a homemade bomb and found a spaceship. Not bad for a lazy weekend.

Nek bounced in the small space of the armband, their version of a nod. "That's about the best estimation so far. Your team is shaping their Guardians nicely."

Mina stepped away as her Thunderbird shook out the last few pieces of blue-tipped tail feathers. As the Guardian stretched up other sheets of metal slid in to push it higher, Mina struggled to gauge how big it was at its full height. 2876 could measure it for her later. For now, she'd let herself settle for Plenty Big Enough. She walked around to see how the others were coming along.

On the other side of her, Emma dodged a silver-edged tail as it whipped over her head. Her Guardian turned and shook itself, releasing a ridge of spikes down its back. It looked reptilian, dragon-like even, but there wasn't any sign of wings forming. She caught Mina looking, "It's a drake!"

Mina gave an apologetic smile. "I don't know that one, sorry."

"I'll explain later." She rolled away from the swipe her Drake took with a sharply clawed paw. It seemed to have quickly taken on Emma's rough and tumble nature, another point to add to the matter of sentience.

Steph was rubbing the large snout of a horse. It gave a relatively quiet whinny as its back twitched, metal plates sliding back and forth as two wings sprouted from behind the shoulders. Not a horse, a pegasus. The wings glimmered with her dark purple. She saw Mina there and gave a small smile, "This isn't like, too easy of an option, is it? Or too obvious?"

"Do you like it?" She watched the tail swish itself into existence. Momentarily distracted and fascinated at how fine those strips of material must be.

"Um, yeah. Kinda. No. I mean - yes, I like it a lot. I love it." Steph ran her fingers over the sheet that was splitting apart to create a mane falling down the side of her Pegasus's neck.

"I think that's all that matters." Mina made eye contact with the Guardian, sort of, being that the eyes were where the pilot would be. That space was currently empty, but there was something in that darkness she felt looking back.

The next Guardian she stepped closer to see fully, there was no helpful glow here because this one wasn't shifting. It remained the very same gigantic, multi-limbed monster they'd been shown before. Fangs poked out of a too-wide mouth, she'd somehow missed those in the hologram before. Probably distracted by the tentacles in the way. There weren't any colored accents to highlight pieces like theirs now sported. Mina had an unnerving feeling that somehow this large of a construct could disappear into a shadow and reemerge in your nightmares. The face was blank, no trace of the animation coming out of the others, leaving it a cold and eerie statue. She glanced at her armband, "I know we've gone over this a bit already, but-"

"No, I understand. We have Capri fully blocked from the system. That includes her Pak connecting to the Guardian. She would need to enter the Guardian personally to regain control."

"So as long as it stays in Outrider and we keep her out, we're good."

"Correct." Nek whirled a bit tighter. "May I direct you to Warden Sean? His stress levels are rising."

Sean was pacing back and forth in front of his Guardian, still a bundle churning around itself. Comp2876 floated nearby with its screen flashing *You got this!*, but he wasn't seeing it. His eyes were screwed up tight and appeared about to rub his forehead raw. She stopped him from almost walking into her. Sean opened his eyes in surprise, looked around to see the other Guardians coming together, and deflated a bit. "This is hard."

"Don't beat yourself up over it."

"There's a lot of options to pick from."

"Then let's try to narrow it down. Was there a particular story you loved growing up? Or even now?"

"So many! But which one to choose? What have we got covered so far?" Sean stepped around her to check out the different Guardians. "You can fly.

So can Steph, bet it can move quick on land too. Though Zane's is probably faster. And Emma," he smiled at his cousin who was still ducking from swipes, "that'll be a tank. Do we need a healer? Is that something Guardians can do?"

Mina saw Nek swirling on their armbands but answered first. "Don't focus on making some kind of optimized team. I think this only works if it's something you connect with."

He went back to pacing. "You'd think that'd make it easier."

Mina blocked his path, grabbing hold of his arms so he'd have to stand still. She'd done something similar for Zane in the past when he got himself too worked up. "Really. I think you're overthinking it. Humor me for a second, get everything out of your head. Forget about all our craziness. Let it all go blank."

"Alright." Sean sighed, shook himself, and dropped his eyes down to the floor.

She racked her brain for what to say next. Mina knew he loved to put on a show, maybe it'd work to pitch it as a sort of sidekick. "Good news! You've completed your quest and gained a companion! Any creature from legend can now be at your side. Name it and it's there. First thing that pops into your head."

Sean didn't say anything, but the mass started to shift. The sound of pieces snapping together emanating from within the form. Something had come to mind. "It's dumb."

"I would put money on the fact that a large part of why Zane picked a jackalope is because it's fun to say."

He sighed and shifted in her hold. "Every Pokemon game, no matter what new types they add, my team always has a Ninetails. Auntie Kay always told the best stories about where her and dad's side came from generations ago. My dad said it was a hobby she picked up in college, obsessively researching our family history. She knew a whole bunch of myths and legends, but I always liked the kitsune stuff best."

Mina looked at the Guardian and saw clear signs of several tails beginning to grow off the back. "Are you close with her?"

Sean grabbed onto Mina's arms. "She's this fireball of energy. Um, was. Had to try everything once. Always some new grand adventure coming up. She was insanely good at getting my mom to let us do crazy stuff. She could even get Aunt Gwen, Emma's mom, to go along sometimes."

She felt a tweak in her chest, catching that adjustment from is to was. "She meant a lot to your family."

Sean smiled at the floor. "She was chaos. Dad calls her a cautionary tale when he wants to put some kind of scare in me, but he always caved to what his big sister wanted. Even when she said she didn't want to do chemo the second time around. She threatened to haunt him if he didn't let me keep up the sleight of hand stuff. She couldn't...she could barely stand at that point and still..."

Mina felt his fingers dig into her harder. She held herself steady, for his sake. "Sounds like you know what you want. Give it a look."

Sean opened his eyes as the long nose of the fox-like creature gave him a nudge. The Kitsune laid down as it came together, legs folding in beneath it. Mina was again fascinated at how thinly the material could form itself to make the appearance of a fur coat; she expected it would still feel soft if she were to touch it. The tails curled around each side. While the eyes were technically hollow, they somehow managed to look kindly at Sean. She wasn't sure how, but she felt like it was smiling.

Mina was fully on Team Sentient when it came to Guardians. She let him pull away and backed off as he stepped closer to his Guardian. Best to let him have his space. On the way back to her own Guardian, Emma caught her eye and mouthed a quick 'thank you'.

Nek whirled and spoke only to her, "Very well done, Warden Mina."

"I think he knew what he wanted. He needed to hear it was okay though."

"Would that Guardian's shape be inappropriate?"

"No, it's absolutely fine. It's just..." Mina looked at her Thunderbird, another blue ripple of energy rolled through the wings. "I kinda get where he's coming from. People from different walks of life meet and make families. It's great! You get a mix of cultures. Sometimes though, you get a couple generations between you and those direct cultures. Bits and pieces get passed along, others get lost in the mix. Then when you try to take part, you can end up feeling like an impostor. Like it's not really yours."

"I'm not sure I fully understand."

"I don't think I'm explaining it right. Sorry. I'm still figuring it out too." Mina took a seat between two talons. "My grandma used the thunderbird to help me not be afraid of storms. That's why it means so much to me. And it's more that she was telling me stories, not the stories themself. If that makes sense. I never bothered to ask for others, to find out what else she knew. Or even ask who taught her. And now I don't even know where to go look if I wanted to now."

"Surely whichever of your parents she was related to could provide details?"

"My mom would never have asked either. She didn't have any connection to that stuff. And so neither did I, outside of those bits from Grandma. Can't even say how much my grandma would have known. She didn't grow up on a reservation or anything. I think she had cousins that did? My mom never kept in touch with any of them. And I didn't, um, handle the funeral well and missed meeting anyone," Mina let the small hitch in her chest ease itself out, leaning further into her Thunderbird before going on, "I never asked Grandma for more and I've been mad at myself about that for a while now. I mean, honestly, she could have made it all up! I wouldn't know. But whatever she had, it went with her."

"Humans are…rather intricate in their nature."

"That's a nice way to say complicated and messy." She looked up to her Guardian, which was flexing its wings. "I know I could find other ways to connect with that part of myself. Maybe even track down that side of my family. I think I will someday, but this is all I have for now."

"I'm sure your grandmother would be proud. Along with Warden Sean's aunt."

Mina looked around at her team again, still cooing over their Guardians as the last few pieces set into place. Steph was tangled up in the mane, but happy about it. Zane was still scratching the ear, the Jackalope's foot thumping in appreciation. Sean was leaning into the snout of his, simply hugging it tight. Emma miscalculated a jump and her Drake's tail caught her ankles. She flipped around in the air once before coming down on her back. Mina was already on her feet when she heard Emma laugh.

Mina dropped back against the leg of her Thunderbird. Daring to believe that they may become good at this. One day. Nek whirled on her armband again. "Your Guardian is ready. May I give you a tour of the control room?"

Mina scrambled, skidding in place for a few steps before finding purchase on the floor. She frantically looked over her Thunderbird, trying to find the way in. Her words came out all squished together in her excitement, "Yespleasewheresthedoorpleaseletmein!"

Nek laughed from the band. "Go around to the right leg, there is a place to set your Pak there."

She did as directed, finding a square spot not covered in the faux-feather texture. The Pak fit perfectly into the space, a teal shimmer pulsed out with the connection. Her Thunderbird let out a call that sounded like her figurine, it echoed off the far other side of the level.

Nek's waves warmed on the armband. "Guardian unlocked. Let me move you in."

Mina was glad to be teleported, she didn't really need the others seeing her cry.

31

Why Have Allies When You Have Minions Like These?

Capri left the Maintenance Crew to their work on the docking bay; they'd perform better with their hands not shaking. Even if it was the only thing giving her joy in all this mess. The chittering from Gregory and Maxwell drifted down, they kept shuffling back and forth between workshops to argue over aspects of the creature. Her Comp provided updates and, somehow between the bickering, they were making good progress.

While back on the main floor, she'd decided to personally inspect the smaller wings that spun off from the main tower. Capri met a couple of automated cleaning Pawns the crew set to work, proving there'd been plenty of resources to keep the base in better shape. Honestly, all you needed to do was turn on the machines and they'd care for the place. Yet that level of effort was too much for this measly crew. Her team would have-

She shook off the thought before it was even completed, a spike of anger threatened to rise all the same. Ridiculous for her to become agitated about cleaning. Chasing around the crew wasn't anything important, simply something to pass the time. She'd have the means to get back what was hers soon enough. Capri was reluctant to accept that Outrider was lost to her. Nek proved they were more than willing to destroy it and themself rather than allow Capri to gain control. But it was her home too. As much as she wanted to rip Nek out, doing so without a nearby replacement would leave Outrider nearly useless.

This was also ignoring the reality of how painful it would be roaming those halls alone, if the annoying children wouldn't submit. Her most likely option was settling for her Guardian, then blowing up the damn ship out of spite. Possibly. It depended on how mad she was once this was over. Her mind kept jumping from one side of the argument to the other, confusing even herself on what she truly wanted at the end of this. She wasn't meant to be doing this alone.

She shook off the wave of…she couldn't even pinpoint the emotion. It left her sour. Perhaps she'd leave Outrider as a relic. A warning. Strip it for parts. The Lenians could craft her something capable of reaching the Collective.

Using the hole a Comp cut as a means of entry earlier, Capri pulled open the door of the larger wing. The bank of generators that filled half the space growled away. What caught her attention was the massive pile filling the other half of the room. The Comp only registered it as a large mass, cold and dormant, before it'd been called back by Capri earlier. She was looking at a pile of Lenian Pawns. Ground fighters, more intended for distraction and to scramble civilians than ever get anything done. She'd counted nearly a hundred of the cube-shaped Pawns before she lost track out of frustration. It was like leaving the Comps on their chargers. Wasteful.

She couldn't shake the anger this time. Her chest felt like a rod was jammed into its center, a tightness stopping her from taking the deep breath she wanted. Capri charged back toward the main room, yelling up from beside the lift, "Are all Lenians truly this wasteful or are you two especially skilled at it?"

There was a long pause before Gregory appeared over the railing. "Sorry, what was that?"

"The stack of Pawns you have sitting in the wing. Did you plan on mentioning those any time soon?" Had she not asked for something to get the impostor team back on the planet? Her head spun a little.

"Oh! Forgot about those. They always insist we keep a number on hand, but never say what to do with them." Gregory looked across to the other workshop. "Turn the oafs on, Maxwell."

"Is creature production not the priority anymore?" he called back without coming out. "Is the mistress fussy?"

"I can come up and show you fussy," Capri answered.

Gregory clapped. "I want to see that."

Something shot out of Maxwell's workshop and clipped the top of Gregory's head. He called out a moment later, "Systems are booting up. What would you like them to do?"

She rubbed the tight spot in her chest, the aching wound there giving her a different jolt of pain, and resisted the urge to bang her head into the lift. "Run diagnostics, make sure they're in working order. Have them at the teleport and ready to go down before the creature."

It was best to keep them on a project, keep them distracted. If killing Nek's new team didn't get Capri what she wanted, let the Lenians send their monster anyway.

Only Gregory's hand appeared over the railing now. "Speaking of the teleport, that may need some attention as well."

Capri grabbed one of the decorative bars on the door of the lift and bent it until the metal snapped off. "Why?"

"It's not like we've gone anywhere. Little dusty out there."

She chucked the hunk of metal straight up the tower, it pinged off the lift cable around the fifth floor and bounced into whatever room lay beyond. "You are…rather frustrating."

Maxwell finally appeared at the railing. "Now you know my pain."

They didn't fear her. They didn't respect her. She didn't know why they were even going along with her orders. Capri felt that rod move closer to the base of her throat, making her breath even shorter. "I will check the teleport. The Comp will advise if you are needed for anything there."

"Sounds good," came from both sides as they ducked back into their respective workshops.

She remained at the lift, fighting to breathe and resettle herself. There was so much to do and no one else here contained any motivation. It's not that she'd imagined finding a new worthwhile team by coming here, but she'd expected a bit more drive. Expected she'd entice them with gaining a win over what should be their greatest enemy. Or that she'd strike enough fear into them to stir them into action. Capri was beginning to believe they were only making the creature out of boredom, there was no telling how much longer they'd follow along.

Capri needed some sort of result from all this effort. From all this trouble. Her friends were dead and her home was lost, there must be a reason for it. She needed to be right. Needed to show the Collective, wherever they were now, that they were right to trust her. And wrong to leave her behind like this. Otherwise, she was in danger of regretting everything she'd done. That was unacceptable.

Amid this anxiety-ridden haze, she made her way out to the glass-encased teleport pad. A few pieces of the creature were scattered about, waiting for further construction once possible. It appeared too small, but they insisted it would become larger once on Earth. Gregory seemed rather proud of their breakthroughs in expandable construction. He'd demonstrated with one of his birds as it grew five times the size before scrunching back into the palm-sized figurine. From what she could tell, it was a larger-scale version of what Comps used to store all their features. Maybe it would be impressive, Capri was worn down enough that her standards were starting to drop.

A small bit of luck, their teleport was more in need of cleaning than repair. Dusting and scrubbing was beneath her, but cleaning off the control console was a task all the same. Something to keep her hands busy. Something to distract from the nerves and shake that rod loose from her chest.

It also helped to watch more pieces of the creature arrive. Pawns were buzzing by to assemble parts, this gave her a tangible progress bar. If only the work inside the base were moving at the same pace. Her Comp's report on the Pawns running diagnostics informed her it'd be several hours before they were all functional. She made a note to herself to better optimize their programming after this.

Isn't it a bit defeatist to already be prepping this place as your own? a voice she decidedly didn't recognize as Jarden asked in her head.

"Can't count on the first plan going right. Last time I did that-" Capri thought of the last moment she and Rin shared. That begging, that pain, and all that blood. "You all ended up dead."

So sad for you, some part of her mind pretending to be Camden snapped back.

That rod in her chest melted away. She pushed a deep, angry breath out. Camden always had a special way of pissing her off. Capri shoved a Pawn as it went by, it bounced off the base of a crane lifting one of the creature's spikes before correcting itself. She gave up the ruse of cleaning and stood watching her monster take shape. It'd be time to go soon enough.

32

Practice Makes a Smidge Less Messy

Turns out that asking people to leave their new giant robots was a rather hard task, evident by how Mina could barely get herself to crawl out of her Thunderbird. She'd managed to convince them to practice moving around, getting a small feel for the basic functions of the Guardians. Since the level was only intended for storing the Guardians, it didn't have enough room to test a wide range, but it was something. Mina could only get a few feet off the ground when trying to fly. But that limitation turned into them figuring out how to move in time with each other, adapting to each other's movements and anticipating what they could as they shifted around the level. As much as she'd like to take credit for thinking of that beforehand, it was purely accidental.

Their synchronized movement only lasted until Emma lined up a shot on Sean and tackled him across the floor. The cousins took swipes at each other as they crashed around. They rolled into Steph, who stomped down a few of Sean's tails and held him in place. Mina was rather impressed by the move. Zane hooked Emma's next tail swipe in his antlers, stopping her from taking the cheap shot on Sean.

"Maybe we don't scratch up the new robots within the first day?" he asked.

They'd all backed off with a laugh. After that, Mina figured they should try doing a little personal training too. She recalled the clunkiness of the hallway fights with Capri. If they could figure out timing in the Guardians, it should be easy enough to do with their bodies. Right?

After a bit of whining, they all joined her at the elevator pad. The glass wall, which Nek retracted while they practiced, dropped back down and the floor lifted them to the center level. Comp2876 switched to a bright *Time to train!* and led the group into another section. They came to a set of doors already sliding open, revealing a round, empty room beyond. The floor was covered in a layer of dingy brown padding that squished under their feet as they walked in. She saw that the walls were covered in the same material. There were scuff marks everywhere, clearly the location of many spars.

Emma was already stretching as they moved into the center of the room. She smirked at Sean. "You remember that old McDonalds on 72nd with the play place? There was that one big room up top."

"The battledome!" Sean laughed. "We'd pull up the mat to block the door so no one could get in and stop us."

Steph's eyes grew wide. "You actually went in that thing? It always looked like it was about to fall over."

Nek rolled into the panel across from them. "We will start simple, make sure you've got a handle on the more basic assistance your suits can give in a fight. First off, they will give alerts of incoming attacks or known weak points on enemies."

"Spidey Sense!" Sean whispered.

"Very copyrighted," Zane countered.

"Warden Warning?" Steph offered.

"Cheat Sheet," Emma threw out.

"Punchpoint," Mina tried. "One word. Like PowerPoint?"

"You can customize your heads-up display however you like," Nek continued, "One suggestion as we begin is to limit your alerts only to your current target. That way a group of enemies doesn't overwhelm you."

"It's important to stay whelmed," Zane said. Emma didn't say anything but lifted a hand to give him a high five.

Nek disappeared from the panel and a video took their place, a hallway filled with several bodies. Mina picked each of them out, thanks to the coloring, as their fight with Capri played out before them. Seeing it from this outside perspective, she realized that calling their ability level clumsy was being kind. It was miscalculations on Capri's part, and a few lucky good hits, that kept them alive. It paused with them all standing over the momentarily incapacitated Capri, before snapping back to the beginning. The encounter played again, but the images shifted. Their figures became less rendered, they all looked flat and cartoonish. They watched Capri miss getting hit by Comp2876, and in turn their next surprise blows never landed, allowing her to put them all down within a minute. The figures reset and moved forward in the fight to show what would have happened if Capri countered Emma's full body slam. The figures reset again and again, highlighting how badly each move could have gone. In every version, in far less time than their actual fight, they were all flat out on the floor. Probably, very likely, very much dead.

"It was all pretty close, huh?" Emma asked.

"These are crude estimates. Worst case scenarios. I don't mean to discourage you." Nek reappeared on the panel. "My team…my last team knew Capri and her skills, trained right alongside her. They all fell to her. I will not see that happen again."

They were quiet. Mina was personally ashamed, talking herself up as a leader this whole time. None were prepared for Nek's honesty. They'd been excited to train in the suits, acting like kids with new toys. They'd been cracking jokes. Forgetting that somewhere out in that big void of space was an enemy ready to end them at any cost. Before going on to do worse to the entire human species.

Mina felt her suit sit heavier on her. "We all want to do right by your team too."

Steph turned to Emma. "Can you teach me that suplex move?"

Emma tipped her head, she seemed to run her own internal simulation. "Not to assume things, but do you do any weight training? We may need to get that going before you try throwing someone over your head."

"Do boxes of coffee count?"

"It's a start, but we'll work up to it. I can teach you a couple of ways to break holds though. Or other ways to knock people down."

"I'll take it!"

They spread out across the floor and watched Emma demonstrate a few tactics, using Sean as a partially willing assistant. Zane offered to switch after a few falls, but Sean insisted that Emma throwing him around was the most normal thing to happen in the last 48 hours. Nek shifted around the room, advising on more ways the suits could help. Mina noticed they did seem to pick up moves rather quickly. Over the next hour, they managed to put each other down several times. Or in the case of anyone against Emma, they managed to make her wobble. Zane got one of her feet off the ground, but only for a moment.

"So you mean all those wrestlers fake the moves?" Mina tried to hook Zane's leg and pull him down. He stifled a laugh at her strain.

"There's still a crazy amount of demand on their bodies." Emma shifted Mina out of the way and took over the move. "And a whole lot of trust and coordination with your match partner. I'll send you some videos."

"Mina knew how to fix alien technology within moments of seeing it." Zane braced harder against Emma. "But was today years old when she learned wrestling is fake."

"Not fake," Emma corrected, sending him to the floor harder than necessary. "Practiced. It's a performance. And plenty can still go wrong."

"Careful where you tread, man," Sean warned as he locked in with Steph.

"Am I about to get thrown over your head?" Zane asked as he pushed himself back up.

"No, but she's got a list of injuries memorized. It's a whole thing. Oh, crap!" He flipped as Steph used a boost from the suit to offset their difference in strength and push him harder.

"People have died!" Emma shouted to the entire room.

Mina looked at Nek, wanting to move the conversation along before this fight got violent. "Do you have any tips for going against Capri specifically?"

Nek spun in place. "I can work something up. We can also practice working together in a fight. Like moving the Guardians around below."

Great minds, Mina thought. Small pat on the back for her.

"Are we going to fight the Comps?" Steph sounded minorly concerned.

"Because 2876 proved they're pretty tricky."

Comp2876 flashed a *Thanks!* to her.

"We have a system in place." Nek's colors sharpened as the lights in the training room snapped off. Smaller, green lights flickered on at the edges of the room. Hazy images of Capri stood around them.

Emma squared up with the one closest to her. "I'm down for some shadowboxing."

The figure sucker-punched her in the gut, Emma doubled over and sucked in a hard breath.

Mina clapped with excitement. "Hard light!"

The figures took a fighting stance. Nek disappeared from the panel, taking their sliver of extra light with them, and reappeared on their armbands. "Remember, it's important to stay whelmed."

33

Monster Assembly Required

Capri leaned against the glass of the telepad and dropped her suit for the first time in hours, enjoying the cool temperature against her back. Her legs were pulled up close to her chest, hands absently picked at loose threads on her shorts. She knew she'd fray and ruin the edges again, no Caro to mend them this time, but that was a future issue. Her stomach grumbled, reminding her that she'd not eaten anything since waking in Outrider. They'd need to assign a few Pawns to grab food while the rest were on the attack, Lenian food would do her no good. One more aggravating task added to this horrible day.

Pawns buzzed around the creature, securing the last few points and running early diagnostics. Her Comps moved in wider circles, keeping their own tabs on progress. With the stack of Pawns inside still sorting themselves out, she estimated only a couple more hours before it would all be ready.

Several parts of her ached from the still angry wounds gained in her previous encounters. But she wasn't going at it alone this time, as lackluster as the Lenians were, and felt sure she'd do away with the imposters easily enough. Then go on to force Nek to bend to her will, burn the whole damn planet if she needed to. Maybe that would get the attention of the Collective, make them finally visit this abandoned corner of the galaxy.

Gregory and Maxwell came stumbling out of the tower. Each with a tablet in hand and rambling about the next steps needed, talking over each other. The pair took on their own orbit around the creature, bickering as they made laps.

"You are overcomplicating this," Maxwell said. "All we need is to-"

"We dress it up, you dullard," Gregory snapped back before he could finish. "A couple of shots to shake the ground, a smidge of smoke beforehand, and it looks to come up from the crater already there. And then goodness, is there something underground? How safe are we? Can you-"

"Creature from below?" Maxwell scoffed. "That's more intimidating than from space? Really? Vast. Endless. Space. Confirming their tiny lives mean even less. Causing endless existential crises and hysteria. Once it lands-"

"I think horns could add some flare." Gregory waved at a design on his tablet. "It would only need an extra hour or so. Be done before diag-"

"If I concede to the horns, will you give up the light show?"

Gregory paused to consider the offer. He fell behind in the orbit and cast a glance up to the head being shifted as Pawns made connections. "Horns really would do good. And a nice filigree overlay."

"No more decorative nonsense! Only horns. Functional. Crude. Intimidating."

"Things can be both. Look at me." Gregory gestured to his adornments.

Maxwell stopped his trudge to double over laughing. His tablet slipped loose and clattered to the pavement.

Gregory was trying to hide his smirk, clearly expecting this reaction. He caught up to Maxwell and snatched the tablet, glancing over whatever was sketched out there. "I suppose simply dropping it in that crater is as good as anything. Their little brains wouldn't appreciate a good production anyway."

Maxwell straightened and gently took his tablet back. "If we forgo the horns, we could use the freed-up Pawns to add some aesthetically appealing details. In select areas."

The two ducked their heads together over the tablets, scribbling out ideas across both screens. Capri didn't know if their arguing or getting along bothered her more. Really, at the moment, it was their noise in general that was upsetting. And the Pawns buzzing on top of that. And the Comps on top of that. And whatever the Maintenance Crew was doing nearby that made them pound very out of time with each other. And the ringing, something was ringing. She realized that the last one was her ears.

She expanded the suit again, snapped her helmet up, and canceled out all noise. The ringing persisted until she filled her ears with static. Capri sat in her quiet, it never took too long for this to settle her. Once she had a better handle on herself, she turned her notifications back on in a text-only format.

The Lenians were looking at her. More accurately, they were taking turns pretending to glance around her. Putting the suit back on must have drawn their attention. She made the nearby Comp transcribe their conversation.

M - Is one Warden worth all this fuss? An old one at that?

Hurtful. She was far from old. She'd been the second youngest on her team.

G - My bruised face can affirm she's plenty of trouble.

M - But when they find out we've-

G - They haven't done more than a courtesy check-in for years. This is at least something new to pass the time.

M - A lot of effort for little reward.

G - There's plenty of chance she gets herself killed down there. Problem resolves itself.

Capri wanted to be offended, but she hadn't done anything to deserve better regard from them.

M - And if not? How far do we let this go? She doesn't even know-

G - If anything, this is better than the last show we picked from Earth.

M - You'd think a ninja nun would at least have decent fights. So bad.

G - The worst.

Capri stopped reading as they fell back into discussing the creature. She sent one of the Comps to watch the Pawns engraving the additional decoration, giving her a live feed across her heads-up display. It was oddly soothing watching the lines be cut into the metal. Her internal progress bar inched closer to completion. Closer to her getting what she deserved.

34

We Have to Stop Hanging Out Like This

Henrie hadn't needed a babysitter in years, but her mom was on hand at the hospital until everything was confirmed clear and she didn't want Henrie home alone or caught in any chaos at said hospital. Her grandparents were still stuck out of town and rather than sit with the new neighbor she didn't know, she'd sent a mayday message and nabbed an invite to Megan's family's apartment. Henrie thought the idea would get vetoed as Megan lived in a building downtown, but as it wasn't right on the edge near The Park there wasn't any kick back. That could also be due to the small amount of sleep her mom was already running on before all the insanity, but she didn't push it. Simply left once she got the okay.

Wouldn't you know it, Mitch felt the same for Sam. Mitch was on some Citizen Crisis Response Team but figured Sam had responded to enough crises for now. They arrived at the same time and were swiftly buzzed into the building by Megan, she texted a **PLEASE SAVE ME** as they rode the elevator up to her floor.

They figured out why soon enough, Megan's mother was very much a hoverer. While she was terrified of what was going on, she'd made them recount their escape from the madness. Gasping and clutching Megan as they went. They thought that'd be it, she left once they repeatedly insisted they were okay, but came back with her phone in hand going over some new conspiracy theory a not-so-great news channel was trying to promote.

Megan gave them sorry glances any chance she got. Her mother kept leaving, they kept trying to talk about anything else, and then she'd reappear with a snack or drink or more unchecked information. After a while, Megan's father came out from wherever he was hiding and shuffled her away. The look he shared with Megan conveying that he was sorry for taking so long to take his turn with her.

Their group had no headspace for conspiracies. Henrie found herself overloaded on serious information. She was instead typing away to the work chat, they'd begun making a strategy for transforming Restoration Cafe into a bunker.

She sent off, **Coffee will be good for bartering with the remaining population.**

That's what I'm saying! Popped in from Sam, who was stretched out across the loveseat. **We'll be sitting on a pile of new currency.**

Are we the bad guys in this dystopia? Steph asked.

I think our supply will afford us the ability to be left alone to our own business. Carter answered quickly. And then after another second, **Here's the thing...**

Megan replied before his next overly detailed message came through. **TBH, I am not above withholding a drink if someone is a snob.**

Oh, I already have a list of those not worthy of our gifts. Michele responded.

Sean may get a better reaction to his tricks. Sam added. Out loud to Megan they said, "I know you're too nice to do that."

Sean sent a gif of Sorcerer Mickey. **They will cheer or they will perish... of thirst. Or go down to Starbucks, I guess.**

So we are the bad guys. Steph affirmed.

But not like, the total worst. Henrie sent. **Mid-tier at most. The hero has to cut their teeth on us and then goes on to the big bad.**

What's our team name? Michele asked.

That got them all going, shooting off names as they all tried to find the best coffee and low-grade crime puns. Megan slid from her chair to sit on the floor, head leaned back into the seat. Carter's long blurb finally popped in, but they pushed it away with their messages. He also started giving names without trying to circle back to his rant. This was nice, it felt normal-ish. But Henrie could tell being cooped up with a worrisome mother all day was becoming more exhausting than escaping an exploding nature park for Megan.

She leaned over closer to the other two. "You wanna stretch our legs a bit? I kinda wanna see how empty downtown is."

"Sure!" Megan immediately pushed off the floor.

"I saw Sax's Pizza is weirdly open," Sam added.

"The owners live above it. It's probably only them in there." Megan looked down the hallway, but pulled out her phone instead, deciding it better to text her parents rather than tell them directly. "I could actually go for Sax's right now."

The three of them quietly left the apartment. While taking the elevator down they all continued to debate the best name for their apocalypse group, but everyone was too attached to their answers to give anyone else's a real chance. It made it easier to handle a national disaster when your focus was finding the best meme to send. For now, anyway.

Henrie put her phone away to take in the relatively quiet downtown once they were outside, falling behind a step or two. Megan took the lead, as this was her neighborhood, in walking them the few blocks over to Sax's. Sam floated between them. The street was near empty, compared to what she imagined traffic was usually like on any given day down here. They passed by a fully empty pocket park squished between a couple of buildings. She expected to catch some hectic employee hunched over their desk in the windows of the office buildings they passed by, bashing away at a laptop trying to finish some project before the world ended or Monday came. Whichever may happen first. But they all were empty too, or at least no one was near the windows. The sign on the parking garage they passed displayed being nearly full, meaning there were people around here somewhere. Henrie also heard some kind of construction work going on a couple streets over, from the bangs she thought there must be some concrete being torn up.

She realized she'd fallen rather behind the other two. Henrie went into a light jog to catch up, meeting them as Sam came to a full stop only a few yards away from the pizza shop.

They tapped away at their phone screen a couple of times. "That's weird. Nothing will load now."

"Yeah, mine is spotty too," Megan said.

Henrie pulled out her phone. "I've got a lot of lag too."

"Of course, this gets through." Megan sighed, tipping her phone to show her mother was calling. She answered after taking a deep breath. "I told Dad we were just going around to Sax's. Ten more minutes tops."

Henrie was close enough that she should have heard Megan's mother, but all that came through was static.

Megan pulled the phone from her ear as the call dropped. She looked back to the other two. "There wouldn't be a reasonable, non-disaster explanation for service to drop again, would there?"

"Something military-related?" Sam asked, looking at Henrie.

She couldn't think of an answer because she was too distracted by the two messages from her mother that managed to get through. **Bunker down. Activity nearby.** More were trying to load, a stack of dot dot dot icons on her screen, but eventually it gave up and asked for her to try again later. "We need to get back inside."

Henrie ran for the corner, the other two not far behind. She picked up that the noises she'd heard before sounded more frantic than a minute ago. On the street ahead cars were screeching to a halt, while others swerved around them and hit the curbs. They even watched one do a full u-turn in the intersection, barely missing several other people, and go back the other way. None of them could see what they were reacting to yet. Henrie could hear it though, rapid firing and the now familiar sound of glass breaking. By the time they reached the corner, traffic jammed up to the point that no one was moving anymore. She ran right into the middle of the crosswalk, joining other onlookers coming out of buildings and cars. Henrie only took in the view down the street at first - a sightline that used to showcase The Hill framed by the taller buildings of downtown. Between her and that space now were several…flying boxes? They shifted and tracked movement on the street. She watched one's underside open up and a vaguely familiar shape unfolded beneath it. Something in her reacted barely fast enough to pull the other two behind a box truck before the flying thing shot into the crowd in the crosswalk.

Not everyone else reacted as quickly. She watched a man take a hit high in his chest and drop behind a car. The drones, that was the only thing she thought they could be, flew overhead. Sending a wide spray of shots into the buildings. Henrie spotted a few break from the group and fly through newly shattered windows. Alarms, and more screams, came from inside. They'd found those weekend warriors.

She kept them down, expecting the drones would take another pass on the street. Given the panic erupting around them, moving wasn't the safest option anyway. People could end up being just as dangerous to them right now. Crashing came from both sides, more glass hitting the ground. Her hands pulsed at the thought of more slivers.

Sam pulled against her. They were staring in the direction of the first man they'd seen shot. "People need help."

"This is not a 'save everyone' situation," Henrie said and realized she was echoing a lecture her dad had given her years ago. Something she'd probably rolled her eyes about at the time, expecting it was something she'd never have to use, but he raised a daughter who prepared for the worst. She knew it sounded cold, but they needed to be smart. There was a fine line between heroes and idiots. Henrie kept her eyes on the batch of drones, now a couple blocks down and still firing wildly. The way they shifted and jerked around, they seemed to be going after anything they saw moving. No real form to their fighting. "They're out to cause panic. We need to hide."

"Do you think this is the same people who blew up The Hill? Or some new and different horrible thing?" Megan asked.

"Which of those is the less evil option?" Sam asked back. Someone called out and they pulled again. "We can't stay here."

Henrie grabbed them, daring to take her eyes off the drones as they turned back up the street to lock eyes with them. "Then help us, Sam."

She heard the drones firing, getting closer again. Sam grabbed their hands and pulled them off the street, back toward the pocket park. They shoved each girl toward a cement bench before diving under their own. Henrie tucked her legs in as the batch of drones shot by on the street.

Sam edged out enough to see both of them. "This may give us some buffer from falling debris."

People ran, stumbled, sprinted, and crawled by the park. Shouts came from above them, pointless warnings to get off the street. Henrie rolled over to see how far they were from any doorway, someone would buzz them in - surely. A piece of her bench chipped away and the bushes behind it shook from hits. The drones must have circled back and taken notice of the unscathed buildings. It was seconds, that lasted hours, as they fired in at the buildings surrounding them. Each teen balled up under their bench. Then it was quiet, well, relatively. Her ears were ringing.

None of them moved. No one called out from the buildings anymore, but there was still screaming. They waited.

And waited.

She picked up more firing and glass breaking on the other side of the apartments behind them. The drones must have moved to the next street. Their own street was now horribly quiet, she hoped because people got away. Unlike them, still stuck in the park.

Megan was muttering under her bench, head pressed against the ground. "It's not far. One quick run. Could make it."

Henrie inched out toward her. "I think we need to stay put."

Megan shook her head, scrapping it against the concrete. "I want to go home."

"We don't know how many are out there. Or if they'll come back."

She knew the other girl wasn't hearing her. Megan took a deep breath before bolting from under the bench. Sam was quicker to follow, hollering for her to wait.

Henrie hesitated, fighting the tightness in her chest, they'd disappeared around the building to the right before she left her bench. She sprinted out to spot Sam catching Megan at the corner and stopping her there. As she reached them, another group of drones appeared up the street. Not coming around any building or out from cover, straight up appeared before her eyes. These moved much slower, hovering over someone walking down the street. The person hopped up onto a car's hood, walking over the length of it, and kept on straight to the next car. The light glinted off their black, glassed helmet.

She had no intention of whoever that was spotting them and once again found herself pulling the other two behind an abandoned car, giving them decent cover on the sidewalk.

"Remember when yesterday was the worst day ever?" Megan cried.

Sam pulled her closer, most likely for comfort but also to muffle her slightly.

Henrie peaked around the edge to track the figure as it passed by over the tops of cars behind them. "Yeah, my mom said this was a quiet little city when we first got here."

"Things change when you leave for a while," Sam said.

She watched the figure, the drones stayed tight on them. They came to the intersection and walked out into the middle. Shoving cars to clear a space around them. Henrie tried to fully process that, shoving cars. Drones fired shots at any person trying to get by. Henrie could hear the figure shouting something, but couldn't pick out the language. The drones spread out to the sides of the intersection, forming a ring around the black-clad figure.

"What do you think they're doing?" Sam asked, leaning toward her with Megan sniffling against them.

"I think they're waiting," Henrie said.

35

Now For Reals

The team settled into their now regular locations around the deck after their stint of fight training. There'd been some initial chatter as they clambered in until Sean, who'd been passively swiping through menus, found the attunement feature for weapons and tools. Their conversation stalled out as they felt embarrassed over how they'd handled Capri's saber. Nek tried to take the blame for not advising on the feature, but they wouldn't allow it. They all started poking around through the suit's options, looking for anything else that would have helped before. Soon the only talking was when one would call out an interesting feature or tip.

After a while Steph pulled the saber from her own Pak, a rather impressive sight to watch it load out from the much smaller device, and took up a spot on one end of the deck to practice a few moves. Comp2876 produced small holograms with targets for her to chase after. Mina angled herself so it looked like she was reading something off her armband and not watching her.

Zane organized their questions, she caught the edits pop in as she pretended to read. He was reworking it to have a page for what they knew and the questions that remained. Then grouping questions that were related, mostly formatting to look nicer. It'd become a mess from them all throwing out questions over that first morning.

Sean was also adding a new section for suit features to their document.

251

Mostly noting if items featured different levels, like the boosts, or were one setting, like the sticky shoes. There were a few other items listed with asterisks next to them, Mina expected that was a personal To-Test list for himself.

Emma was the only one with her helmet up. She told them she was optimizing the heads-up display. Making different layouts for, what she thought, could be more common scenarios. Sharing them with the group as they were finished. Mina was impressed with her knack for the designs and updated to one that featured Comp updates meshed in with the team's channel.

Nek idly rolled on the main screen. They weren't speaking or triggering any functions on the consoles, so Mina wasn't fully sure they were there. She didn't know if Nek had a "room" elsewhere in Outrider. Maybe it was the deck, maybe they were intruding, but she felt awkward to ask as they'd been sitting here for twenty minutes already. For now, she added it to the list to ask later. Comps were flying around Outrider doing the remaining repairs, Nek was likely directing tasks down there. A set buzzed by outside as they moved to another section of the outer hull needing patched. The swarm was impressive to see working together. To the point that it was increasingly odd to see Comp2876 alone, but it remained with the Wardens whenever possible. Always ready to jump on any request.

Mina stretched her well-used legs and wondered what a nap in the blanket fort would feel like. The thought was broken by every screen on the deck flashing white. Everyone, besides Emma, shook their heads as their vision cleared. On the main screen, next to the now whirling Nek, was breaking news about an attack currently going on in downtown Hurst. One helicopter feed showed a far-off angle, people scrambling from a street.

Another feed, a livestream, loaded in. The person was running down 15th street and there was shouting all around them. The camera caught something flying overhead, the block shape stopped suddenly and turned back, appearing to look right at the phone recording it. The person dived for the ground as the thing moved closer. The livestream cut out.

"What were those?" Steph got closer to the screen. "They don't look like

Comps."

Nek split across the consoles. "Lenian Pawns."

"Lenian?" both Zane and Emma asked.

Information loaded into their armbands, but no one took time to read as Nek continued to swirl even tighter. "Original projections estimated others would reach this sector around now. With our recent issues, I never got around to…This is my fault, Wardens. I should have-"

Mina leaned closer to the main display. "Hey, it's okay. Not like you've had nothing going on to distract you. Time for us to earn these Paks. Can you send us all at once?"

"Helmets up. Setting your drop point now."

The weightless feeling ran over her again before she dropped into a street, the others around her. It took a moment to situate where they were. Oddly, it was the grease and cheese of Sax's pizza that grounded her first. They looked around, but none of those Lenian Pawns were here.

"We protect that pizza at all costs." Sean pointed to the painted window of the restaurant that now sported a spider-web crack across its length.

"Focus," Mina said. "There is actual Earth saving to do."

Steph pointed down the street, saber still in hand, to a row of Pawns waiting there. Pings popped on their heads-up as she did. "Found them."

Zane shook himself. "Yup. Let's go be cool."

"Already are," Emma said.

Nek appeared in a corner of Mina's display, presumably in all of theirs. "Lenian Pawns are simple in design. Main objective is to keep them from grouping. You've all learned quickly so far, keep that up."

Mina took off in a run toward the Pawns, a boost having her at a faster pace than she'd ever do alone. The others were close behind her. Windows from a floor of the office building on their left exploded out, sending debris falling to the street below. She looked up to see another set of Pawns, they'd set a trap.

"Keep an eye on the other side," Mina called out. "Don't get surrounded."

The Pawns aimed straight for them, taking shots as they neared. The Warden's scattered, not giving them an easy line on the group. Mina pressed against a truck and watched as the Pawns spread out as well. She managed to tag a few for the group. One weaved through the cars and took a shot at Zane, who reacted with a punch as it passed by. It ducked under a box truck and popped up to go for Steph, who was ready for it with the saber. A chunk sliced off the Pawn and it spun out into a nearby shop window.

"So she's stealing 2876's duck and cover moves too," Emma called out. "So lazy."

"This is the person who called us children twenty times in one fight," Sean pointed out. "She probably doesn't think this will take too much effort."

Mina shifted to track another Pawn and pulled up her Pak's inventory. A small recon drone, a set of cuffs, a blaster, and two sais. A couple of them did target practice earlier, but she'd passed and didn't feel like learning on the move now.

"Cowabunga it is, I guess." Mina loaded out the sais.

"Oh shit," she heard from below her. Followed by a camera shutter going off.

Mina looked down to see a woman, scuffed and scraped, poking out from under the truck with phone in hand. She pointed toward an alley between two buildings. "Please move off the street."

The suit automatically distorted her voice, making it sound sort of tinny, almost too overprocessed. She would tweak it later, but for now she was happy with simply not sounding like herself.

The woman crawled out and made the short run for the alley. A Pawn appeared over the top of another sedan aiming for her, but Mina lunged between them. She swung high with both hands, sais jamming into the casing. Sparks flew down around her. Mina felt smug until her feet left the ground. The Pawn was shorting out, but still pushing for the alley and taking her on the ride. It tipped from her weight, the force swinging her legs up toward the wall of one of the buildings. With a thought she turned on the extra hold in her boots. The Pawn pulled her a few more steps until Mina gained enough traction to yank it back with another boost. Slamming the Pawn into the wall that she was standing on. She took a sideways jump and landed upright on the ground.

The camera shutter went off again. Several times. The woman was now crouched behind a dumpster, doing a photoshoot of Mina.

"Keep going!" Mina yelled and the woman listened. Back stepping to the sidewalk, she checked on the others who were all tied up with their own Pawns. There was still the row down the street, none from that line moved when the Wardens appeared. She marked the spot again for the rest. "I think Capri is down there. Push that direction as you can."

Mina followed her own order, moving up the sidewalk. Glass and plaster crunching to dust beneath her boots. Shots came from behind her. She turned enough to see another batch of Pawns take out several sets of windows on a hotel on the other corner. There were shouts from the people inside who must have taken refuge in the lobby. Mina's stomach clenched, they wouldn't squeak this one by with as few casualties. The line of Pawns buzzed between buildings, going farther into the city.

"They're too spread out," Sean shouted.

"We can't ignore them for the sake of Capri," Zane added.

Mina wanted to disagree, Capri was the threat. Probably the one commanding these Pawns. Somehow. All she knew about Lenians was that they were a Collective enemy, so she wanted to know how that partnership came about. But Zane was right too. The Pawns were attacking anything that moved, there were still people hidden all over the streets.

Nek whirled tightly on the screen. "That is not advised."

"What's the plan then, Nek?" Mina asked, thinking Nek was reading her mind. She felt at a loss.

"Sorry, I wasn't speaking to you. Comp2876 has an idea."

"Their plan worked out pretty well last time," Zane said.

Mina turned back toward the line of Pawns, about to tell the others to focus on Pawns and leave Capri to her until she realized there were small spots of light beginning to fill the street. They each expanded and solidified into a Comp. A notice popped, telling her that nearly the entire swarm was now with them.

"This is unusual," Nek said.

"New planet, new tactics?" Steph asked as Comp2876 pushed up close to

Mina.

We contain Pawns. Wardens stop Capri!

"Let's do this." She watched Comps drop their blasters and peel off after the Pawns. High above their heads a pair of Pawns tried to outmaneuver some Comps, which looked like a twisting flock of birds as they stayed tight on their target. They disappeared over a building, but the pops she heard seemed to mean they'd caught their quarry. If they won today, they'd have to devise some sort of cleanup system. Alien robots couldn't just end up with anyone.

"Yeah, this all started because you stole one," she said to herself as she kept moving toward the even still unmoving line of Pawns. Mina spotted Zane on pace with her as she passed a truck. He unloaded a set of blasters from his Pak. They looked beefier than the model she carried, maybe those hit a bit harder.

Down the line Steph stepped out, saber clutched in hand. Emma was beyond her, shaking Pawn parts off a morning star. Sean was on the opposite sidewalk, she'd seen his staff before him. They came up to the intersection between different battered cars. As she expected, waiting in the middle was Capri, sitting on the roof of an SUV and staring them down. The line of Pawns dropped to hover at eye level, blocking the Wardens from her.

"Fight us, you coward!" Emma shouted.

"We want to contain the situation," Mina reminded her. "Not escalate. Remember we have what she wants."

Capri took her time sliding off the roof to stand on the hood. "You've done some practice. How cute. Still making Comps do the heavy lifting though. Disappointing." She waved a hand, the Pawns lining the other streets moved in. "You need more training with the Pawns. You haven't even seen their best trick yet."

The row in front of them opened, their casing pulling back and rougher circuitry exposed. And then, the bit that broke a part of Mina's mind, all that wiring and hardware moved. Pieces snapped, twisted, and elongated in every which way they shouldn't. She watched cables rebundle along these new configurations, which then latched into attachments on different

Pawns. Casing slid back into place as armor pads. A row of now humanoid figures dropped to the ground and stepped toward each Warden.

The entire change took seconds, she'd play it back slower some other time. Her heads-up display updated with the name MegaPawn over the new constructs. Mina made a mental note to ask if that was a translation thing or if Lenians were that lazy with their naming. For now, she fixed her grip on the sais and squared up to her, she really hated that name, MegaPawn.

36

Teamwork Makes the Framework

Comp2876 did a pass of the streets alongside a set of Comps, they tagged and chased Pawns as they could for others to come in behind and destroy. 2876 noted the tally of Pawns dropped at a satisfying rate with the swarm now upon them. Their numbers dropped as well, but not as quickly.

2876 pulled off and joined a different group as they banked around a corner after two Pawns. More Comps came from over the roof of another building, pushing the Pawns down toward the street. 2876 and others opened fire, sending pieces of Pawns falling to the ground.

Comp2876 registered the ping of civilians at a nearby vehicle. It dropped, commanding the others to follow suit. They formed a line between the people and the nearest doorway.

Please follow!

The Comps all repeated the message. The humans appeared unsure, but one finally broke off, stayed low, and moved out across the street. They followed 2876 to the door, which it held open.

Please remain away from windows!

The person gave a nervous jerk of a smile as they passed by. The remaining group bolted across after seeing the first make it safely, the final one managing a small thanks as they entered the building. Comp2876 let the door fall shut, requesting two Comps remain close so no Pawns made an attempt for the people inside. The task was accepted as soon as it touched the framework.

2876 left to check on others, it wanted one full pass on their loose perimeter before focusing back on the Wardens. Nek pressed hard through the framework about ensuring no Pawn got too far away. It flitted between groups as they set upon their targets, ending with a set heading back to where Capri was making her stand. 2876 noted three more civilians crouched behind another car. It watched as a Pawn reformed to replace a limb Warden Sean cleaved off with a spike protruding from the end of his staff.

"They keep replacing parts!" Warden Sean called out.

"Aim for the center," Nek advised, "They're connected under that casing. The limbs are easy enough to dispatch after that."

Warden Emma followed the direction, slamming her morning star into the center of a MegaPawn. As expected the limbs fell away and she broke each in turn. Warden Zane shot two down from his position atop a vehicle. Warden Mina pinned a Pawn midair with the sais as it attempted to shift, but lost one as the Pawn spun off. Warden Steph stepped in to cut the legs out from under another MegaPawn.

Capri clapped from her stance on a vehicle. "Took you long enough to figure that out."

She ducked from the bolts Warden Zane sent her way. Comp2876 provided a couple more, leading into where she'd moved. One hit, Capri twisted to glare up at 2876. It watched her unload the charged saber from her Pak and pushed back before she could send a bolt its way.

"Go! Go! Go!" hissed out from below 2876.

It looked down, the civilians were not far off below. One dashed for cover at another vehicle. That one waved the others over, trying to get them to move. The second dashed right away, the third hesitated but followed suit. Comp2876 tried to assess their best exit, but many of the nearby buildings were heavily damaged already and not verifiable as safe. It pushed further up the street for more options.

"We have to book it for my building," Third said.

Second shook their head. "It's too far!"

"We can't stay here! They're fighting almost on top of us."

"We need to make smart moves," First said. "Wait for another break."

Not that they would be the only moving targets, other civilians were running in all directions again. Pawns had stirred them out of whatever hiding spots they'd previously found and the Comps struggled to wrangle them back in. Some, civilians and Comps alike, did not make it all that far. 2876 figured out a partial route for the three civilians, but the plan was interrupted by another set of Pawns coming around a corner. It reached out through the framework to pull Comps back to its location.

"This is a crap plan," Warden Emma shouted back at the intersection.

First leaned out from their cover, 2876 tracked their eye line to see Capri turning toward Warden Emma.

Capri laughed, "Are you getting tired? That weapon looks heavy for a child your size."

"I'm going to shove my driver's license down your throat the next time you call us kids." Warden Emma cut through another Pawn, gaining a step on Capri.

"What did the other one say?" Second asked, pulling First back to cover.

"It didn't sound like any language I know," First said.

"How can you hear anything over everything else here?" Third asked, curling into a tighter ball.

Warden Sean stepped up next to Warden Emma. "Maybe we look into anger management classes again after this."

Second tugged at First. "They seem distracted enough now."

First hesitated, long enough that Third was the one to make the move from their cover. Second went next and First followed right after. They dashed out to another nearby vehicle pushed halfway up on the sidewalk. They all pressed into the side away from the Wardens.

It was the same path 2876 had estimated, but their timing was off and a Pawn spotted them moving. The Pawn veered off toward the car. None of them moved, they were still too focused on the fight behind them. Comp2876 pushed toward them and saw Warden Emma break from the group as well.

2876 knew the Pawn would make it to the civilians first and let off a few bolts in hopes of drawing attention, but it kept on. It watched First brace for impact, their hand landing on a length of rebar. Their fingers tightened around the rod. The Pawn sent a couple of shots that hit the car. As it came overhead, First jumped straight up and swung the rebar high. All they managed was to clip the blaster hanging down, but it was enough contact to cause the Pawn to spin away, its next few shots sinking into a wall instead of the civilians.

Warden Emma ran over the length of a larger vehicle, jumped with a boost off the hood, and dropped onto the top of the Pawn before it could fully correct itself. The force sent both smashing into the street, bits from the Pawn scattering around. Warden Emma picked it up and ripped a few more pieces off, then looked back to the Wardens. "You might be right about the anger class thing."

"Henrie, move," Second commanded as they grabbed First from behind.

Comp2876 tracked with them as Second pulled both First (Henrie) and Third up the street behind them, weaving around all the debris and a few people. First (Henrie) glanced back, saw 2876 following but then looked past it. Comp2876 registered that Warden Emma was still watching the set as well, until the other Wardens finally broke the MegaPawn line and moved in on Capri. As the civilian group turned the corner, 2876 noted First (Henrie) pulling out a phone and snapping a picture. Nek pressed through the framework to keep eyes on the Wardens, it turned back to the fight at hand.

37

Epic Guitar Riff

Mina felt relief as they pushed in on Capri and Emma circled back. Those three people were the last on the street from what any could see, Comps having escorted the rest away. Other than the few dead she could make out from here.

This was rough, but it was working. Capri's grip on the charged saber tightened, looking angry that she might have to join the fight again. Mina shuffled her inventory to have the cuffs ready to pop. New Pawns were joining to make MegaPawns around them. It felt unending, but Mina kept their estimated tally up on her display. If they all kept at it, Capri would run out of Pawns to throw at them soon enough.

She watched Emma use a boost to launch off another car's trunk and smash a replacement Pawn out of the air as it closed in on Zane. He gave a quick nod to her and took the opening to shoot at Capri.

Steph gained another foot on Capri. "Nobody else needs to get hurt here. I'm sure Nek will be fair with you."

Capri only laughed.

Nek spoke through their suits, in both English and whatever language Capri was using, "There was more room for forgiveness before you betrayed your team. Your fate will be in the Collective's hands, but I swear you will make it back to them for trial without further harm."

"I am a hero with the Collective." Capri lunged for Steph. Their sabers clashed together a few times before Capri shifted to a low swing, knocking one of Steph's legs out from under her.

Steph hit the ground hard, and barely recovered in time to roll away from the MegaPawn that closed in for a kick. She was caught between the legs of the machine but punched through one of the knees. Then stabbed up into its center as it fell toward her, the remaining limbs fell and shot off to reform with another Pawn.

Capri moved on to Sean, dodging each swipe from his staff. He took a chance on a spin for more force, but she caught the strike and pulled him close. "You're practically screaming your moves for me."

"That's because you're supposed to be looking at me." He tipped back, the motion pulling her forward. Right into the two blasters Zane lined up while she was distracted, several shots connected before Capri tossed off Sean and dropped behind the cover of another car.

Buzzing came from behind them, another set of Pawns with Comps hot on their tail. Mina felt stuck in a loop, but at least the Pawns weren't actively destroying the city or killing people anymore. She needed to find that one with her other sai stuck in it, she could only do so much with one. Part of her attention shifted to directing Comps. Her, Nek, and 2876 were each pushing through the framework now. The act was harder than Mina expected. The pulse of a headache ran over the right side of her head from the strain as she called a group back to her.

"This only gets worse if you keep fighting," Capri called over, she was now leaning against an upturned car. Watching them become surrounded by another set of MegaPawns. Mina couldn't tell if this was her trying to look casual or her running on reserves already.

"I don't know, stopping you seems like a good way to end it." Sean jabbed the staff up at a passing Pawn, the spiked edge impaled through the center. He chucked it toward her.

"Your fight doesn't end with me." She sidestepped the dead machine. "Put any thought into where this all came from?"

Steph glanced at her armband. "Lenians. Am I saying that right?"

Capri groaned, something their suit didn't need to translate. "I swear you all are-"

She dropped the sentence as Mina's sai pinged off her helmet. Mina decided they weren't her thing. It'd been a decent throw though. As her Comps arrived Mina dropped the blaster from her Pak.

"You…you just suck." Intimidation was not her strong suit, oh well. She shot. Fifteen Comps followed, along with 2876 and Zane.

The others pushed in toward Capri's crouched figure. Pawns swooped in as cover but were torn apart by bolts.

Nek spoke through them again, "Surrender and your compliance will be rewarded."

There was an angry scream that cut through all their firing. They'd pissed her off again. Good. Mina knew it was to their advantage, expecting she'd become rash and reactive. That's when she'd make more mistakes.

The cry continued as Capri charged over the car she'd used as cover. Her suit was again damaged and torn. Mina thought she saw pieces turn to wisps of smoke for half a second. Capri charged the saber and aimed for Mina. Mid-swing, one blink to the next, she was gone. The Pawns and MegaPawns began blinking out around them next. Mina spotted even fallen machines disappearing from the street.

"Did we do it?" Steph rushed forward to the space Capri once filled.

"Where did she go?" Emma hopped back on a car's roof, spinning to check down the streets around them.

"Do the Comps have eyes on her?" Mina asked out loud, but also to the framework.

Nek swirled on her display. "It appears the Lenians recalled their Pawns. Capri along with them. We can't track it. Comps are confirming an all-clear now."

Emma kicked the already cracked windshield below her, sending glass back into the car. "We had her!"

"So that's a no on being the end of it." Sean leaned on his staff.

"She did kind of say that herself." Zane dropped the blasters to his sides, clearly ready to be done. "When she was talking about the Lenians before."

"Bad guys can't be right."

There was a boom from off behind them. Probably some collateral damage of a building collapsing. Mina figured the city could put it on their tab of property destruction.

"They can be right. The problem is that they don't go about it in the right way," Emma countered.

Mina looked at her armband, Nek's tight waves whirling. "Can they teleport farther than we can? Can we start a search for their base?"

"My estimates show it must be within the solar system. Pluto might be a stretch, but can't be fully ruled out." Nek spun tighter than they'd as yet seen, almost bundling up into a ball on their bands.

So that was a no on the search. Mina gave a tap to the band. "But we stopped her for today, right?"

It was Sean who answered, looking up the street that faced The Park. "No. No, we didn't."

A billowing cloud of green smoke rolled down from a building cloud bank above the newly minted Hurst Crater. Something was moving inside the smoke. As it shifted, the wall dissipated. Slowly revealing the towering, ruby colored, figure within. Except Mina couldn't piece together what it was supposed to be. She wasn't the only one confused.

"It's like a porcupine and, uh, I don't know, an alligator had a baby. But also a robot," Zane slowly put together. A new sentence for human history.

"Someone took a hedgehog and made it evil. And a robot," Emma said.

"They saw a sea urchin and thought 'let's give this some extra appendages and a face from nightmares'," Mina offered. "As a robot."

There was another set of booms above the monster, more of the smoke shifting away in the wake of them. Nek was in their ears. "Guardians landing."

Mina got a brief glimpse of the Guardians surrounding the monster, towering figures of glinting dark metal filling the rest of the crater before her helmet blurred over. She found herself secured into her Guardian's seat. The monster stood in the center, shifting slightly to keep an eye on each of them. Made easier by the fact that, she could now see, it featured several sets of eyes pointing out different directions. What were they really going for with this thing? Blackened edges of the crater crumbled under the Guardian's weight, but each kept their balance. All of them were staring down the robot creation that sneered back, she knew someone needed to start this fight. With a twitch of her hands, the Thunderbird was off the ground. The talons made a swiping pass at one pair of the creature's eyes.

"Is there a way to filter out metal-on-metal sounds?" Steph tried for a kick to the creature's head, but it crouched from Mina's passing and she only hit air.

One spiked arm slammed into Emma's Drake, pushing it down to the ground but she twisted back and dug teeth into the creature's leg. Mina grabbed at the spikes on its back and snagged a few between the Thunderbird's talons. With them in hand, foot technically, she flew straight up. She very much enjoyed having the room to fully flex her wings. Emma let go before she also left the ground. The monster squirmed trying to break free from her hold, but wasn't able to reach high enough. Blue crackling energy rolled over her wings, Mina sent the monster back to the crater with a crack of lightning behind it. The monster landed hard, shaking the crater and caving in more of the edge. Its spikes jammed into the ground, anchoring it down further. Zane was there waiting to hop on top and caught one of the arms in his antlers, he pushed it into the ground. Sean moved in close enough to grab the other arm with three tails and slam it down. Steph and Emma took up positions at its feet, putting their full force down to keep it pinned.

"Nobody say it," Mina whispered to herself as she hovered over them. "Please, please, nobody-"

"That seemed-" came Steph across the comms, but she was cut off by a sudden jerk from the creature throwing her into Emma.

It grabbed one of Sean's tails in its snout and twisted, chucking him into Zane. Emma recovered first and moved to catch one of the now free arms in her Drake's jaws, but the monster snapped off its spikes from the ground and rolled away in time, leaving a bare silver patch along its back. The creature roared and clenched one arm, sending three spikes shooting out toward Steph's Pegasus. The hit sent her skidding across the crater into the far wall. Spikes set deep in her Guardian's side.

"Steph!" they all shouted on the comms.

"Okay! I'm okay," she got back quickly. "Was upside down for a second, but okay. Fun fact, it kind of hurts when the Guardians get hurt."

"I'll add it to the list." Zane took a chance to thump the legs out from under the monster.

It shifted to avoid the hit, putting itself back in the middle of the crater.

"I want what's mine," Capri's voice called out from the monster, which topped off the message with a growl of its own for good measure. The voice sounded wrong, not a match for the recreation their system used.

"Guardians are reserved for Wardens." Mina dropped down talons first, aiming to pull off more spikes.

"And again," Emma said, "to reiterate, you are not one anymore." She squared up in front of the creature. Drawing attention by whipping her tail around with the threat of a hit.

Mina clamped onto spikes across its other arm, pulled back hard, and ripped them out. Metal scrapping and crunching as she did, maybe they did need to work on that sound filter. The monster didn't react in pain, she realized it hadn't to any of the hits they'd landed so far. There wasn't enough space on it for the kind of control room they were using, she didn't think Capri was here. "I think it's just a robot, if anyone was having moral dilemmas about fully putting this thing down."

"Don't have to tell me twice." Emma took the opening to pounce, caught it in the gut, and slammed it back into the ground. Front claws sinking into the shoulders.

Sean grappled the legs with his tails while Emma's back claws dug into the middle of the monster. Zane gave a thump to its head. The mane on Steph's Pegasus proved more dexterous than expected and pulled the spikes from its side. Once fully recovered she slammed her hooves into one of the hands for good measure. Sean stretched out so far that he hooked the edge of the crater in his front claws, pulling until a leg broke away from the monster. It sputtered around after the break, long enough to make Mina almost rethink the 'just a robot' thing, but did stop moving eventually.

"We have an audience growing," Zane said as Sean set himself up to pull the other leg off.

Mina looked toward his Guardian and saw a set of helicopters coming in. The Comps hadn't pinged any during the fight in the city, must be new arrivals. Maybe it was because they'd cleared downtown. Her display lit up with Comps tagging others nearing all around the crater. A few were news, a couple private, and the rest looked military - ready to take aim. *Could have used the hand earlier*, she thought, but realized they likely would be aiming to take down the Guardians as well.

"Can we get on their channels?" Mina asked Nek.

They whirled her display. "You're connected now."

She saw the new comm symbol pop up and switched over. Mina pushed up toward the first helicopters Zane pointed out. "Please stay back. We're handling this situation."

"Identify yourself!" shouted back several people, Nek must have connected all of their channels. There was then cross shouting not directed at her, mostly the military people demanding others leave the area.

She let a little energy crackle over her wings to pull their attention back. "You all should leave. We can stop this. It's too dangerous for you."

"Who are you?" several voices asked and was followed by:

"What are you?"

"Stand down."

"Is that a jackalope?"

Mina let out an angry sigh and pulled back, she cut the connection with their channels. She pulled up a function Nek talked her through back on Outrider. "Everyone stay near the center of the crater for a minute."

Zane's antlers were in the ground, pinning the monster's other arm down. "Not really able to go anywhere. Oh, hey wait, I found a button." The antlers detached, keeping the arm pinned, but allowing Zane to straighten out. He jumped and gave the monster another thump in the head. "Nevermind. All good. Staying put."

The Guardian was tied in with her thinking, making it simple to set a path that followed the crumbling edge of the crater. She hit a button that she'd internally labeled Go Too Fast. A better name would come later. Her Thunderbird took off, picking up speed with each pass around. The helicopters pushed farther and farther back as she went. Mina closed her eyes after a few laps, remembering mid-action that she wasn't a huge fan of rides dependent on g-force.

"They're backing off," Steph called out.

Mina broke her spin and rose to the middle of the crater, impressed with the boom that followed her up. Her small cloud bank hung over the Guardians, misting over the tops of their heads. She reopened her connection to their channels as she dropped back through her cloud. "Let us handle this. We're here to help."

Several turned to leave, a few remained steady at their new position. The Thunderbird stayed high, turning slowly, keeping an eye on them as the team worked below.

Mina shut all her comms off and took a moment to make sure her head was still on straight. Once she knew her stomach was staying put, she lowered her Guardian and spoke to the team, "Remind me to only do that in moderation."

"You can throw up, it's fine," Zane said.

"That'a boy," Emma cheered as she clawed into the chest of the creature. "Not so chatty now are you, Capri?"

The monster stopped putting up much of a fight. Its jaws would snap at limbs that came close, but with its movement so limited it couldn't do much damage. Not to mention the several dents the Jackalope's kicks put into its head.

"I want what's mine," came out of the monster again, but the voice was grainy and garbled. They'd heavily damaged whatever speaker system was inside and soon the monster stopped moving altogether. Mina was now certain the voice was Lenian work, not Capri directly. Zane's antlers pulled from the ground and snapped back to the Jackalope's head. They all released their holds and took a step back. An unseen force pushed them even further away, making a wall around the monster.

"Lenian callback," Nek reminded the group.

"Is it possible to track it given the size?" Mina asked, fairly sure of the answer already.

"Sadly no." Nek filled more of the display, their waves a bit looser. "Comps have confirmed the city has no active Pawns. All Lenian forces have withdrawn."

"And Capri with them," Emma added.

Mina turned her Thunderbird back toward the city proper, there were small tendrils of smoke rolling out of a few buildings, various sirens still going off. "What's the city looking like?"

The display filled with updates, most from the immediate area of attack. Several spots were indeed on fire, but first responders moved in once the fight shifted to the crater. Military teams were doing their own sweep of downtown. Several took shots at Comps as they passed.

"I feel like we should go back in," Steph said. "Give a hand."

"They'll shoot us first," Emma said.

Mina swiped through the various feeds. Trying to organize the amount of information coming in was futile, but she was determined. She knew they were waiting for her to make a call.

As a Comp passed over several bodies in a street, somewhere they hadn't even been, Sean gave a hard sigh over the comms. "I don't know if we did this right."

"I don't know if there is a way to do it fully right. Capri was after destruction." Mina looked over her images of battered people and crumbling buildings. "She wanted us backed into a corner and desperate to give in to her. We did the best we could. She didn't get anything she wanted."

"I think our best move is to let the proper authorities handle this part," Zane said. "They have to realize we stopped the real bad guy."

Nek's waves loosened further. "I believe Warden Zane is correct. Today was a lot for all of us. Our own repairs are needed. Transporting to Outrider."

As Mina felt the now familiar fuzziness come over her. Knowing she was being pulled off the planet, she started to breathe a little easier.

38

I'll Take a Nap Right Here

Capri came to in the suite of the Lenian tower, when exactly she'd lost consciousness in the first place was a mystery. Along with how long she'd been out. More parts of her hurt than when she'd gone down to that annoying planet. She wondered what, if anything, was left of the medical pack in her escape pod. It was doubtful that there was anything in this decrepit place able to work on flesh-based bodies. As she tried to push off the couch, her head spun and sent her falling back to the cushions. Perhaps the damage was a smidge worse than expected.

"Outstanding performance," Maxwell spoke through the intercom system set into the wall. "You're welcome for the rescue, by the way."

"But we did give them a show," Gregory added.

"Made a good fuss."

"But weren't they supposed to give you a Guardian?"

"And be easy to defeat?"

"Those pesky children."

She pulled the blaster from her Pak and shot out the speaker, relying on her suit's targeting system to do most of the work. Her arm fell heavy to her side, no ounce of energy left in her. They'd get theirs soon. For now, Capri sunk into the cushions and let the darkness of her defeat envelop her.

39

We Got This

The city of Hurst shut down for the next three days, along with a decent portion of the world. For Hurst directly, it was partially for cleanup crews to do what they could downtown. Partially to allow everyone to hold their breath for another robot vs robot-monster smackdown. And mostly to give them all ample time spent glued to their preferred device to consume information as it was discovered.

The internet was flooded with pictures of the various robots seen around Hurst. There were already polls going for best action shots of Comps and Pawns running on multiple sites. Pictures of the Guardians were even easier to obtain from nearly anywhere in the city due to their size. Those were plastered on the green screened background of most armchair reporters. Within the first hours after the fight, there was once again 'experts' on all the main news channels theorizing about the meaning behind the Guardians appearances. Mina thought some were reading way too much into it, especially anyone taking a crack at Zane's, but at least those were generally entertaining.

Fewer images were found of the team, not many people caught them in action. Mina thought the one from under the truck was unflattering, but the alley ones made her look cool. She also enjoyed the discussion around their chosen colors. People were determined to not take 'it's their favorite color' as an answer. Most were using the colors in place of their names. The team agreed to take that up as well, a safe enough alternative for when they were on Earth and in the suits.

Early on, the conversation leaned toward them being also the enemy, the lesser evil of an enemy. No matter that they fought against the monster and the Pawns that were blatantly attacking the city. No one could agree which group was responsible for The Hill incident. The mystery only grew due to the disappearing act they'd all pulled once the fight was done. Leaving the city in dismay.

From what Mina could find online no one was talking about Capri, or as they would know her as, Black. It was likely most caught in the fight were too distracted by Pawns to notice her. Or mistook her as one of the mystery team members, which left Mina itching to find a way to slip that information to the public. Warn them about the still present danger.

On day two, someone beat her to it and the conversation shifted in their favor. Henrie, the new girl Emma saved and promptly started crushing on, typed up her entire experience on the street and attached one image of the group. Taking the time to point out that the figure in all-black was not one of the good ones. She'd sent this anonymously to a local news station, of course, but the Wardens all knew. Emma was rather pleased with the recounting. In the hours after its publication, more stories came forward. Some even complimented the 'polite, little, red robots' that ushered people into safe locations.

Yes, there were deaths and injuries and millions of dollars in property damage. But if you're fighting battles at that actual scale, some chaos is inherent, right? It wasn't their fault. Mina was telling herself that, at least. Seeing her team no longer vilified helped. She wanted to keep that confidence going. They needed people to trust them if they were going to continue to defend Earth against Capri and whatever else was out there. The list of known Collective enemies was something she still needed to dig through. That was a task for another time because on that second day she had a different plan for her team.

The result came out on the third day, their mystery team reappeared. In video form, at least. Nek uploaded it directly to several news stations' websites and social feeds at the same time. None were so far able to trace where it came from.

Their team of five stood in the training room - which with some proper lighting was made to look a bit more void-ish. Their banding vibrant against the washed out background. Zane did some nifty quick work. None of them spoke, they only stood looking toward the camera. All of their helmets were up, lights glinting off the smooth surfaces.

She'd asked Nek to do the talking. Their large swirling ribbons appeared on the panel behind them. "We are Wardens. Our mission is to protect life across the galaxy from those that would wish them harm. While we have been in this fight for some time, it is new to your system. As seen by the attack on Hurst, our enemies are aware of your planet and its potential. We are here to stop them. To protect Earth."

The video changed to show several of the images they'd been looking at for two days. Nek's voiceover came back in, "We owe an apology to the city of Hurst. To those who have suffered losses during this encounter. The lives lost can not be replaced with platitudes. We will not attempt to do so and insult you. We vow to do better. As this fight will not be the last. Know that we are here to help."

Zane decided to stay on Henrie's picture for a bit, they all looked pretty good in it. "Information of our mutual enemies will be shared as we can. Working together will ensure darker forces will not prevail here."

The video came back to the team in their void. "We know this trust will need to be earned and will take time. We want to prove ourselves to you. We hope you give us the chance."

Snap to black, that was it. Mina privately hyped Zane up about his work on the video after it was done. She learned from Steph that Henrie was in a bit of shock that a potentially robot, potentially alien, absolutely badass crime fighting team featured her picture.

She thought about taking a break from the internet after it went up, maybe actually fully resting for the first time in several days, but needed to know what everyone else was saying. There'd always be neigh-sayers, but most were hopeful. Even more stories like Henrie's came out. It also didn't take long for people to start lying about being personally saved by a Warden or Comp. But what could you do?

The longer things went on without anyone knocking on any of their doors, the better she felt. But she couldn't dwell on that, or Capri reappearing, or the several listings now claiming to have pieces of broken robots for sale, because she was late to meet her friends.

Steph wiped down the front drink bar as Mina entered. The front room was nearly full, a glance toward the back showed the same there. Sean was cleaning up the toppings racks, he spun every bottle between his hands. Emma was tracking Henrie, who was delivering drinks to customers, from a stool at the bar. She and Zane slid into the two empty spots next to her, with Mina in the middle.

Steph smiled at her and started to make her normal drink. They'd had a long few days of learning the basics of being a superhero, having a first huge fight, and then obsessing over what the world said about them. Their group was ready for a little normalcy.

Nek understood they couldn't disappear from their lives. There was going to be a lot of teleporting in their future. And coming up with cover stories. And maybe more sleepovers in the blanket fort.

Mina looked around the cafe again. "Mitch wasn't wrong about people missing their coffee."

"We weren't the only ones needing back in our comfort zone." Steph passed over the scone Zane was eyeing. "It's been all hands."

"Even new hands." Sean smirked at his cousin.

The other three also looked at Emma, who was taking a long pull from her cup. She finally took a breath, clearing away a bit of whip from her mouth. "Sorry, what'd you say?"

Sean leaned in closer. "Your damsel headed to the back if you want to change locations."

Emma flushed and looked down at her smartwatch, a special edition Mina put together to cover the armband they'd all taken to wearing full-time. "Did Nek say something?"

The screen flashed to Nek's waves. "I didn't."

Emma jumped and covered the screen. "I didn't...oh man."

"Henrie is the one who wrote the first post defending us, correct?" Nek said from under her hand. "I can run a scan on-"

"No!" Emma shouted at the watch.

Mina leaned against the counter. "Cool in combat, bad at dating."

"Sounds familiar," Zane whispered before taking another bite of scone.

Steph smiled past them and gave a loud greeting to the people coming up behind the group, letting them know to shift to safer topics. Zane laughed around his mouthful at the stunned Mina and dazed Emma.

She softly shoved her best friend and turned on the stool, looking over the full cafe. Her team, her friends, all around her. This felt good. This felt right. While the list of work to be done still spun around in her head, the urge to bury herself in work was strong, Mina kept herself grounded in the cafe. She felt the weight of her Pak, hidden away in a pocket. The same weight she was sure the others could feel. It was heavy, but it came with a lot less fear than a few days ago. Then this morning even. Hurst was adjusting to this new reality and pushing forward. The world was too.

Mina took a deep breath. Allowing herself this small moment to simply feel excited. They were going to save the world.

A bottle of caramel drizzle bounced across the counter next to her. Sean, who must have missed a toss to himself, came diving after it next and hung halfway over the counter. Emma jumped out of the way and spilled most of her drink over the both of them. Zane laughed and started choking on his scone. Causing Steph to panic. She jumped up on the counter, trying to figure out how to do the heimlich on someone his size.

Maybe, she amended. Maybe they would save the world.

Acknowledgments

To be honest, while writing this I'm still getting my head around the idea of putting a book out there. At this point, the brain is short on words. Forgive me if this is quick. I promise to work on it for next time.

Thank you Mom and Dad, for not saying 'no' just 'be smart about it'.

Thank you Tori and Tesa, for the Write Nights. Body doubling for the win.

Thank you Stephanie, for letting me ramble to you about superhero teens for so very long. (That's why you got one named after you.)

Thank you to everyone who decided to hang out with Mina and her team, especially if you're reading this bit. Escapism is my preferred survival mechanism. If I did this right, Outrider was a fun little place to hide for a minute. Be safe out there. Text me when you get home. Which you can do at the following:

Instagram/Threads: @brazeetara

TikTok: @tarabrazee